All or Nothing

A MAPLETON NOVEL

DIANA DEEHAN

Copyright © 2024 by Diana Deehan

All rights reserved.

No part of this publication may be reproduced, distributed, or transmitted in any form or by any means, including photocopying, recording, or other electronic or mechanical methods, without the prior written permission of the publisher, except as permitted by U.S. copyright law. For permission requests, contact diana@dianadeehan.com.

The story, all names, characters, and incidents portrayed in this production are fictitious. No identification with actual persons (living or deceased), places, buildings, and products is intended or should be inferred.

1st edition 2024

TITLES BY DIANA DEEHAN

Mapleton Series

Make or Break (FREE copy at www.dianadeehan.com)

Fight or Flight

Now or Never

All or Nothing

Love or Leave

For Pauly—
Thanks for not murdering me IRL.
Maxine

ONE

Willow Spencer was pretty sure she'd lost her mind.

She sat in the back seat of a cab, watching the pretty little town pass by, and wondering why on earth she was returning to Keller's Pub.

Maybe it was the weather putting her in a more agreeable mood. When she had left Churchill two days ago, a thick blanket of snow and ice had covered the town. But Mapleton was warm, and the leaves on the trees were just beginning to burst into bright oranges and reds that looked kaleidoscopic through the sunlight. It made her smile, even after the crap she'd gone through the day before.

She watched the quaint main street pass by, lined with cafés and bookshops and clothing stores. It was so different from her hometown. It was big and busy and beautiful. She knew by most people's standards that Mapleton was a small town, but it was four times the size she was used to.

"We're here," the cab driver said as he pulled to a stop.

She sighed in annoyance as she opened the door and stepped out of the cab onto the sidewalk. She thanked the driver with a smile, but as soon as she started toward the door, her annoyed scowl was back in place.

The door to Keller's stuck out like a sore thumb along Main Street, clearly under construction with a paper Coming Soon sign in the front window and no sign above the door.

The rest of Main Street looked like a photo from a magazine with its pretty storefronts that led down to a sparkling lake. Even though the trip had been a bust, she was still happy about the change of scenery, even for just a day or two. She had been super excited at the idea of trying something new, right until Lurch had swung that door open and shooed her away like a rabies-riddled rat.

God, that guy was such a dickhead.

She sighed again, wondering why she'd come back. Actually, she knew why. It was because she'd already come this far, and she was a nosy bitch and wanted to see how they were setting up their brewery so she could get ideas of how to set up her own.

Not that she would open her own place soon, but a girl could dream.

It also didn't hurt that her contact person, a guy named Adam, had called and apologized. She just hoped that the giant ass from yesterday wouldn't be there.

She pulled the handle, surprised when it smoothly eased open, unlike the day before. She stepped in and immediately spotted *him*.

The asshole.

He was impossible to miss. When she'd first laid eyes on him, she'd actually thought he was good looking. Not that she cared; she was happily engaged. Nevertheless, it was impossible to deny the objective hunkyness of the guy.

He was a thousand feet tall with intense dark eyes under slashes of dark eyebrows, and he had gigantic biceps covered in tattoos. Then he opened his mouth.

He was just another asshole.

Surprisingly, he wasn't scowling as he had been the day before. Actually, he had no expression whatsoever. His face was like an icy wall; hard, cold, and completely unreadable.

"Hi, you must be Willow. I'm Adam."

To her right, only a few feet away, a smiling face caught her attention. She hadn't even realized anyone else was in the room. She took Adam's outstretched hand in hers and gently squeezed.

"Nice to meet you," she said with a polite smile, then threw a pointed look over his shoulder at the giant dick across the room.

See, Neanderthal? This is how normal people interact when meeting for the first time.

He gave her a blank look as if he could read her thoughts and walked over, surprising her when his knuckles didn't drag on the ground. He came close, then extended his huge tattooed hand.

"Max."

She glared at him, waiting. Was that it? Nothing else? No apology?

God, what a dick.

She left his hand in the air and looked back at the non-dickish one.

"I'm so sorry for the confusion yesterday," Adam said. "It was my fault. I was going through some personal things, and I sent my crew home early. Max thought you were on the crew."

She cocked a brow in the asshole's direction. Why would he think she was part of a construction crew? Then she remembered her clothing. The standard outfit everyone wore from the catch-all store in

Churchill. It made her blend in there, but she had to admit she looked way out of place in an upscale little town like Mapleton.

It hadn't really occurred to her to dress nicely for the interview, and even if it had, it wouldn't have mattered. These were the only clothes she had.

Her last interview had been a decade ago for her current job, and her boss, Doug, hadn't batted an eye at her attire when he'd hired her. But to be fair, he bought all his clothes from the same store, so they had basically been wearing the same outfit.

Given all that, she supposed it wasn't that huge a leap for Max the Asshole—Maxhole—to assume she was a construction worker.

But she didn't have to forgive him for it.

Especially if he wouldn't apologize.

She threw one last glare at him, then tried to forget he even existed, and focused on the nice guy.

"I hope everything is okay," she said to Adam.

He smiled back. "It will be. Let's get started."

He led her through a hallway and into a small office that someone had hastily thrown together, and she sat down on a brown leather chair, questioning why she didn't feel any nervousness. Probably because she'd already written this job off. Maybe Shane was right to tell her not to bother with this and stay home with him instead, but if nothing else, at least she got a change of scenery and some warm air.

Not to mention the tasty drive-through pumpkin spice latte she'd tried for the first time that day.

Adam followed her through the door, and to her dismay, Maxhole followed. They sat across from her.

Adam began telling her about the brewmaster position they were hiring for and how they wanted someone with good taste and a lot of experience to head it up, create the beer, the brew schedule, everything. They asked her some basic questions, presumably to see what her level of experience was and whether she could run a brewery. Which she obviously could. She'd been working at a brewery for over ten years, had gone through the steps to become a brewmaster, and had been desperate to get out from under Doug's thumb for some time.

But she wanted her own brewery, not someone else's.

Maxhole sat silently, staring at her, watching her every move as she answered Adam's questions. She would have found it intimidating had she not already hated him so much.

"Do you have questions for us?" Adam asked.

She glanced over at Max's intense dark eyes and back, then asked what she'd been wondering since he'd opened that door, but she was sure she already knew the answer. "Who would be my boss?"

Silence met her for a moment, then Adam finally spoke.

"Max is the owner and general manager."

Willow gave a nod. That's what she thought.

"What's your role?"

"Investor."

Willow fought the urge to shake her head and say *Never in a million fucking years.* She already had a controlling dick for a boss. The last thing she needed was an even more controlling, even bigger dick.

Huge dick.

Stop thinking about dicks.

She shook her head and had started standing when Adam stopped her.

"Would you like to see the brewery?"

Oh yeah.

"Sure," she said, finally feeling a tinge of excitement. At least she'd be able to tell Shane that something came of this. He had been less than enthused when she told him she was going away for a few days for an interview. At least now she could put his mind at ease that she didn't want to take the job. She knew it would be a long shot to talk him into moving away from Churchill with her, anyway.

She followed Adam and Max out of the office, through the dismantled dining area, and into the taproom. Then stopped dead in her tracks and stared up with her jaw going slack.

It was as if she'd just stepped into a greenhouse.

The ceilings were high and all glass, with lights strung up that gave it a glow. The floor was wood, as was the bar that spanned the far wall. Behind the bar, they had already fitted a long row of taps and mounted three screens on the wall above to display the beers.

"We started in the taproom," Adam said. "It isn't quite finished yet, but we're getting close. The plan is to plant trees in the corners to grow to the ceiling so it feels like you're outside even in the winter. The glass panes on the ceiling open in the warmer months."

"Wow," she said, at a loss for more words. It was incredible. Better than anything she could have dreamed up herself.

"Through here is the brewery," Adam said, gesturing to an opening behind the bar and leading them through. "It's ready to go. We have state-of-the art—"

She stopped listening.

The place was enormous. And immaculate. This was not the rundown crappy place she had spent almost every day for the past ten years in. They had sunk some serious money into this.

The tanks were shiny and new, with built-in touch screens to automate the process. She walked through the wide row between the fermentation tanks, checked out the storage tanks and the mash tuns. She was in complete awe.

"Where's your canning line?" she asked.

"We've got a mobile service that cans for us," Max said.

She nodded, then remembered that she hated him, and turned around again. They had to do the canning themselves in Churchill, and it was the only part of the process she didn't really love.

"So," Adam said, "what do you think?"

"I think that if I ever got to open my own brewery, it would be exactly like this."

"Your own brewery?" Max's deep voice, hard and unfeeling, came through, and she realized what she'd said.

She tried to shrug it off but couldn't stop herself from thinking about it. Realistically, she'd never be able to open her own brewery. She had some money from an insurance payout she got after her mom died, and her Nana had encouraged her to invest it and keep it to herself, so she'd done just that. In the fifteen years she'd been with Shane, she'd never told him about it, and it had grown into an enormous sum.

But the money was practically irrelevant.

She could never open her own place in Churchill. It was too small a town to support two breweries, and all the locals already loved what she brewed at Tipped Canoe. Not to mention that distribution from a town with no external roads was impossible.

But the logistics were hurdles she could jump. The real problem was talking Shane into moving. He never wanted to leave.

"It's incredible," she told Max, forgetting for a moment that she hated him. Her mind became consumed with more important things, like the realization that her dreams would never be achieved. "I wouldn't change a single thing."

She looked around again, basking in the disappointment that she would never own a place like this, then wondered whether they were actually going to offer her the job.

She had been so certain she would never work for Maxhole, but now that she saw the brewery, she had to admit that she wanted this job.

Like, badly wanted it.

Finally having control would be amazing, and she knew she could make remarkable beer. She'd have to deal with Maxhole, but she already knew how to put up with Doug, so how much worse could it be?

She glanced at Max, who was still glaring at her, unreadable.

She rolled her eyes.

It would be nice to get out of Churchill for a while, have a little adventure before she and Shane got married. She'd only left twice since she moved there to be with her father after her mom died. Once to visit her Nana in Ottawa when she was nineteen, and now for this interview.

She wanted to get out and see some more of the world, maybe go to a concert or see a Blue Jays game.

Something.

Anything.

Willow exhaled, reminding herself that she was in a job interview and couldn't cry. "I should probably get going. My flight is in a few hours."

Adam nodded with a polite smile. "Thank you so much for coming, Willow."

Willow smiled back. "Thanks for having me."

"We'll be in touch."

With a nod, she said goodbye and turned to leave. She didn't know how they were feeling about her, but she *knew* she wanted this job, even if Max would be her boss. She'd just have to wait and see whether they offered it to her.

She stepped out onto the sidewalk and looked back at the pub, then down to the pretty lake. If they offered her the job, she'd try her best to talk Shane into moving with her. Maybe he'd be willing to step out of his comfort zone, even for just a little while, and have an adventure with her.

Her shoulders began slumping, and she ordered them to stop. Stranger things have happened. Maybe there was still hope.

TWO

"We'll let you know," Max said through gritted teeth.

He waited for the door to close behind their last interview, then turned to look at Adam with an eyebrow cocked.

"Where'd you find that buffoon?"

Adam snorted a laugh. "I guess he's a no?"

"Waste of fucking time," he said, walking back to his office and opening his laptop.

Adam followed and plopped himself into the chair across from him. "At least we know we've exhausted all our options. You updating your spreadsheet?"

"Yes," Max said and could practically hear Adam's eyes rolling in their sockets.

"Is there anything you don't record on a spreadsheet? Do you tick a box every time you take a dump?"

Max ignored him, continued working his way down the list of things he was looking for in a brewer. "How are things going with Chelsea?" he asked, hoping to change the subject.

Adam sighed. "I met with the therapist last night. It's going to be okay. I'll win her back."

Max nodded. If anyone could do it, it was Adam. He was good at articulating his feelings. Women found him charming.

Max didn't have the same easy way with people. "How's Cara?"

Max sighed. His sister was the only person he was close to, and that's only because he had to raise her on his own after his dad bailed and his mom had to work three jobs. And even then, there were plenty of things he *never* talked to her about.

"She's still hung up on that mullet-headed loser."

Adam shook his head. "I thought she hated him."

"Apparently, nothing compares to him, according to the Sinéad O'Connor playlist that runs on repeat from her bedroom."

"Yikes," he said, then dropped his gaze to his feet. "But I get it."

Max fought off an eye roll, continued clicking along his spreadsheet. The people in his life were driving him wild. He filled in all the fields for the fifth and final candidate who'd just left and hit Print.

"You're overthinking this," Adam said. "We don't need a spreadsheet to know who the best woman for the job is."

Max glared over his fresh spreadsheet, still warm from the printer. They'd only interviewed one woman. Willow Spencer. And she fucking hated him. He wasn't sure he'd ever pissed anyone off as badly before. And he'd pissed off many people.

It had basically been his job for the past decade.

But looking at the numbers in front of him, it was clear as day that Willow was the best candidate for the job.

"Let's see," Adam said, plucking the paper out of his hands. "Just as I thought. Pretty little redhead with the dagger eyes for the win."

"She can't stand me."

"Can you blame her?" Adam said with a laugh.

"She'll never accept this job."

Adam considered this. "I worried about that, too. But I'm not so sure. She seemed to warm up when she looked at the brewery. Plus, she was talking like she wants to leave the job she has now."

"She said she wanted to start her own place."

"Yeah, but this might be a step in that direction for her. The better question is whether you can handle her."

Max stabbed Adam with a look. He had yet to meet someone he couldn't handle.

Adam shrugged. "She doesn't seem like she's going to take any shit from you."

"I don't want someone who takes shit."

"Okaayy . . ." he said, unconvinced.

Max shook his head. "I just want someone who can make good beer. She can glare at me or ignore me or call me a prick all she likes as long as she keeps making beer that sells."

"So you want her, then?"

Did he want her? It'd be absurd not to. She had tons of experience, an impressive track record, and when she wasn't snapping at him, she seemed pleasant enough. He supposed it couldn't hurt to offer the job to her and see what happened. He just wished he'd got off on a better foot with her.

Or that she sucked so he wouldn't want her, anyway.

"Yeah," he said, turning to Adam. "Call her, and offer her the job."

The moment he said it, he felt a weight off his shoulders. This was the last key position they had to fill before they could get everything set up for the grand opening. He wasn't convinced she would accept, but he had to at least give it a shot. She was clearly the best person for the job.

"Okay," Adam said. "I'll make the call in the morning."

Max placed the spreadsheet in his folder, closed it, and neatly stacked it on the shelf in the corner of the room. He needed to work on getting the office into shape. He hated working out of such a disorganized space.

"I gotta get going, but I'll be back—"

"At the butt crack of dawn, I know," Adam said. "When does Chef Luis get here?"

"Tomorrow," he said, closing his laptop and sliding it into his bag.

"Got it. I'll just go through the kitchen one more time before I lock up so it's up and running for him."

"Thanks. Let me know what Willow says," he said and found hope bubbling up as his words came out. If she said no, he'd have to choose from one of the subpar brewers on his spreadsheet. He quickly swept it aside, knowing hope and worry were useless emotions, and carried on to the door. He had too much else to think about, and he'd promised Cara he'd make her favourite dinner when she got back from her classes.

He'd just have to wait and see what Willow said, even if the thought of his future being in her hands made his skin crawl.

THREE

Willow shivered as she stepped out of her car and grabbed her suitcase from the back seat. Churchill was colder than it had been when she left, and the snow was twice as high. She walked up the front step to the home she shared with Shane and warmed from the inside at the sound of barking coming from behind the door.

"It's me, Barley. I'm home."

Barley barked louder as she juggled her keys in her frozen fingers, trying to find the keyhole in the dim light. She'd nearly got it in when her phone rang, and she stopped what she was doing, shamelessly dropping everything to see whether it was Adam offering her the job. But when she pulled the phone from her bag and looked at the display, a photo of her and her nana filled the screen.

"Hi, Nana!" she said while unlocking the door and bracing for impact.

"Willow, are you home?"

"Just got here," she said as Barley attacked her leg. He was a small but mighty corgi who had definitely missed her.

The feeling was mutual.

She dropped everything and went to her knees, hugging him while scratching his neck until he calmed down.

"Oh good," Nana sighed. "I've been worried. You didn't call to let me know you made it home safe."

"My flight was delayed a little. Are you okay?" she asked with a smile. "You sound like a pony."

Nana laughed. "A little horse?"

Willow snorted. "Yes."

"I'm fine. I'm just getting over a cold. Tell me all about Mapleton."

Willow filled Nana in on everything from the pretty little town to the wretched asshole who told her to get lost—but who owned the stunning brewery she loved.

"I visited Mapleton once," Nana said. "Back in ninety-three. Maybe Ninety-four. Some girlfriends and I went on a wine tour, but I can't seem to remember much of it."

Willow snickered. "Because you were loaded the whole time?"

"Yes."

"You wild thing."

Nana barked a laugh. "Speaking of wild things, how's that fiancé of yours? He must be happy you're back."

She calmed Barley down with a belly rub and snuggled her cheek into his soft, furry little head. "I haven't seen him yet. He wasn't happy when I left."

Nana let out a disapproving hum. "I know you two have been joined at the hip since you were teenagers, but you can go where you want, Willow."

"I know. It's just that things are still a little . . . strained between us."

"Well, maybe you shouldn't have—"

Another call beeped on the line as her Nana launched into a lecture, and Willow pulled the phone back from her ear and checked the display.

Adam Vale.

"Nana"—she cut her off—"the guy who interviewed me is calling. I gotta go."

"Okay. Let me know what happens."

"I will," she said, hanging up and accepting Adam's call. "Hello?"

"Hi, Willow. It's Adam from Keller's in Mapleton."

"Yes, hi," she said, hoping beyond hope he would offer her the job.

"Did you get home okay?"

"Yup, just got back."

Come out with it.

"Thanks again for coming. Your experience and talent are impressive. We would love for you to join our team."

Willow silently bounced up and down, earning a head tilt from Barley, who nudged her hand with his nose to make her continue the belly rub.

"That's great," she said.

"I've had an offer of employment drawn up, and I'll email it to you so you can look it over. If you have questions, you can call."

"That's great," she said, then slapped her forehead.

You already said that, doofus.

"Great. I'll be looking forward to your call."

Don't say great again!

"Cool," she said, then shook her head at herself.

"Cool," he said, and she could see his face in her mind, laughing at her. "Bye."

"Bye."

She hung up and screamed in excitement as Barley jumped up and down, barking. She stared at her empty inbox for a few minutes, begging for the mercy of a notification, before the realization hit that she was desperate to be offered this job.

Obviously, she didn't love her job at Tipped Canoe, but in reality, could she even consider accepting a job in Mapleton?

She looked around the simple living room she shared with Shane. He'd lived in Churchill his whole life; his entire family was there, and he'd always been clear that he never wanted to leave. And she never wanted to leave him. She'd loved him since she was fourteen.

Maybe this had been a terrible idea. She'd gone across the country to interview for a job she knew she could never take. It was selfish and wrong.

She had just bowed her head in defeat when the notification of a new email arrived with a loud ping. She hit the icon, opened the email, clicked on the attachment, and forced herself to read through line by line until she saw the salary they were offering.

Her heart stopped as her eyes doubled in size.

Holy shit.

That was more than she and Shane made now, combined.

A little sound of disbelief escaped her chest. If she accepted this, they could move to Mapleton, and he wouldn't even have to worry about finding another job. She could definitely pay all their living expenses herself.

He was always complaining about his job. Maybe he would move there if it meant he could just relax, take up a hobby or something. Even if it was only for a year or two.

She looked at Barley. "You'd love it there, Barls. It's warm. And there's a beach with no polar bears."

Barley licked her hand, and she decided she'd at least try to talk Shane into it.

· · · · ● · ● · ● · · ·

Willow sat on the worn-out plaid couch with Barley in her lap, staring at the old wooden clock hanging on the wall above a gigantic set of moose antlers from Shane's last hunting trip. It was fifteen minutes past his normal arrival time.

She tapped her toe impatiently, trying to rein in her racing heart, and inspected the antlers with disdain for the hundredth time since he'd first hung them there. Decorating with dead animals wasn't really to her taste, but the house was just as much his as it was hers, so who was she to tell him no?

If she was being honest, it was actually more his house than hers. It had belonged to his uncle, who'd died in the corner of the living room on a reclining chair that matched the couch. Shane had been eighteen and bought the house to live in. It had been right around the time when her father had announced he was moving to Northern British Columbia for a new job, and Willow had moved in with Shane so she wouldn't have to leave. Since then, everything in the house remained as it had been when his uncle owned it, including the couch.

At least he'd thrown out the chair.

She stood from the couch, hugging Barley to her chest and pacing the floor.

Seventeen minutes now.

Ugh.

She caught a draft from the rickety window and shivered, remembering the greenhouselike taproom that was practically tropical compared to Churchill. If the brewery she worked at now had a taproom like that, every local in town would spend every evening in there. She closed her eyes and imagined being in there, surrounded by people drinking her beer, and a smile spread across her face.

Suddenly, the door opened.

She spun around with a big smile to see Shane step in through the door.

"You're back!" she said, placing Barley down and going to the door.

"You're back," he said, his deep voice vibrating in her chest. He dropped his lunch pail on the floor and opened his arms.

She stepped into his chest as his cold arms came around her back, and his familiar scent of body wash and motor oil filled her nose. She used to hate the way being a mechanic made him smell and how his hands always looked dirty, but eventually, she got used to it, and now it made her feel at home.

He pulled back, then looked around the house. "It's clean again," he said with a lopsided smile. "I'm happy you're home."

Willow nodded, a little annoyed that when she'd left four days ago the place had been clean, and it was a mess by the time she got back, but that was just what guys were like.

At least he'd fed Barley.

She shook it off and waited for him to ask her how it had gone. But instead of saying anything else, he bent and unlaced his boots, threw his jacket over the back of the chair instead of hanging it on the hook, then walked to the kitchen without his lunch pail.

Ugh.

She rolled her eyes as she picked it up and followed him in just as he was taking the top off a bottle of beer. If she could get him to agree to going with her to Mapleton, she would make him all the delicious beer he wanted. And it would be significantly better than the stuff Doug forced her to brew week in and week out.

She watched as he pulled some leftover pizza from the fridge and shoved it in his mouth. "Aren't you going to ask how it went?" she asked.

He stopped midbite, swallowed, and looked at her. "How did it go?" he asked in a dry voice.

She withered a little, but squared her shoulders, and refused to be defeated that easily. "It went really great. The brewery is amazing, state-of-the-art equipment, and the taproom is like a tropical paradise."

Shane's dark eyebrows scrunched up, and he took a deep pull from his bottle.

She braced herself. "The owner just called. They offered me the job."

Shane huffed out a breath and shook his head. He stuffed the rest of the pizza in his mouth before turning away from her and walking to the bathroom with his beer.

She followed, undeterred. He'd always hated change, so she knew to expect this from him. First, he would ignore it and hope it would go away; then, he would get annoyed; finally, he would talk her into changing her mind.

But not this time.

"Just please hear me out, Shane."

"I'm not moving, Willow," he said, pulling his dirty shirt off his back and turning on the shower. "I told you that before you left."

"It's a lot of money. You wouldn't have to work."

He stopped, stared at her. "You told me you wanted to stay here, too. When we got engaged."

She looked down at her empty ring finger, remembering the horrible circumstances that had surrounded their engagement. She'd forgiven him for all of that before she'd said yes, but as much as she'd tried, she could never forget.

She had told him at the time that she wanted to marry him and stay in Churchill, but that was before she saw what she could achieve in Mapleton. She tipped her chin down to her chest as the guilt swirled.

"Kyle and Nikki are coming over," he said, ignoring her and stepping into the shower. "They'll be here soon."

Willow turned and walked out of the bathroom without another word. He was impossible to negotiate with. She wasn't sure anyone on earth was as stubborn as him. But he had a point.

She sat on the couch, and Barley immediately curled into her lap just as the door opened and Nikki walked in.

"Willow!" she said, toeing off her shoes and plopping down on the couch next to her. "Thank God you're back."

She smiled as her best friend stretched out next to her, completely at home. She loved living so close to her best friends. If she and Shane left, they wouldn't have Nikki and Kyle in their lives, and that would be awful. Maybe staying in Churchill was for the best.

Logically, it made sense to stay, but she couldn't seem to stop the disappointment from swirling in her mind. She felt like a sprinter who'd just broken their ankle before a big race.

She shook her head, trying to focus her attention on all the good things in her life.

"I missed you, Nik. Where's Kyle?"

"He's just dropping something off in the garage. Are you okay?" she asked as she stared at Willow's face, clearly sensing that something was wrong. "You look upset."

Willow wondered how to answer or whether to even say anything about the job offer before she and Shane figured it out. Although, according to Shane, it had already been decided. She'd be turning down the job and staying in Churchill.

Forever.

Nikki glanced at the bathroom as the shower turned off, then back at Willow. "Were you guys fighting about Bunny367 again?"

Willow squeezed her eyes shut at the sound of that name. She had been deeply in love with Shane before she found those explicit messages hidden on his phone from that fucking Bunny367. She could still remember the embarrassment and heartache when she packed her bags and showed up at Nikki's doorstep, asking for a place to stay.

And the relief when Shane came to her a few days later and told her it would never happen again, then asked her to marry him.

Willow shook her head. "No, it's not that. I got offered the job in Mapleton, but Shane doesn't want me to take it."

"Well, no," Nikki said with a laugh. "None of us want you to take it. What would I do if you left?"

Willow took in Nikki's pleading brown eyes. "It's not like we'd have to be gone forever."

"I know, but I don't want my best friend and maid of honour to leave," she said, closing the distance between them on the couch and pulling Willow into a hug.

She didn't really like the idea of leaving her friends and hometown, either, but she just wanted something—anything—exciting to happen. Or even just something to work toward. Going back to work and making boring beer after boring beer now that she'd seen Keller's Brewery was going to be demoralizing.

"You and Kyle could come to Mapleton and visit. It's really beautiful there."

Nikki shook her head as she pulled two giant resealable bags filled with wedding paraphernalia next to her. "I want to have a baby right after the wedding," she said. "Will you help me make these centrepieces?"

Willow nodded as Kyle walked through the door and Shane came out of the bedroom, cleanly dressed. His entire demeanour had changed. He was now wearing a big smile as he greeted his best friend.

A much bigger smile, Willow noted, than he'd had for her.

She watched as Nikki showed her how to fill a vase, just how she wanted it, and tried to wipe her mind of Keller's Brewery. This was her home, and these were her people. She loved it in Churchill. She had agreed to marry Shane and had forgiven him for sexting with Bunny367. Now she had to live with the consequences.

Besides, the grass wasn't always greener on the other side. Maybe Mapleton was actually horrible. And she *knew* working for Max wouldn't be great.

She was probably better off staying where she was, with her friends whom she loved, and working on her relationship with Shane. If they could just get back to where they'd been before the cheating, she'd be happy.

She excused herself from Nikki and went to her bedroom for a quick moment, pulling out her phone. Then she called Adam and declined the offer.

FOUR

Max walked into the fully finished kitchen an hour before anyone else was supposed to be there and found his new chef, Luis, in the cooler with his back to Max.

He raised his brows, impressed.

From the moment he'd hired Luis, Max had known he'd be a good fit. He'd already built the first draft of the menu and was working to test it all in the coming weeks. He was hardworking, ambitious, and decisive.

Max admired those traits.

Especially after spending all last night with his sister as she bawled her eyes out and destroyed a half gallon of ice cream while googling ways to get the fool who'd dumped her to give her another chance. It was refreshing to be spending the day with someone focused on useful endeavours.

Max left Luis to his work for a moment as he made his way through the rest of the kitchen to ensure everything was in working order. Adam had told him last night that the kitchen was complete and his crew would work in the dining room, but Max wanted to be certain.

People had accused him of micromanaging in the past, so he usually came in early to avoid being called out for it.

"Morning," he finally said.

Luis turned toward him, and that's when he noticed that Luis was holding a tablet and carefully filling out a colour-coded spreadsheet.

Max's shoulders relaxed.

"Good morning. I came early to get started," he said in his thick Québécois accent. "Okay?"

"Of course. Do you need anything from me?"

"Yes," Luis said, clicking a few more times on his tablet, then turning it toward Max. "Here's the menu I'm going to test. I made a few changes from the first draft I sent you."

Max read through, his eyes snagging on the only line he actually cared about. When he'd hired Luis, he'd had only two pieces of input about the menu: make sure they were profitable, and make sure his grandmother's cabbage rolls were on it.

But Luis had put cabbage roll under sandwiches.

"What's this?"

"I had an idea to make your cabbage rolls more pub-friendly and more profitable. I'm going to test out a cabbage roll sandwich."

Well, that sounded pretty fucking delicious. "Like a meatball sub?"

"Exactly!" Luis said, his hand flying upward.

Max had never met someone so animated when they spoke. He chalked it up to passion, but he was pretty sure Luis waved his hands even when he spoke of the blandest of things.

"We could have the thick brioche bun," he continued, his eyes squinting and his hands in front of his face as if layering an imaginary sandwich. "A delicious cabbage roll, but made into a patty, with stewed cabbage and a mouthwatering tomato sauce. Beautiful."

Max nodded, a little uncomfortable with the look on Luis's face, but mostly impressed.

"We could serve with a coleslaw or potato salad. Easy, delicious, higher profit margin."

Max smiled. "Perfect."

Luis threw his hands in the air, an over-the-top smile stretching across his face. Man, this guy fucking loved being a chef.

The door swung open, pulling their attention, and Adam strolled into the kitchen. Max's brows rose.

Adam wasn't supposed to be there until later in the afternoon.

"Problem?"

Adam nodded. "Morning, Luis," he said.

Luis waved dramatically, then returned to his tablet.

"Office?"

Another nod and Max followed Adam out of the kitchen, into the office, and closed the door.

"It's looking better in here," Adam said, taking a seat.

Max had spent a day painting the walls, building some proper shelving, and organizing the desk. It was time well spent. Now he could actually concentrate.

"What's up?"

"Willow called," he said.

Max stared, waiting for Adam to elaborate. "And?"

Adam shook his head.

"Fuck," he said. "Did she counter with a different offer? Did she want more money?"

"No, she said it was personal and that the offer was generous and she loved the brewery, but the timing wasn't right for her to move."

Max rolled his eyes, immediately spinning his chair toward the shelf behind him and reaching for a binder.

"What are you— Not the spreadsheet again," Adam said, rubbing his face.

Max opened the binder, took out his spreadsheet, ignoring Adam. The other four brewers they'd interviewed weren't as great as Willow, but he needed to choose someone. They were running out of time. "What about the first guy?"

"No."

"Third guy?"

Silence. He looked up at Adam, who was staring at him as if he'd lost his mind.

"Who do you want, then? We're running out of time."

"Obviously, I still want Willow."

Max slapped the spreadsheet onto the desk and sat back in his seat. This conversation was killing him.

"Cool. So we'll kidnap her, then? Burn down the brewery she works at? Kill her whole family so she has no reason to stay in Churchill?"

Adam narrowed his eyes. "You know, it's a little concerning how fast you jump to arson and murder. This is why people are afraid of you."

"No one's afraid of me. And unless you have an actual solution, I'm going to do this my way."

"As it turns out, I thought of something yesterday."

"You knew about this already yesterday?"

Adam nodded as if this shouldn't matter.

Max inhaled slowly, trying to summon patience. "Why didn't you tell me yesterday?"

"I wanted time to think about it without you being all . . . well, you."

"And did you come up with a plan?"

Adam nodded. "I think we need to adjust our offer."

Max shook his head and reached for the spreadsheet, but Adam slapped a hand on it.

"If she doesn't want to move here, and she's always wanted her own place, and we desperately need a brewer ASAP—"

Max's eyes went wide. "Are you fucking— No," he said, shaking his head. "Murder is a better plan."

"I haven't even finished."

"I know exactly where you're going with this. You want to sell the brewery to her, have her run it from Churchill."

Adam smiled and gave a nod.

"Obviously, that's a no."

"Why?"

Max rubbed at his temples. "I'm not selling off half my business to some stranger. I barely tolerate working with you."

"You're taking this independence thing too far," Adam grumbled under his breath.

Max shook his head, not wanting to reopen their long-running debate over Max's control issues. Max had originally wanted to go it entirely alone, but he agreed to partner with Adam because he could secure more funding and get cheaper labour. As it was, they'd built a contract where Adam was a silent partner—though not as silent as Max would like—and a plan for Max to buy him out slowly over five years after opening.

"The whole point of me running my own business-es is because I don't want to deal with other people. Otherwise, I would have just taken any job. Now you want me to sell part of my business to a person I don't know? What if she sucks? How will I fire her if she's the fucking owner?"

Adam sighed. "Look, I know why you're doing this, and I know how much of a controlling freak you are. But the financial pressures are mounting. We need to open in six weeks. Delaying will cost too much. Our margins are razor thin as it is. She can take some financial pressure off."

"And she'll keep all the brewery revenue."

Adam reached into his pocket, pulled out a folded paper, and handed it to Max. "I had my guy run the numbers. We'll come out on top if she takes over the brewery."

"You ran numbers without me?" he asked, taking the paper.

"Well, I know how much you like numbers, and we're running out of time."

Max unfolded the sheet and looked through the lines.

"She could come for a month to get the place off the ground. We'll get her beer recipes, and the quality she can offer, not to mention all the systems in place for her staff. And she'll get to go back to live in the Arctic like she apparently likes."

Max sighed, annoyed that the numbers actually looked good. Maybe it wasn't as bad an idea as he'd thought.

Adam kept his pitch rolling. "You can be supervisor of the brewery and overlook things once she's gone so you won't be completely losing control over it. You can make sure it's still running the way you want."

"I hate it."

"Why don't we discuss it with her and see if she would be interested? Maybe she'll say no, and then we'll have no choice but to pick from your spreadsheet. Unless you'd rather have one of those guys?"

Max glanced at the list, disgusted. "Maybe I can find more brewers to interview."

"Look, there's a reason all the brewers we interviewed sucked. It's because brewmasters who are really talented and hardworking open their own breweries."

He definitely had a good point there.

"We got lucky with Willow because she's stuck. She can't open her own place in Churchill. If she was from here, she'd have already opened her own place and been our competition. It's better to have her on our side."

Max rolled his neck. "I still fucking hate this."

Adam shrugged. "I think she'll do even better if she has some skin in the game."

Max went through the paper as Adam waited. It would be nice to have some financial pressure off. He hadn't planned to go so deep into debt renovating the place. He had wanted to open as it originally was, and slowly, as their margins increased and they turned a profit, update things. But Adam thought bigger and had convinced him to open fresh with a place that would attract a good crowd.

Maybe selling the brewery to someone with that much talent would be better for his pub than keeping the brewery and having someone subpar making beer.

"Fine."

"Fine?"

"Yeah," Max said. "Make the offer. Maybe she won't accept."

"I think you need to make the call."

Max's eyebrows shot up. "Yeah, that's an even better plan. She probably won't even answer."

Adam rolled his eyes. "I've been wondering if her hatred toward you is one reason she said no. Maybe if you called and made amends, she'd agree. Just try to be nice."

"Nice?"

"Yeah," he said as he stood. He made his way across the office to the door. "Just remember to smile while you talk to her. People can sense smiles over the phone."

Max glared at Adam as he laughed and walked off.

He looked at his phone, then dropped his head. This was going to be a fucking disaster.

FIVE

"What are you doing?"

Willow nearly jumped out of her skin at the sound of Doug's voice behind her. She quickly covered the doodle she'd drawn of a bunny with a fatal gunshot wound in its head in her worn out old notebook.

"Nothing," she said, hopping up from her stool and following him to the metal table in the back of the brewery, where he sat most days keeping up on the bookkeeping and whatever else he did.

Honestly, he did little around the place anymore. Willow had been running the place for the last few years. Yet she still made the same amount she always had while he raked in more and more every year.

She shook her head. At least there were some advantages. He knew not to piss her off, because he needed her too badly. Also, she took time off whenever she wanted.

It would be nice if he'd let her experiment a little more with new beers, though.

"Doug," she said, placing her notebook on the table where he'd just sat.

He looked at it, then up at her, already knowing what she was going to ask. "No."

"Oh, come on," she said, flipping it open. "I made this one at home in my test tank. It's a triple IPA, and everyone loved it, and we already have the perfect hops in the storeroom for it."

"You're brewing the pilsner today," he said, staring down at his phone.

"It's so boring."

"Boring makes money. Make the pilsner."

She scowled at him. "You used to be cool."

"You try being cool with two sons away at university."

She stayed where she was, wondering whether there was anything she could say to make him change his mind, but she already knew the answer. He was all about the bottom line. He didn't care about trying new things, making something unique or interesting; he just wanted to make his "bread and butter" beer that he knew would sell, and sell well.

"Why are you looking at me like that, Willow?"

"I'm bored."

He set his phone down, met her eye. "Look, you've been incredibly helpful in improving our recipes. But our locals want the pilsner, and the ale, and the lager. I already let you have four beers a year, one per quarter, and yes, they do well with the tourists. But the locals don't want Hazy Mango Triple India Pale Ale, or whatever the hell you have written in that book. What you brew at home on your own is up to you, but when you're here, you need to be making what I tell you. If you can't do that, then . . ."

Willow rolled her eyes. "Fine."

"So, you're going to . . ." He waited, looking over the rim of his reading glasses at her.

"Make the fucking pilsner."

He smiled before turning back to his phone. "Good."

She turned and walked through the old brewery toward the mash tun to get started. When she'd first walked into Tipped Canoe as a naive nineteen-year-old, she thought the place was incredible. Her creativity went wild, and she wanted to make every different beer there ever was. But Doug had quickly shot that dream down, and she ended up in a routine where she'd make what she was told until she wanted to rip her hair out. Then she'd beg him to let her try something new.

Until she got that phone call from Keller's Pub.

She wondered what it would be like to work for Max. He was probably just as controlling and small-minded as Doug. Maybe worse.

She glanced over her shoulder at Doug, then back at her mash tun. Max was significantly easier on the eyes, at least.

Not that it mattered. But it was hard not to notice.

She wondered what beer they would brew first. She'd have made something awesome and unique. Maybe something that appealed to locals but also felt like something you'd drink on a tropical vacation to go with the greenhouse vibes in that taproom. God, she wished she was in that stunning brewery instead of this one.

She checked over the tun, making sure it was sanitized, then took her malted barley to the crusher to get it in a finer crush. She could do these steps in her sleep at this point.

She'd just turned it on when she felt her phone vibrate. She pulled it from her pocket and didn't recognize the caller.

But it was a 905 number, and she remembered that was from Mapleton.

"Hello?"

"Hi."

The deep voice skated through her ear and vibrated down to her spine, the same way it had when she'd first heard it, leaving no doubt in her mind who it was.

"It's Max. From Keller's. In Mapleton."

"Yeah, I know," she said with a breathy exhale. She mentally slapped herself.

"How do you know?"

She cringed, thankful he hadn't tried to video call her. "I guess I recognized the grumpy timbre of your voice."

"Grumpy?" he asked. "I have a smile on my face. I was told you'd pick up on that."

What?

She let out an exhale that was dangerously close to a laugh. "Are you fake smiling?"

"Yes," he said in an overbright, definitely fake way.

She held in a laugh. "Do you ever genuinely smile?"

"Occasionally."

Willow raised an eyebrow in disbelief as she shook her head. "When was the last time you genuinely smiled?"

"Three days ago. I was watching an episode of *Friends* with my pathetically heartbroken sister."

Willow paused, trying to wrap her mind around the idea of him smiling. Not to mention how unexpected it was to hear him say something personal. She'd figured he was a firmly closed book.

"Was it when Ross and Rachel broke up? Did that just warm your bitter heart?"

Max grumbled, and it sounded dangerously close to a chuckle. "That's more on brand for me than the truth, so let's go with that."

Willow laughed loud, then looked back at where Doug still sat staring at his phone, not paying any attention to her, thank God. "No, be honest. What part was it?"

Max's breathy sigh sent shivers over her skin. "It was when Rachel and Chandler ate cheesecake off the hallway floor."

Willow laughed. "I remember that part. I love that episode."

Silence.

"Same."

More silence.

Awkwardness settled on her. The conversation felt . . . intimate. And wrong. If Shane knew she was talking on the phone with a guy that looked like Max, and laughing, and feeling spinal shivers, he'd lose his shit. Despite that, she silently hoped he'd keep talking so she could bask in the cadence of his voice in her ear.

But she encountered a never-ending silence instead.

"So," she said, hoping to break the tension. "Did you call just to chat, or . . . ?"

Max cleared his throat. "No. I wanted to discuss a new offer with you."

Willow's smile dropped as her heart sank like a stone. She looked around until her eyes landed on her notebook filled with dreams that would never materialize. She wanted to get over it, not revisit it.

"I'm not—"

"Just hear me out," he said before pausing for an eternity. "Please?"

It couldn't hurt just to hear what he had to say, could it?

She blew out a breath. "Okay."

SIX

Max's ear filled with Willow's breathy sigh as she said, "Okay."

An image of her from their interview filled his mind. Her sharp, mossy eyes piercing him the second she'd walked into the pub. God, she was a pain in the ass.

A beautiful pain in the ass.

It probably wasn't helping the situation that there was nothing he loved more than a good pain in the ass.

He lounged back in his office chair and crossed an ankle over his knee as a smirk pulled at his lips. "So that's how I get you to listen? Say *please*?"

"Ugh," she said in a haughty little tone, and his smirk morphed into a smile. "Yes, Max." His nerves flared as she drew out the x in his name. "Polite manners get a polite response. Is this your first time interacting with humans?"

Why did an image of her dressed as a school-teacher and smacking his hands with a ruler come to mind?

A movement caught the corner of his eye, and he turned to find Cara standing in the doorway, staring at him in shock with her jaw unhinged.

"Are you . . . smiling?" she asked.

He rolled his eyes and shooed her away, but she didn't move.

"Just a minute," he said to Willow, then muted the phone as she asked whether he needed time to compute.

He fought a smile as he got up and walked to the door.

"Who's on the phone?" Cara asked with her arms crossed and a gotcha look on her face.

He closed the door without a word, locked it for good measure, then went back to his desk and took Willow off Mute.

"Computing complete. My programming won't allow me to discuss my history of human interaction."

Willow snorted. "Will it allow you to get to the point of this conversation?"

His smile doubled, and he rubbed his face, annoyed with how much he liked how sharp she was. What the hell was he thinking agreeing to this?

If the numbers worked out and it made good business sense, one could argue for selling her the brewery. But did he really know her well enough to commit to this?

No.

And now that he was talking to her alone for the first time since he'd run her off, he was realizing she was a little too . . . easy to talk to.

And way too pretty.

Funny, too.

Searching for focus, he shook his head. He'd made this decision, and he'd come this far in the conversation. He wasn't about to hang up and block her number now. Besides, that wouldn't solve his problem. He needed a brewer—a *good* brewer.

And fast.

He cleared his throat. "You're a pain in the ass. But you're also exactly what we're looking for, so we're willing to adjust our offer."

"Okaayy . . ." she drew out, waiting.

"Adam said you weren't comfortable moving, but how would you feel about buying the brewery off of me and running it from Churchill?"

That shut her up. She actually became a little too silent, and he didn't know what she was thinking. He could imagine her pretty little elfin face, brows raised, green eyes rounded. A contrast to the scowl that would've turned her porcelain skin pink.

Fuck.

This had a lot of potential to get very messy for him.

"Uh," she said.

He waited. No other words came, so he carried on.

"You could come here for a month, get the brewery off the ground, hire some workers that can do the day-to-day, then go home. I can oversee it while you're gone. It's the best of both worlds."

Dead silence.

"Hello?"

"Yeah, sorry, that just sounds . . ."

She trailed off back into silence, and he wanted to reach through the phone and snap his fingers in front of her face.

"It sounds like the best thing you've ever heard?" Max said, filling in the blanks for her. "You have to go pack? You'll be on the next flight out of that icy tundra?"

She gave a breathy, disbelieving laugh. "Actually, yes. Well . . . maybe. I'm not sure."

Max rolled his eyes. "Glad I'm potentially partnering with someone so decisive."

"Easy, Maxhole."

His eyebrows shot up. What the hell did she just say?

"Maxhole?"

"Yeah. That's what I call you. I'll need some time to think about this."

"What the fuck have I got myself into?" he muttered out loud but to himself. "Fine, Wishy-Washy-Willow. You've got two days to figure this out."

Her huff skated over the line through his ear. "I am *not* wishy-washy. You're pishy-pushy—"

"Forty-eight hours," he said, cutting her and her breathy voice off. "Starting now," he said, and hung up.

Maxhole?

He sat back in his chair, the smile on his face almost permanent now, and completely out of his control. He wondered what to even hope. That she'd say yes? Or that she'd say no?

He shrugged and opened his laptop, trying to shift his focus to work. He'd thrown the ball back to her side of the court, and it was up to her now. If she didn't get back to him in two days, he'd hire someone from his spreadsheet and forget all about her and her pretty little attitude.

SEVEN

Willow pulled a lasagna from the oven, slid in some garlic toast, and quickly tossed a Caesar salad, hoping to get dinner on the table before Shane got home so she could warm him up before dropping the bomb.

Was it wrong to bribe Shane with his favourite meal so he'd hear her out?

No.

At least, not as wrong as flirting with Max over the phone had been that morning. But it wasn't really her fault that he seemed to get a kick out of her attitude. It *was* her fault that she couldn't get his voice out of her head. The way it raked up her spine should be illegal. If the whole owning-a-pub thing didn't work out for him, he could make serious bank narrating erotic novels.

She shook off the thought. She had bigger things to worry about than sexy Max with his sexy voice. Like coming clean to her fiancé about the amount of money she'd had in a secret bank account, and how she was going to use that money to buy a brewery.

In Mapleton.

With Max.

She inwardly cringed. This was going to be tricky.

The door opened, and in walked Shane.

"Hi!" she said in an overbright tone.

He glanced at her and lifted an eyebrow.

Too much. Calm down.

"I made lasagna."

"Cool," he said, taking off his boots, dropping his lunch pail, and making his way to the fridge, same as always.

He'd always been one for routines.

She smiled as he passed her, feeling awkward and wondering whether she should give him a hug or a kiss, but he just grabbed a beer and turned toward the bathroom.

She deflated as the bathroom door closed behind him and the shower started running, wishing things were easy as they'd once been, but she shook it off. No sense dwelling. Plus, he'd feel better after he was clean and warm.

She took his lunch pail to the kitchen, finished dinner, set the table, and was sitting waiting for him by the time he came in.

"How was work?" she asked, easing in.

"Work," he said, sitting at the table next to her and shovelling the food into his mouth.

She waited, wondering whether he was going to ask her how her day was and give her an opening, but no. He looked up at her, found her staring at him, stopped chewing.

"What?" he asked.

"Um," she looked around. Where to begin? "I was hoping we could talk."

He huffed an exhausted breath out. "Fine, but you'll have to make it quick. Kyle and Nikki are coming over."

"Again?"

He stared at her.

"Okay . . ." she said, bracing herself. "I got a call today—"

"This isn't going to be about that brewery in Mapleton again, is it?"

Willow pulled in a calming breath. He was so impossible to talk to sometimes. "Well, I'm leading up to that—"

"Because I thought we were done with all that."

She waited to see whether he had anything to add before continuing. Being cut off was getting a little annoying. "I know we already decided it was a no, but that was before—"

"I'm not moving there."

"I'm not asking you to," she said back, matching the coldness in his voice.

"You're not going, either."

Willow reined in her temper. Yelling back and forth never got them anywhere. God, he could be so fucking stubborn. "Can you please just listen to me?"

He dropped his fork, put his elbows on the table, and rested his chin on his hands. "Not if you're gonna go on with this bullshit about uprooting our lives so you can risk everything on some pipe dream that you're not even capable of, no."

"Shane . . ." she said, staring to argue, then stopped as his words sunk in.

Not even capable of?

He didn't believe she could run a brewery? Not even someone else's brewery? He didn't even know yet that she wanted to own the business, and he already believed she couldn't do it.

And that's when it hit her.

He didn't believe in her. Maybe if he thought she could do it, he'd have been more open to moving to Mapleton. But he *thought* she'd fail.

What was even the point of telling him about Max's offer? He definitely wouldn't agree.

But he was so wrong.

Sure, she struggled to take control of certain situations, and she could be full of self-doubt from time to time, and the thought of firing someone was enough to send her into a panic. But those were things she could overcome.

She blinked, fighting back tears as she processed how little her fiancé believed in her and thought about all the years stretching ahead of her, going to work day after day, making Doug's pilsner and picking up Shane's lunch pail from the floor. It was as if she'd bought a one-way ticket to hell, and now that she was on the train, she couldn't get off.

What would happen in five years? Would she have kids on this train with her? Ten years?

There was no end in sight.

The brewery in Mapleton was a fucking lifeline, and she was about to pass it at full steam.

She couldn't let that happen.

"Don't cry," Shane said, the coldness in his voice still there.

It was more of an order than words of comfort, and something inside her snapped.

"What I was trying to say is that . . . Nana is sick." *Oh fuck. Here we go.* The lie came so easily, it almost scared her. As soon as the words were out, it started taking over her mind, taking on a life of its own, forming a complete fabrication that pumped the life back into her.

"Oh," he said, sitting back. "I thought you wanted to talk about the brewery."

Willow shook her head, trying to make it believable.

"Is she okay?" he asked.

Yes.

"No," she said, giving a sniff as if her nose were running.

It wasn't.

"She has . . ."

A sore throat.

"Pneumonia."

Shane sat back. "Shit. Is she in the hospital?"

Willow shook her head. "She's at home, but she needs help."

Just then, the door opened and Nikki and Kyle came in.

Fuck.

"Mmm, lasagna?" Kyle said.

Willow fought off the panic and kept her head down. What a nightmare.

"What's going on?" Nikki asked.

"Willow's nana is sick," Shane said.

Willow inwardly cringed but covered it up by pulling off the bandage and finishing this off. "I'm going to go stay with her for a while. Help with her housework and groceries and get her to her appointments, stuff like that."

"For how long?"

Willow turned to Nikki, eyebrows raised, surprised she had piped up before Shane.

"I mean, you'll be back before my wedding, right?"

She wanted to roll her eyes. Nikki was her best friend, one of her only friends, actually. She loved her and wanted nothing but the best for her, but sometimes, she could be incredibly selfish.

"Yeah, I'll be back before then."

She looked over at Shane, whose eyebrows had bunched up. He was so hard to read; she didn't know whether he was on to her lie or annoyed that she was leaving.

"When are you going to leave? You just got back."

"Next week," she said, figuring that would be enough time to tell Max yes, get the ball rolling on the paperwork and financing, and get the supplies she'd need ordered and delivered there. "I won't be able to get a flight out 'til then."

Shit. She was going to need to book a flight to Ottawa, not Toronto; otherwise, he would know she hadn't gone to Nana. And how was she going to get a hotel in Mapleton without giving a credit card? She only had joint accounts with Shane.

She'd have to get a credit card attached to her secret account. Or find somewhere that would take cash.

The thought of sneaking around filled her with a thrill she both loved and hated. She was probably just so desperate for a change of pace from her ordinary life that she didn't care that she was doing something wrong.

Besides, it wasn't *that* wrong. She would rather have caught Shane lying about having a ton of money and starting a secret business than sexting Bunny367.

"Okay, I know how much Nana means to you," Shane said.

Willow smiled. She got up and hugged him, but it was awkward, as always. They just hadn't got back to being comfortable with each other. Maybe their relationship could grow if she were happier, and starting this brewery filled her with a joy that she wasn't sure she'd ever experienced before. It also filled her with some fear and pressure, but it was still better than boredom.

She bent and picked up Barley, hugged him close. "Wanna come with me?" she asked. She'd hated leaving him behind last time, and this was going to be for weeks. Plus, she liked having him around when things got overwhelming.

"Isn't Nana allergic to Barley?" Shane asked.

Shit.

Think of something, think of something.

"I don't think you can bring him around her when she's sick with pneumonia," Shane said, misinterpreting her look of dismay. "He'll be fine here."

Willow looked at Barley, hating that she was going to walk away from him. But she'd come this far, and she couldn't think of another way out of it.

"Okay," she said, holding Barley close. "I'm just going to go call Nana, tell her the good news."

She turned and walked to her bedroom, hugging Barley tight, and knowing that all the lies and the time spent away would be worth it in the end.

EIGHT

"Have you heard anything?"

Max looked up from the bench where he was lacing up his skates. It was Thursday night, hockey night with his friends, and he needed badly to hit something.

"Not yet, but her deadline is looming."

Adam laughed. "I can't believe you gave her two days."

"I'm not fucking around with this. We need a brewer. Now. Yesterday—"

Max's phone rang from the pocket of his hockey bag next to him. He pulled his laces tight, grabbed the phone, and checked the number.

"It's her," he said.

"I'm gonna leave you alone to answer that," Adam said, then skated off.

Max stabbed the button. "Hi."

"Hi, Max?" Willow's voice came through soft, distant.

That was weird.

"Are you . . . whispering?" he asked.

"No," she whispered.

He rolled his eyes. "Why?"

"I said I'm *not* whispering."

"I know a whisper when I hear it."

"Well, if you can hear it, then it must not be a whisper," she said, getting more ruffled.

"Now you're whisper-screaming."

She huffed out an annoyed breath. "Are you always so—"

"Perceptive?"

"We're just wasting time with all this back and forth."

"If you just told me why you're whispering, we could have avoided all this."

Willow let out a noise that landed somewhere between a growl and a hiss, and Max's smile doubled. Something about pissing her off brought him great joy. Probably because she was making his life hell by refusing to take the job as it was offered. She deserved some comeuppance. And he was all too happy to deliver it.

He caught two figures standing still in his peripheral vision and turned to find Adam and Ethan staring at him, smirks on their faces.

He glared back and fixed his face, wondering how he kept getting caught enjoying himself every time he was on the phone with her.

He stood and turned his back to them. "Why are you being so cagey?"

She sucked in a breath. "I'm not, and it's none of your business."

None of his business? It was a completely valid question. Why the hell was she whispering? He checked the time. Eight o'clock at night. What were the chances she was at her other job and her boss was within earshot?

Not that great.

Before he could press and ask more questions, her whisper filled his ear.

"I'm in," she said.

Max's brows shot up. "You are?"

"Yes."

His stomach dropped out as his mind released the pressure it had been under all day. He thought he might throw up. Or sag against the wall. Or jump out of his skin at the thought of seeing her again.

He was annoyed that she was clearly keeping this a secret from someone. And keeping him in the dark about the secret.

Did it really matter, though? Probably not. His problems with the brewery were solved, at least temporarily. Even if she turned out to be completely unhinged, she could make good beer, and she'd only be there for a short time.

He sucked in a breath, and his lungs filled a little easier than the last few days.

"Good. I'll have Adam email you the details. You'll have to sort out financing on your end, and I'll see you here in about . . . a week? We're on a pretty tight schedule."

"Fine," she whispered. "Talk soon."

The call went dead, and he started shaking his head. He dropped the phone into his bag, grabbed his stick, and turned to find his entire team staring at him.

"We've got a brewer."

"Willow's in?!" Adam yelled, his smirk becoming a smile.

Max nodded.

"Thank God!"

"Yeah," he said with a frown, still not sure how to feel. She was too shifty and hard to read. "I want a clause in the contract that if she bails, the agreement will be null and voided."

Adam considered Max's words, a furrow forming on his brow.

"And," Max said, without waiting, "if she decides she wants to sell down the road, a third party assessor will fairly evaluate the brewery, and she'll sell it back to me for that price."

Adam's brows shoot up. "Anything else?"

"If I think of something, I'll let you know."

"Are you sure you're going to give her control over this?"

Max shook his head. "No," he said, then stepped onto the ice and skated off without another word.

He needed the game to start so he could hit the puck and blow off some steam. There was no point in dwelling on Willow anymore. He'd just have to wait until she got there and got to work before he could tell whether this partnership was a good idea or the worst decision he'd ever made.

NINE

After twenty hours of flights, driving, and more deception than she'd engaged in in her whole life, Willow finally saw the big blue Welcome to Mapleton sign and nearly jumped out of her skin. It had been a torturous journey—literally and figuratively.

The last week had been non-stop secret calls and emails between her, contract lawyers, financial institutions, and everyone else. Once all the funding had gone through and the purchase agreement for the brewery had been signed, then the real trouble started.

First she had to let Nana in on her secret and ask her to rent a car, since she'd need a credit card for the rental and didn't have one in only her name, which had set Nana off on a twenty-minute lecture about "growing a pair of tits and telling him the truth."

Despite her disagreeing with Willow's methods, Nana had turned out to be an awesome hype-girl and made her feel as if she *could* definitely do this. She'd rented her a car that had been waiting for her at the Ottawa airport when she arrived.

But once she got on the road, she'd quietly panicked the entire drive from Ottawa to Mapleton, second-guessing herself and wondering what the fuck she'd been thinking. Maybe Shane was right; maybe this was stupid. She'd sunk every dollar she had into this. What if it failed? She couldn't turn off the negative chatter in her mind, no matter how loud she turned up the music.

That is until she reached the Toronto traffic and found herself in survival mode.

She'd never seen so many cars and highways in her life. Or had so many near-death experiences. Once she'd made it to the Niagara QEW, and traffic calmed, and she was no longer fearful that Shane would get a knock on the door telling him his fiancée died in a car accident in Toronto and the last conversation they'd had was her lying to his face, she'd calmed down a little.

She even gained a little confidence. If she could make it through that hell, fuck, she could do just about anything.

She pulled into Keller's Pub feeling better than ever, parked her rental car in the back, and walked in. Before coming, she really should have gone to the room she'd rented for the month, unpacked, and taken a shower. And called Shane. But she just couldn't wait any longer to see her brewery.

She pulled open the back door that led into the brewery, stepped in, and nearly died. It was even better than she remembered. Her eyes landed on a set of keys on a table, and she picked them up and held them against her cheek as her eyes filled with tears and a laugh bubbled up out of her throat.

She stood frozen in place, laugh-crying until the excitement took over and she couldn't stand still anymore and started dancing around, jangling the keys. She would've danced around the whole place if a door closing behind her hadn't interrupted her.

She whipped around to find Maxhole standing in the brewery, his hands in his pockets, leaning against a table, watching her.

She straightened her shirt and tipped up her chin. "Hi."

"Hi," he said, his deep voice buzzing between them. He strolled toward her, eating up the distance in a few strides. She'd forgotten how big he was, and how menacing. His whole vibe was no-nonsense, direct, immovable. "Happy?"

She snorted a laugh. "No," she said, and he narrowed his eyes, a smirk forming on his lips.

Holy shit.

That was the first time she'd seen his mouth do something. He'd only ever had a blank, slightly angry expression on his face before.

She shook it off, looked around the room, and her excitement bubbled up again.

"This is mine," she said, touching the fermentation tank closest to her. "So is this," she said, picking up a brew valve. She could feel the need to dance start up again just as the door opened and a strikingly beautiful girl walked in with short dark hair and big doe-like brown eyes. She stopped next to Max and came up to his chin.

Willow only came up to his shoulder, at most.

"You must be Willow," she said with a warm smile. "I'm Cara, Max's sister."

Willow looked between them and could see an obvious resemblance, despite the fact that Max was robotic and Cara seemed human.

"The *Friends* fan?" Willow asked.

Cara's smile grew. "Yes, that's me," she said, glancing over at Max and giving him a pointed look as he stared blankly, not showing any sign that he had a single feeling in his whole body. "I wanted to come say hi. I've heard a lot about you."

Willow's brows shot up. "You have?" she asked, glancing at Max.

Cara nodded and was about to say something when the door behind them opened again and a short man with a round belly came walking in.

"Bonjour," he said. He came in close, took her hands in his, and kissed both her cheeks.

"This is Luis," Max said. "Our head chef. He'd like to collaborate with you on some menu pairings."

Willow smiled. "You're Québécois?"

"Oui, Montréal," he said with a nod.

"My Nana's from Québec City, but she lives in Ottawa now. I used to visit with her when I was young."

Luis smiled. "I have family there, too. Beautiful place. My kids love it, too."

"How many kids do you have?"

"Three. They're adjusting to the move well. We all love the beach here."

Willow nodded, smiling. And the guilt crept in a little. Luis moved here with his family. He didn't lie to them and take off. But maybe his wife and kids were more reasonable than Shane.

"I'm looking forward to trying your beer. Perhaps we can meet next week to discuss our menus?"

Menus. Right.

Panic set in as she looked around the room. She needed to make some beer that would sell consistently and easily, but she wanted to do this her way. The problem was that she didn't know what the best way to do it her way was.

Now she was barely making sense.

Maybe she should go take a bit of time first. Get settled before she got to work. Call Shane and tell him everything was great so she could stop the guilt from invading her mind.

"I'm gonna get going," she said, hoping the self-doubt and panic hadn't been obvious in her voice. "I need to move my stuff into my new room, get settled."

She'd heard once that procrastination was really just anxiety that you'd do an awful job. Maybe that's what she was doing, but it didn't really matter. She only had so much time, and she needed to get clear and intentional about what she was going to do. Make a brew schedule that would work, and above all else, make something that the locals would love.

But she didn't know what locals in Mapleton even liked.

In an ideal world, she would've had enough time to wander around town, try out some places, and test out a bunch of beers, but she was under the gun.

"Don't you think it would be a better idea to brew?" Max asked, making a show of looking at the fancy watch on his wrist.

Willow's heart raced. She didn't want to tell him, of all people, that she was feeling anxious or didn't know where to start, so she stayed quiet and put a scowl on her face to mirror his.

"Where are you staying?" Cara asked, breaking some tension.

She turned away from Max. "I'm renting a room at this old mansion. Monroe Manor."

"Oh, Chelsea's place?" Cara asked, glancing at Max. "I didn't know she was renting rooms."

"It's two in the afternoon. On a Tuesday," Max said, his scowl deepening, gigantic arms folding across his barrel chest.

Willow rolled her eyes. "Telling time isn't that impressive for a robot, I'm afraid."

Max's frown deepened. "We have deadlines. Soft opening in two weeks."

"Two weeks, three days," Luis added.

Max rolled his eyes. "I already booked canning. We need beer."

"Soft opening?" she asked.

"Yeah," Max said, annoyance bleeding into every word. "We're having a friends and family night where we can try everything out before the grand opening, test the menus, make sure everything works properly."

"Oh," Willow said, her mind turning. That might be the perfect time to test out beers. She could make a few batches and a poll to see what people liked the most. But which ones to make?

She turned toward the door, lost in thought.

"Don't you think it's a little irresponsible to lose more time?" Max asked, pulling her attention back to him. "You're already here."

She stared at him as her mind changed the visual of him into Doug.

Make the pilsner.

"No," she said, a smile taking over. God, it felt good to be at work and say no, and for it to actually mean something. "This is my brewery. I will decide what I brew."

Max raised an eyebrow. "I don't care *what* you brew. Just that you brew *it* before the canning company gets here. You also need to decide on can size and designs and names. There's too much to do to just walk away in the middle of a workday."

As much as she refused to admit it out loud, Max had a good point. There were a hundred billion things she needed to do. And she wanted to do them, and would do them. But first, she needed a little time to settle in. She'd likely come back later that day and get to work. It's not as if she'd be able to sleep that night, anyway.

She could explain it to him and smooth things over. That was in her nature. But Max wasn't her boss, and he was definitely the type to bulldoze a person. She wanted to set a clear boundary with him, right from the start. This was her brewery, and she would run it the way she wanted it. Not him.

She looked away from him.

"It was very nice to meet you, Luis. I look forward to collaborating with you, but it will have to wait."

Luis nodded.

"Cara," she said, getting her attention. "I like you."

Cara's natural smile doubled. "Same," she said.

"Max," she looked up at him. His eyes pierced hers, and her bravado tripped over itself a little, but she held on. "Please move."

He stayed exactly where he was, so she brushed past him, and out the door she went without another word, feeling like a million bucks.

TEN

Un–fucking–believable.

Max watched Willow walk away, her long red hair flowing behind her, and he wanted to scream. Why the fuck would she think it was a good idea to walk away?

He figured she'd get started right away. They didn't have time for whatever the fuck she was off doing. Plus, she'd already ordered and had delivered all the things she'd need. So what was this all about? And why was she being so cagey?

What was she hiding?

"I'm going to get back to work," Luis said behind him and scurried off.

At least someone was doing what they were told.

"Max?"

He blinked, trying to drain some annoyance from his features before turning to Cara. "What?"

Her eyes lit up, and the corner of her mouth lifted. "Did you think she was going to tell you she liked you, too?"

Max rolled his eyes. It was nice that Cara was finally looking more like herself, and he didn't mind if she was smiling at his expense, so long as she stopped feeling down all the time, but he just couldn't stop this nagging feeling in the back of his mind that Willow was keeping something from him.

"How long does it take to brew beer?" Cara asked.

"Two weeks, give or take."

"Well then, there's time," she said. "Besides, it *is* her brewery. If she never makes beer, that's up to her."

"We have a partnership, according to the contract. And if she doesn't hold up her end, I take over."

Cara's brows shot up. "Don't you think you're being a little too . . ."

Max stared at his sister. "A little too what?"

"A little too Max about this whole thing," she said, waving a hand in his general direction.

He narrowed his eyes. "No. I'm not being too Max, whatever that means. She needs to be working. You can't build a business without being at that business."

Cara scoffed. "That's not true. Isaac Newton was just laying around in an orchard all day and he discovered gravity. I really think this is going to be fine."

Max shook his head. "It's not just that. I don't trust her."

"Why?"

Why? Well, the whispering when he spoke to her last was the first glaring red flag. Also, she was thrilled with being there but hadn't just taken his first offer to work for him. She seemed defensive about choosing what she was going to brew, but he'd made it very clear from the start that he *wanted* her to take control of the menu. That's why he wanted to hire her, because she knew what she was doing with beer. She also just had a general demeanour that seemed very secretive. And she was fighting for control while being very indecisive.

He didn't know what to make of her.

"I don't know," he said, not sure where to even start and wondering whether he was making a bigger deal of this than he really needed to.

Cara looked upward, shaking her head. "She seems nice. And normal. Far more normal than you seem right now."

Maybe. But still. If she was staying at Monroe Manor with Chelsea, and especially Ben, he needed to know she wasn't a criminal. For reasons he could never explain, the moment he'd met Chelsea, he'd felt a sort of protectiveness toward her, same as Cara. And he wouldn't be able to rest if he was the reason some horrible person ended up murdering them all in their sleep.

"Didn't you once tell me that Paul Bernardo seemed nice and normal?" Max asked, satisfied when Cara's holier-than-thou expression dropped. He knew at some point all those useless facts she was constantly saying would pay off.

He pulled his phone out, found Adam's contact, and hit the Call button. Better to be safe than sorry.

"Max, how's it going over there?" Adam asked when he answered.

"Willow just got here. Something feels off. She said she's staying with Chelsea."

Silence. "Yes."

Max rolled his eyes. "Did you run a background check?"

"Weird," Adam said. "That's the second time I've been asked that today."

"Who else asked?"

"Natalie. She called me early this morning all hyper, just like you."

"Why?"

"Apparently, Willow asked Chelsea if she could pay her in cash. Chelsea told Natalie, who freaked out about red flags and murderous roommates, and called me."

He'd always known Natalie was smart. "And?"

"And yes, I had Uncle David run a thorough background check on her. She's squeaky clean. Not even a parking ticket. Though I imagine people don't get many parking tickets in Churchill."

"She's hiding something."

"Maybe, but she's not hiding being a murderer. I gotta go."

"Bye," Max said, hanging up, staring at his phone, wondering what the hell she was hiding.

"What did Adam say?" Cara asked.

"She asked to pay Chelsea in cash, but her background check came back clean. Maybe I should go over there and find out what the hell she's keeping from me."

Cara's eyebrows shot up. "You can't do that, Max. She's not your employee, and even if she was, she doesn't have to tell you all the details about her life. Maybe if you became her friend—"

Max rolled his eyes, turning to walk away.

"Do not go over there and yell at her!"

"I'm not."

"Then where are you going?"

"I'm going to place an ad for brewers. She needs at least one person working here, and I want to make sure it's someone hardworking and not flaky. If she drops the ball, I'll need someone ready to pick it back up. I'm not gonna let her drag all of us down."

"Okay," Cara said. "I'm going to get out of your hair. Just try to be nice to her. I think she's great."

Max shook his head. "Where are you going?"

Cara plastered on a huge smile. "None of your business."

Max watched her leave, annoyed that everyone wanted to keep him in the dark about everything. Whatever, he had more important things to do than worry about everyone else.

He had an ad to post.

ELEVEN

Willow pulled on a pair of jeans and a hoodie, then settled onto the pretty white chair at a vanity in her new room.

She'd chosen this place to rent because Chelsea seemed normal and accepted a cash deposit instead of a credit card. But she would've chosen it, anyway. It was a beautiful old house, and the room Chelsea had put her in was gorgeous.

It was the kind of bedroom she would have dreamed of growing up in if she'd allowed herself to dream as a child. Instead, she'd grown up in a broken-down apartment until her mom was too deep into her addiction to make ends meet. Then she was shipped off to Churchill to live with her dad.

She could still remember her first night in her new room at her dad's, settling onto a futon in the corner of his spare bedroom while he'd promised to order her an actual bed and some new sheets. He'd been happy that she was there. In fact, he'd wanted her to move there sooner, but her mom had refused to part with her until she had no choice.

The next day, she'd met Shane at school, and finally, after years of uncertainty and constant moving, she'd felt secure and at peace.

That is until Bunny367 came along.

Now here she was, on her own for the first time in her life, in a strange town, far from home, far from everyone she knew, and under false pretenses.

She sighed as she dragged a wet towel from her hair and ran a brush through the damp, tangled strands before giving it a quick braid. She had done everything she needed to and only had one more excuse to not get to work: Shane.

She stabbed the green button on her phone before she could change her mind, and waited while it rang, hoping he wouldn't pick up. Lying would be easier over voice mail.

Probably.

"Hey."

Shane's deep, familiar voice buzzed along the line, filling her with dread.

Shit.

"Hi," she said, trying desperately to come up with something to say that wouldn't technically be more lies. Not that it mattered at this point. She was neck deep in deceit. "I made it here."

God, what the hell was she doing?

"How's Nana?" he asked.

"She's grea— Uh, gross," she said, slapping a hand to her forehead.

Sweat trickled down the back of her neck, and she grabbed the front of her hoodie and aggressively fanned herself.

She should come clean. What would be the harm in telling him the truth now? She was already there. The lie had done what it needed to do. But he wouldn't be okay with being lied to. He'd be angry, and she might lose him, which was the very last thing on earth she wanted.

He was her everything. Had been for half her life.

"Oh," Shane said.

Willow took a deep breath and exhaled. She only had to keep this up for a while. Once he saw how successful her brewery was and how much money they were making, she would come clean, and he would forgive her.

He'd have to.

"Yeah," she said, clearing her throat. "She's coughing and hacking up phlegm, and there's snot everywhere. She's super gross."

Sorry, Nana.

"Well, it's a good thing you're there, then."

Willow flopped face first onto the bed and cringed. "Mm-hmm," she said, wanting this over. "I better get going. I'm going to make us some dinner."

"Okay, I'll talk to you soon, then."

"Love you," she said.

"You too," he said, then hung up.

She pushed her face into the pillow and let out a scream, then sat up, took a breath, and told herself to get a grip. The only way out was through, and the best way through would be to make her brewery an enormous success.

She forced herself to stand, gathered her keys and purse, and left the room. She needed to get started on her version of Doug's pilsner. A delicious, easy-to-drink ale, or maybe a smooth lager. If she could get two staples brewed tonight, they would be ready for canning in two weeks when Max said they were coming.

Ugh, Max.

She'd deal with him later.

She'd nearly descended the stairs when Chelsea and a man she'd never met before came around the corner from the kitchen and met her at the bottom.

"Willow," Chelsea said with a pretty smile. "Did you settle in?"

"Yes," she said. "It's a beautiful room. Thanks again for letting me stay."

"Of course. Can I introduce you to someone? This is Ethan. He desperately wanted to meet you."

Ethan stepped forward with his hand out and a kind smile on his face. He was tall and good looking in a geeky boy-next-door kind of way.

She took his hand with a smile. "Hi."

"Hi, it's great to meet you," he said, shaking her hand. "I'm a huge fan. Your beer is fantastic."

Willow's jaw dropped. "You're a . . . fan?"

Ethan nodded. "Actually, we met a few years ago at Tipped Canoe, but you probably don't remember. I drank about five pints of your black lager. It was so good."

A laugh burst out of her. She started feeling incredibly awkward at the idea of having a fan. Like a real live person, outside of Churchill, who cared about her beer.

"Wait," she said. "Are you the reason Adam contacted me?"

"Yeah. I've been going up to Churchill for years now, and I always bring a couple of cases of your beer back."

"Oh, what kinds?"

"Well, the black lager is my favourite. It's a perfect balance of flavours."

Willow nodded. It had taken her over a year to convince Doug to switch the hops to improve it.

"Thanks," she said.

"Your red ale is perfect, too. But if I'm being honest," he said, pushing his glasses up, "the pilsner isn't your best."

Willow's face split in two. "Thank you," she said, tossing her hands in the air. She'd never felt so vindicated in her life. "I've been trying to get my boss to change it for years. He's very stubborn."

Ethan smiled. "I'm so happy you're here. Now I can have your beer anytime. What are you planning on brewing first?"

Willow sighed. "That's the question. Tonight, I'm probably going to do a lager, maybe the black. And I think an ale. I've been working on a triple Belgian ale that's pretty good. But I'd really like to make something special for the locals. And maybe some test batches for the soft opening."

Ethan nodded. "Well, if you're looking for something that will resonate with locals, there's a peach ice cream stand in town that's been here for over sixty years. People here love it."

Willow's eyebrows shot up, and the wheels in her head started turning. "I made a milkshake IPA for a friend who loved Neapolitan ice cream once. It turned out great."

"A peach ice cream milkshake IPA?" Ethan said with a smile. "Sounds incredible."

Willow smiled, a little overwhelmed. She'd become accustomed to naysayers, not . . . fans. The word *fan* still seemed weird, but he'd said it, not her. She was on top of the world at the idea of having a fan, but it also brought pressure.

What if she made something he hated?

"Thank you," she said, turning toward the door. "I better get going. I need to . . ." She trailed off, her mind whirling so fast with all the things she needed to get done that she couldn't even finish her sentence.

"Are you going to the brewery now?" Chelsea asked, glancing at a clock on the wall. "It's getting kinda late."

"Yeah," she said, her mind everywhere else but there. "My new partner is kind of dickish, to be honest. He was ready to have a hernia when I left."

Chelsea and Ethan glanced at each other, then burst into laughter, and Willow realized what she'd done.

"Oh no," she said, feeling her cheeks flame. "You know him, don't you?"

Ethan nodded. "We've been friends since we were kids. Don't hold it against me."

Willow stopped herself from saying she didn't think Max had any friends, although she figured he probably did. People that looked like Max didn't need personalities. He could easily get by on his sexy-foreboding good looks.

She cleared her throat, wondering how to remove the foot lodged down there. "I shouldn't have called him dickish. It's just that he can be a little . . ."

"Aggressive, controlling, unbearable?" Chelsea supplied.

Willow bobbed her head up and down.

"He's not one for niceties," Ethan said. "But he's a good person."

Willow narrowed her eyes at him. "If you say so. Anyway, I better get going. Thanks for all your help."

"Anytime," Ethan said with a nod.

She turned to the door, opened it up, and found Cara standing on the porch, fist poised in the air to knock.

"Cara?"

"Hey, Willow," she said, then leaned to the side. "Hi, Chelsea, remember me?" she asked with a smile.

"Of course I do," Chelsea said. "What's up?"

"Well, I heard you rented a room to Willow, and I was wondering if you had any more rooms available."

Chelsea's brows shot up. "You want to move in?"

Willow smiled at the idea of living with Cara. She seemed so fun, and Willow had only ever lived with her mom, her dad, and then Shane. Living in a house with a bunch of girls her age seemed like something out of a movie.

"Yeah, I *need* to get out of my brother's house."

Willow snorted. "I can't imagine living with *him* is easy."

"He's impossible," Cara said. "All he does is hover over me and tell me how much he hates my ex. It's suffocat—"

Her words died as she stepped into the house and spotted Ethan.

"Oh, Ethan! Didn't see you there . . ." she said with a cringe on her face.

"Does Max know you're defecting?" Ethan asked, his eyes narrowing behind his glasses.

It seemed like Cara had more than one "brother."

Cara shuffled her feet. "Not exactly."

Ethan crossed his arms, and the three of them fell into an uncomfortable silence.

Willow felt as though she'd been dropped into a private conversation where she didn't belong, and she had an itch to get out the door. She hated how curious she was to know what they thought Max would do once he realized his little sister, whom he was clearly extremely protective of, was leaving his house.

"I better get going," she said before anyone else could say a word.

They said bye, and she left the door, forcing her mind off of her curiosity about Max, and onto the peach ice cream beer. She hoped Cara would work it all out and be her new roommate, but mostly, she felt bad that Max might put up a fight about her leaving. Hopefully, Cara would put him in his place and do what she wanted.

She smiled as she got to the car and breathed a great sigh of relief, knowing there was no one waiting at that brewery who could say no to a peach milkshake IPA.

• • • • • • • • • •

"You can do this," Willow said to her reflection in the rear-view mirror after she pulled into the parking lot and killed the engine. "You *must* do this."

She left the car and unlocked the back door to the brewery. The place had already been abandoned, and she was the only one there. She let herself in, locked the door behind her, and immediately pulled out her notebook.

All of her tried-and-true recipes were in there, including the milkshake IPA. She scanned the recipe and realized that she'd need some extra ingredients if she was going to make that peach ice cream beer. Definitely lactose to make it sweeter. Some peach fruit puree, vanilla beans, maybe some cinnamon would be nice.

She searched her purse for a pen, then the brewery, but found none, so she went off to steal one from Max's office.

Her office?

She shrugged.

Their office.

She gave a satisfied nod, made her way out of the brewery and into the hallway, then through the door to the office. She was shocked when she flicked on the light.

Max had fixed up the place, and it was perfect. Better than perfect. It was immaculate. It looked like a showroom. Everything was in its exact place, neatly organized on the desk. He'd even tucked his chair in.

Carefully moving around the desk, she reached a shelf with neatly lined-up rows of office supplies and grabbed an unopened box of pens. She ripped it open, took a pen, and placed the box back, careful to leave it exactly as she'd found it. She should leave;

it felt as if she was invading his privacy, but she just had to try out the desk chair. Just once.

She pulled out the enormous chair and sat, wondering where he'd found a chair that size. It was soft leather, comfy, and huge. The cool leather engulfed her, quickly warming up under her body. She gave it a little twirl with her feet, unable to keep the smile from her face.

A chair like that made a person feel important. Maybe that's why he was so domineering. This was his own personal kingdom, and he seemed to thrive on ruling with an iron fist. She smiled, remembering his face when she'd walked away that afternoon. He was used to telling people what to do and having them fall in line.

What would he think if she referred to this space as *theirs*? He'd probably go ballistic on her, hoping that she'd scream in terror and run back to Churchill.

Fat chance, Max. She spun in his chair, a wicked smile on her face.

You're procrastinating again.

Right.

She got up, left the room, went to the brewery, and got to work. She had beer to make for her fan. Maybe one day she'd have fans, plural.

But it wasn't just the people that would drink her beer that she needed to impress. She also needed to impress Shane, and more importantly, she needed to prove him wrong.

TWELVE

Max was standing at the stove in his kitchen, cooking an omelette, just as he had every morning for the last four years. He never tired of the same morning routine as other people did. He woke up every day at five, worked out in the home gym he'd built in his basement, then showered, dressed, and made eggs.

And he liked it that way. It was comfortable. Easy. And he didn't have to think about it, which was probably the best part about the routine. It gave his mind a chance to worry about more important things. Like finding brewery staff.

He flipped the omelette out of the pan and onto his plate, buttered his toast, and filled his coffee cup before sitting down at the table. He was just about to dig in when an email notification came through. When he looked at his phone, he found a response to the ad he had placed the day before for a brewery worker. Perfect.

His ad had actually generated a fair number of responses, which put him slightly at ease after his flaky brewer had stormed off in a huff the day before.

He quickly replied, confirming the time for an interview that morning, and gathered his things. The sooner he got to work, the better. He had about a million things to do before lunch.

"Are you leaving already?"

He spun to find Cara walking into the kitchen, headed straight for the coffeepot in her bathrobe and slippers.

"It's only six, Max."

"Some people take their careers seriously," he said with a smirk, earning himself a glare.

In truth, his little sister had always taken her schooling seriously. She'd been labelled gifted when she was in grade three and had very lofty goals for her future. Goals that she kept putting off by staying in school for so long. But he had to admit, he would be enormously proud of her when she finally finished her PhD in astrophysics.

He threw his laptop bag over his shoulder and headed for the door.

"Wait, Max," Cara said. "Can I talk to you for a minute?"

Max stopped and turned to Cara. She was standing awkwardly at the counter, staring at her feet.

"Don't look down," he said for the billionth time in her life. She was brilliant, to be sure, but unfortunately, she seemed to lack confidence. If she could somehow find that confidence, she'd be a force no one could push around, and Max would sleep much better at night.

"What is it?"

She picked her chin up the way he'd taught her to and looked him in the eye. "I'm moving out."

Max scoffed. "Like hell you are." There was no possible way he was going to allow her to move back in with that fucking guy. She shouldn't even be talking to him. Zero contact was the only way to go. "I'm gonna fucking kill that kid—"

"No," she said, shaking her head. "I'm not moving back in with Cooper. I'm renting a room at Chelsea's."

Max's face blanked. "Why?"

She shuffled around some more. "I'm really grateful you let me stay here, but I just think I need to be a little more independent."

Max cocked a brow. "Why?"

She rolled her eyes. "This is happening, Max. I'm moving out today. I won't be here when you get back."

He narrowed his eyes at her. "You're going to be living with Willow?"

Cara's face lit up, and Max had to rein in his temper. "Yeah. Not just Willow, Chelsea and Jae, too. And Natalie's next door. I think it'll be great for me to be out on my own and to have roommates my age. Besides, you like Natalie and Chelsea."

"Yeah, I *know* Natalie and Chelsea. All I know about Willow is that she's . . . secretive."

Cara rolled her eyes as she turned to fill a cup with coffee and pull a spoon from the drawer. "Maybe you should get to know her. She's your business partner now, like it or not."

Max huffed an annoyed breath.

"You seemed to like her when you were talking to her on the phone," she said, pointing at him with the spoon. "You even smiled."

Max thought back to that conversation and had to admit she was easy to talk to. But that didn't mean he wanted her to live with his sister. He supposed it was better than her moving back in with that little shit, but not much better. She should just stay at his place, where he knew she was fine and, most importantly, where she wouldn't dare bring fucking Cooper over.

Was she doing this because he was being too overbearing? Probably. As much as he hated to admit, it wasn't really his place to tell her what to do. She was an adult. And he liked she was sticking up for herself, telling him how it was going to be instead of doing what he told her to do.

Besides, how bad could Willow really be?

"Fine," he said. "But you can come back anytime you want. Night or day, you call me."

Cara nodded.

"I gotta go," he said, and she waved bye.

He got in his car and drove to the pub, eager to see when Willow would arrive for the day so he could get to the bottom of her secrecy. Maybe he was being a little too nosy before, but now that she was going to be living with his little sister, he had to know what she was hiding.

When he pulled up, the sight of her rental car already parked in the lot took him by surprise. He didn't know what he'd been expecting. Probably that she'd show up at noon, or not at all.

He walked in, and instead of going straight to his office to get started for the day, he dropped his bag on the bar and went through the connecting door that led from the tap room into the brewery.

The moment he walked in, he spotted her passed out at a table. He cleared his throat, but she didn't even twitch.

"Morning," he said a little louder than usual, hoping she'd wake up.

Again, nothing. She was like a corpse.

He came a little closer to where she sat in a chair, her folded arms resting on the table in front of her, and a pool of bright-red hair surrounding her pale, freckled face.

"Hello?" he said.

She didn't budge. Her back continued to rise and fall in gentle, peaceful breaths. He forced his eyes away, wondering when she'd got there and whether she'd actually accomplished anything or had just fallen asleep. He was on his way over to the fermentation tank when she suddenly popped up, startled.

She glanced around, caught him in the corner of her eye, and screamed.

Max rolled his eyes and waited for the ringing in his ears to stop.

"Oh God, sorry," she said, catching her breath as she pushed the hair from her face. "What time is it?"

"6:17."

"In the morning?"

Max's eyebrows narrowed. "How long have you been here?"

She ignored him, pushed herself up from the table, and dashed to the tank closest to her. She grabbed hold of the lever on the hatch and pushed but couldn't get it to budge.

When she started throwing all her weight behind it, Max took pity. He came over, reached over her head and grabbed it with one hand, then pulled, releasing it easily.

She glanced up, her eyes staring at his biceps next to her face for a moment before continuing up to his face. "Thanks," she said, then blinked those beautiful pale-green eyes away from him.

She measured something and poured it into the tank before pressing some buttons. Finally, she closed the tank and sighed against it in relief.

"Everything okay?"

She pushed her wild red hair back from her face again. "Yes. I should have put the hops in an hour ago, but it will be okay. I set an alarm, but I must've slept through it."

"Have you been here all night?"

She narrowed her eyes. "Yes."

"Why?"

"Why do you ask?"

Max threw up his hands, exasperated. "You won't even answer a simple question now?"

"I don't owe you any answers. I can come here when I want, I can brew what I want, I can leave when I want," she said, her little hands fisting before resting on her pretty hips.

God, she looked hot when she was all pissed.

He mentally slapped himself, took a deep breath, and changed direction.

"Of course you can. I'm not trying to stop you from brewing beer. Trust me, that's the last thing I want. I'm just trying to understand why you're being so secretive."

Her narrowed eyes seemed to ease a little, then her hands dropped from her hips, and her shoulders relaxed. Finally, she slumped back down in her chair.

"Sorry," she said.

His eyebrows shot up. "Sorry? For what?"

She shrugged. "For being difficult, I guess. I'm just . . . dealing with some things right now. This is all overwhelming."

He sat down next to her, then looked her over. "Do you need help?"

Her eyebrows shot up. "No, I'm okay. I have a brewing plan, so I feel better about all this," she said. "It's just . . . personal stuff."

He narrowed his eyes at her. "What kind of personal stuff? Are you doing something illegal? Are you on the lam? Are you using this place to launder dirty drug money?"

She burst into disbelieving laughter. "Launder money?"

He stared at her, eyebrow cocked.

"Max, I don't even fully understand how laundering money works."

His face relaxed as he decided she was probably telling the truth. She didn't look like a criminal as she shook her head and smiled. She looked pretty as fuck, with pink cheeks and creamy skin down her throat. Even the sleep gunk in the corner of her eye didn't lessen the effect.

"What is it, then?"

"Are you always this persistent?" she asked, rolling her neck.

He continued to stare.

"Ugh, fine. I'll tell you," she said, shaking her head. "It's not even that big a deal."

He crossed his arms, waiting, trying to suppress his smile as she threw all that attitude his way.

He should probably try to figure out why that did it for him. Something about a woman who was smart and strong and challenging was incredibly attractive to him. It always had been.

"I lied to my fiancé and told him I was going to Ottawa to look after my Nana, but I came here instead."

Fiancé?

She was engaged?

Fuck.

He liked it better when she was a drug lord.

He ran a hand through his hair, annoyed with himself for being disappointed, and tried to focus on the issue. "Why didn't you just tell him?"

"I tried to, but he doesn't want to leave Churchill."

Max shook his head. "Okay, but why didn't you tell him about buying it?"

"He kinda shut it down before I could even explain. I don't want to . . . lose him."

Max stared, trying to make this person match up with what he knew of her. She was so sharp with him. He never would have imagined she'd sneak around and lie just to spare some feelings.

"You don't want to lose someone who doesn't care about you?"

Her eyes shot up at him, horrified. "There you go being a Maxhole again. He loves me, and I love him. We've been together forever."

Max gave his head a shake. What she did with her personal life wasn't his business, but this seemed really messed up. At least her story checked out; the paying in cash and whispering. He hated she was a liar, but at least he didn't get the sense she was lying to him. Still, didn't that make it even worse?

"He's going to find out."

"I'll tell him, eventually, once the brewery is up and running successfully and he can't naysay me anymore."

Max shook his head. He told himself to take a step back, keep his distance, but one other question hung over his head, and as much as he tried to let it go, he couldn't.

"How did you pay for it without him knowing?"

Her shoulders slumped forward. "I got an insurance payout when my mom died. He didn't know about it."

"How long ago?"

"Ten years ago."

Max nodded. "I'm sorry about your mom."

"Thanks."

"Is your Nana actually sick? Please don't tell me you abandoned her when she needed you."

Willow's head tipped to the side as she assessed him. "She just has a little cold. She's fine."

Max nodded. "Fine."

She looked up at him with raised eyebrows, looking nervous.

"What?" he asked.

"That's all?"

Max looked around, then shrugged. "What the hell else is there?"

"You're not going to yell at me? Call me a liar, tell me I'm a horrible person?"

Max narrowed his eyes. "Seems like you get enough of that from your guy already. I think you handled the whole thing badly, but I'm not going to judge you for doing what you needed to do."

She looked down, lost in thought.

"Just don't lie to me, and we're cool," he said.

She looked up at him with a nod. "Just out of curiosity, how would you have handled it?"

"I'd have looked that fucker in the eye and said, 'I'm out. We're done,' and then I would have left."

Her eyes widened. "Have you ever been in a long-term relationship before?"

"No."

A notification pinged, and he remembered about the interview he'd set up.

"We have a guy coming in at ten for an interview. He has some experience at a brewery two towns over. You need help in here. And we need someone reliable once you're gone."

She nodded. "Right. Good."

He turned and walked out, annoyed that she was getting under his skin. He wished he could get a hold of that dick she was engaged to and force him to treat her better. The guy seemed like a toxic asshole. But it wasn't his place.

He shook his head and silently reminded himself that she was not his problem. She was only a business partner. Someone who could make beer that would sell.

And he had much more important things to focus on.

· · · · ●· ●· ● ● · · ·

The door to Max's office opened, and Willow sauntered in and fell into the chair across the desk from him. It had been a few hours since he'd found her sleeping in the brewery, and she looked rundown. Why she hadn't just worked during the day like a normal person was way beyond him.

He looked at his watch. Ten minutes to ten. At least she was early for the interview. Maybe she wanted to go over the resume, talk about what kind of experience they were looking for.

"You did a lot of work in here since my interview," she said, ending on an enormous yawn that made her eyes close and her nose crinkle. "Thanks for fixing up our office."

Max's train of thought skidded to a halt.

Did she just say . . . ?

"Our?"

She crossed her arms on the desk in front of her and placed her cheek against them. She could barely keep her eyes open, but she had a small smile tugging at the corner of her mouth. "Mm-hmm," she said. "Ours."

He wanted to be annoyed, even waited for the feeling to bubble up, but it never came. "You were in here last night."

"How'd you know?" she asked, looking up at him with squinted eyes. "Do you have security cameras in here?"

"Pen box," he said, pointing with his thumb over his shoulder to the shelf along the back wall. "You opened it like a raccoon."

She looked over his shoulder, and he knew when her eyes landed on the ragged box because they brightened and her smile doubled. She was pretty even when she was tired, with her heavy eyelids and pink cheeks.

He shook it off, annoyed at how attractive she was, but even more annoyed at himself. He should hate that she'd been in there, rummaging around and making a mess of his space. But he didn't. It had actually made him laugh that morning when he'd walked in and seen it. Why would anyone open a box like that?

"Have you ever shared an office with someone before?" she asked.

"Yes."

"Someone that wasn't as organized as you?"

He thought back. "No."

"Is this the first business you've started?"

"No."

"Other pubs?"

"No."

She stared at him, waiting.

He stared back. "What?"

She rolled her eyes. "I came in here early to find out more about you. I keep fishing for more information, and you won't give it up. It's frustrating."

"I was hoping you were coming in here to find out more about the guy we're interviewing."

She shook her head. "I'll find out more about him later. It's you I want to know about."

"Why?"

She shrugged. "I feel like we've had an unfair exchange of information. I told you all about me this morning, and I think you owe me now. Are your parents still alive? It seems like it's just you and Cara."

He shook his head, reached for his mouse, and pulled up a fresh spreadsheet that he would need for their interviews. "I don't talk about my personal life to strangers."

"I'm not a stranger."

He shrugged. "Well, I don't talk about my personal life to friends, either."

"I'm not your friend."

He stopped and looked up at her. "Fine. I don't talk about my personal life to pains in my ass. Better?"

Her pretty little mouth fell open in mock offence. "I prefer to be called a business partner. And you know that you're a pain in the ass, too."

He held her stare for a moment before narrowing his eyes at her. "I wish I could fire you."

Her face split into a gorgeous smile. "Well, you can't. Tell me about your other businesses."

He checked his watch. Five minutes before the interview. "Fine," he said with a forceful exhale. "I started a consulting business as soon as I graduated."

"What kind of consulting?"

"Business consulting. Companies would hire me to sift through their overhead, find places to cut, and then cut them."

Her eyebrows shot up. "When you say 'cut them,' do you mean fire people?"

Max nodded. "People will pay good money to avoid doing their own dirty work."

"Oh," she said, leaning back in her chair. "That sounds soul-destroying."

He shrugged. *Soul-destroying* was a dramatic take, but not *that* far off. Some people were really hard to fire. "You just have to learn to compartmentalize."

A crease formed between her eyebrows. "Do you still do that?"

"Compartmentalize?"

"No," she said. "Consulting."

"No," he said. "I bought a laundromat when I had enough capital. The previous owner had established it well, and it was profitable from the start. I own three now, plus two car washes, a strip mall, and two warehouses. Those businesses *would have* bankrolled this pub, but I partnered with Adam, and he had a whole fucking vision."

Willow smiled. "It *is* beautiful."

"It's expensive," he said, still annoyed that he'd let Adam talk him into gutting the place. The pub's busy location and loyal customer base in town had been what attracted him. It would've been just fine if they took over, put in a better chef and a better brewer, and slowly upgraded as profits allowed while remaining open to the public.

What he was doing now was way too risky for his comfort zone. It made him feel as if he were on a treadmill that kept getting faster and faster and there was nothing he could do but try to keep up.

"Why laundromats and car washes?"

Max gave a shrug. "They're cash cows. Low maintenance, low overhead, and I could negotiate a good price from the previous owner because no one wants to own a laundromat. Most people want to start a glamorous business that they can brag about. They care less about their bank account and more about their ego."

"But you don't?"

He shook his head. "I don't give a shit what people think of me as long as I can take care of myself and my family."

Her pretty eyes went a little wide. "What about your parents?"

Max's face went hard with no effort. "I don't talk about that."

Silence filled the room as Willow's eyebrows shot up. He hadn't realized how easily the conversation had been going until he shot it down.

"How do you do that?" she finally asked, her eyes narrowed on him.

"Do what?"

"Shut down. It's a little scary how fast you shift."

"It's a little scary how comfortable you are with asking deeply personal questions to strangers."

"Ah," she said, pointing a finger at him. "Not strangers, remember?"

Max blinked away, glanced down at his watch, then at the door. Where the hell was this guy?

"Come on, Max," she said. "Can't be worse than a heroin-addicted mother."

He met her eyes and found no judgment there, no pity, and actually considered telling her. He'd told no one about his parents before, not even Ethan or Adam. But that was probably because they'd grown up normal, and he hadn't.

She quietly stared at him with her curious pale-green eyes. If there was anyone on earth he could tell this to, besides a therapist, it was probably her. From the sounds of it, she'd grown up just as fucked as he had. Maybe even worse. Plus, she'd be out of there soon, back to Churchill.

With a defeated shrug, he took a breath and gave her the quick-and-dirty version.

"I thought my dad was dead until he turned up when I was eight. He'd left my mom when I was a baby, but she kept sleeping with him until she wound up pregnant with Cara. When Cara was four, he left again. That time was for good. My mom had to work three jobs, so I took over Cara."

Her eyes went round. "So you were twelve?"

"Yeah," he said, pulling out his phone and checking to see whether the guy had notified him he'd be late. Opening up to Willow hadn't been as bad as he'd thought, but it still left an uncomfortable weight lodged deep in his throat.

He swept all his childhood baggage back up and shoved it in a box deep in the corner of his mind. "He should be here by now."

When Willow didn't respond, he glanced up to find her eyes full of pity. It made him recoil.

"I guess it makes sense why you're so—"

"Sorry!"

A commotion at the door cut her off, and Max was relieved he wouldn't have to hear whatever she was about to say. He stood as the guy came in, panting and sweaty, with a long, angry red scrape down the side of his face, from his temple to his jaw.

"Sorry I'm late!"

Max fought off an eye roll, already totally annoyed with this fucking guy. Max could have avoided being sucked into telling Willow about his childhood and seeing that look in her eye if he had been on time. Well, maybe. She was very persistent. She'd probably have cornered him eventually and forced him to tell her. It was probably better to rip the bandage off.

"I'm Max," he said, reaching out a hand.

"Willow."

She shook his hand next, smiling as they all took their seats.

"How do I pronounce your name?"

"It's Jer," he said. "As in Jeremiah."

Max lifted one brow as he looked down at the guy's resume, wondering why he wouldn't have put his full name on it. "You put your nickname on your resume?"

"No. Most people call me Jer, so why put Jeremiah when I'm going to ask you to call me Jer, anyway? Also, Jer isn't my nickname. My nickname is Jer-bear, but you can't call me that."

Max stared at him, wondering if they should even bother interviewing him. Jer-bear was already a no for Max. Curiosity had him glancing down at the guy, wondering what the hell he'd been thinking when he chose his outfit for this interview. He was wearing a neon purple T-shirt with a picture of a cat in a martini glass on it, acid-wash jeans he'd rolled up to show off white socks, and green Converse high-tops. He looked like a cartoon character on his way to a high school dance in 1983.

"Are you okay, Jer?" Willow asked, her voice caring and soft. "Your face is bleeding."

"Oh," he said, pressing a dirty hand to his cheek. "That's why I'm late. There was a squirrel trapped in a bird feeder on my way in. It freaked out when I tried to let it out, ran up my face to the top of my head, and jumped."

Max snorted, then schooled his smile off his face when Willow looked at him.

"Please sit down," she said. "Can you still do the interview, or should we postpone?"

Postpone? No. This guy would not be coming back. Max needed someone in there that was responsible, and serious, and capable. He'd basically be running the place once Willow left.

"I can do it now," Jer said, taking in Willow's eyes with a softened face as if he'd just fallen in love.

Max cleared his throat. "You said on your resume that you've been working at Wildwood Brewery for six months. Can you tell us about the responsibilities you've had there?"

Jer answered the question, running through a laundry list of things he took care of. Willow asked a few follow-up questions, and Max actually started wondering whether he impressed Willow. She seemed to actually like this fool.

In a last-ditch effort, Max gave him one more question. "Can you tell us how you would handle a problem on your own?"

Jer nodded, and his face took on a serious look. "Many people think you can manifest a solution to your problems, but I think that's bullshit," he said.

Okaayy.

"No, what you need to do," he continued, leaning in closer, "is raise your vibration higher so you're above the problems. That's the best way of handling a problem on your own. You gotta rise above it."

Are you fucking kidding me?

Max glanced over at Willow, who was smiling indulgently at Jer, as if he were her child in a piano recital who hadn't hit a single correct note, but she was still immensely proud of him. What the hell was happening here?

"Thanks so much for coming, Jer," Willow said.

Max sagged a little, thankful that Willow was pulling the plug on this waste of time.

"I'm worried about the squirrel scratch. You need to get to a clinic."

Jer stood, nodding, then gave Willow a hug. When he pulled back from her, he took a step toward Max, then thought better of trying to hug him, and let his arms drop to his sides. "Thanks for the interview. Sorry again that I was late."

Max fought off an eye roll. "We'll let you know."

He waited for Jer to leave, then started filling in his spreadsheet. Not that it mattered. Jer was a hard no.

"I loved him!"

Max paused, his fingers in the air above his keyboard, itching to make X's down the columns. "What?"

"He seems great. Didn't you think so?"

Max stared at Willow. Had she blacked out during that nightmare? "No. He's a court jester."

Willow's eyebrows shot up. "What?"

Max shook his head. "Jer-bear is a no. There's been a lot of interest in this position. We're moving on."

The silence that followed his statement should have sent up red flags, but Max ignored it. That is, until Willow stood and swiped Jer's resume from the desk in one fluid motion.

"Jer-bear is a yes," she said with a flip of her pretty red hair. "I'm hiring him. And I'm going home to get some rest. And I won't be in tomorrow."

It took several seconds for Max to process all that. "Wait a minute," he said, getting her to stop at the door and look at him. "What about the other interviews?"

She tipped up her chin, looked down at him over her nose, and said, "Jer and I will interview them. You're not needed anymore."

With that, she turned and sashayed out the door, leaving Max gaping at her back, wishing for the millionth time that he could fire her ass and send her packing back to the Arctic.

Thirteen

Willow opened her eyes to a room filled with dim sunlight. It took her several disoriented minutes of staring at the bedside clock before she realized it was five in the afternoon, not morning. She'd been sleeping for . . . holy shit balls. Fourteen hours.

She sat up, reached for her phone. Before passing out, she'd told herself that she would call Shane in the morning, but she'd missed morning. By a lot. She dialed his number as she pulled her hair from its tie and reached for her brush.

"Hey."

"Hi!" she said. "I miss you."

"You too. I can't talk. I'm at work."

"Oh," she said, taken aback. He always talked on his phone at work. Maybe he was having a bad day. "Everything okay?"

"Yup."

Willow rolled her eyes. She didn't know why she expected anything different from him. He wasn't really one to talk about feelings or ask her how she was. He'd never asked her about her day. She should have been happy that he wasn't asking questions that would just force her to tell more lies, but it would be nice if he at least gave a shit about her life.

"Okay," she said, dropping her chin to her chest.

"Talk soon," he said and hung up.

She stared at the phone as the call disconnected. What the fuck was that? They hadn't talked in two days, and he just rushed her off the phone? Maybe it was unfair to expect otherwise. He would normally work all day, then come home, and they would spend some time together. If she hadn't lied and left, she'd be there with him, so the breakdown in communication was probably on her.

She shook it off, trying to focus on the positive. And there were plenty of positives to focus on. She'd called Jer and offered him the position, which he enthusiastically accepted. And she now had a proper brew schedule that she'd created before she fell asleep, as well as four test beers that she would brew on Jer's first day for the soft opening.

Everything in her work life was going along nicely, unlike her personal life. But it wasn't the end of the world that she and Shane had hit a rough spot. They'd been together long enough that this sort of thing was bound to happen. She'd get them back on track once she returned.

She fixed her hair, got dressed, brushed her teeth, and headed downstairs, where she found Cara, Chelsea, Ben, and another girl she hadn't met yet sitting at the big island in the middle of the room.

"Morning!" Cara said.

Willow laughed. "Morning, sorry I slept so long."

"You can sleep as much as you want," Chelsea said with a smile. "This is my sister Natalie. She's married to Ethan."

"Oh," Willow said, shaking Natalie's hand. "I met Ethan a couple of days ago. He gave me an idea for a beer I'm going to test out."

Natalie nodded, a wry smile on her face. "I know. He hasn't shut up about it for days."

Willow laughed. "He seems great."

"He's the best," she said with a dreamy look. Willow wondered whether her face ever did that when she spoke about Shane, but she refused to think too deeply about it.

Chelsea smiled. "Newlyweds," she said.

"Ah." Willow nodded. Maybe that was it. She needed to actually marry Shane before she felt that way about him. The thought depressed her, so she shook it off and turned to Cara.

"You must have moved in while I was sleeping," she said.

"Yup. Max said you worked through the night, so I didn't want to wake you up. He was annoyed."

Willow rolled her eyes. "Is he ever *not* annoyed?"

"Doesn't seem to be," Cara said.

"He's driving me wild," she said, turning to the cupboard for a glass and filling it with the tap. She let out an exhale, remembering what he'd told her about his childhood. "At least I understand why he's so controlling now, though. It must have been really hard for him to take on the responsibility of raising you when he was only twelve. And no offence, but your dad sounds like a huge asshole. Do you remember him at all?"

Silence fell over the group, and she took in the faces of the other women in the room and realized she'd put her foot in her mouth.

Again.

Cara stared at her in shock, her jaw nearly on the table in front of her. Chelsea's pretty smile had disappeared, and her eyebrows were sky high. And Natalie glared at her with slitted eyes, as if she were inspecting her under a microscope.

"Sorry," Willow said. "I didn't mean to get so personal."

Silence continued, making Willow shift between her feet. It hadn't been that bad, had it? Maybe she just felt more at ease talking about shitty parents than everyone else.

"He told you about our dad?"

Willow met Cara's eyes and realized that she wasn't offended. She was shocked.

"Yes."

"Holy shit," she said, sitting back in her chair. "He's never even told *me* about our parents."

Willow shuffled her feet, feeling incredibly awkward about the whole situation. "Well, if it makes you feel better, I forced him," she said. "Maybe I shouldn't have."

Natalie raised an eyebrow, then gave a quick glance to Chelsea and Cara before zeroing her sharp gaze on Willow. "Max wouldn't do anything he didn't want to do, even if you tied him down and peeled back his fingernails. You didn't force him."

She looked over at Cara. "What did he tell you about your parents?"

She shook her head. "When I was younger, he'd say our dad wasn't worth talking about and that I should forget about him. He's always been very good at controlling his emotions. Probably a little too good at it."

"So, he was, like, a dad to you?" Chelsea asked.

Cara nodded. "He was at all my math tournaments and space science competitions. He even taught me how to throw a punch. Now he just lectures me about Cooper."

"Is Cooper the reason you were heartbroken and watching *Friends*?" Willow asked.

"Yeah," she said, looking down.

"What happened?" Natalie asked.

Cara blew out a tortured breath, making Willow's heart squeeze. She knew how hard breakups could be.

"Why don't we all go out for dinner?" Willow asked. "You can tell us about it."

Cara perked up a little. "Really?"

Willow nodded. "Yeah. It's easier to talk when there's food and drinks and we don't have to cook. Are you guys free?" she asked Chelsea and Natalie.

Natalie nodded. "I can come, but I can't stay long. I'm leaving on tour early tomorrow."

"Adam's coming over after hockey," Chelsea said. "But Ben and I can come for a bit, too."

Willow beamed. "Perfect! Is there a good place around?"

Cara shrugged. "Well, the best place for a drink was the place Max bought. Unless you wanted beer. Their beer was disgusting."

Willow laughed. "I'm working on it."

"There's a cool dive bar two towns over with a good vibe. The Misty Moose. I think they have karaoke tonight, and I won't run into any of my friends."

"Why don't you want to see your friends?" Chelsea asked.

"Cooper kept them in the breakup. My whole life is a disaster."

Willow nodded. "I know the feeling all too well."

"Really?"

"Yes. I'll tell you about it later," she said, then looked down at her thick old jeans and flannel shirt. "Do you think I could borrow something to wear?"

Natalie nodded. "I have just the thing," she said. "As soon as I saw your hair, I thought you'd look gorgeous in purple. I have the perfect dress."

"Dress?" Willow asked, then remembered it was warm in Mapleton. "Sounds great. I was actually hoping to go shopping while I was in town. And maybe do some fun stuff, like go to a concert or something. I've never been to a concert."

Cara's smile doubled. "I don't know about a concert, but we could go see a comedy show. And I'm down for shopping anytime."

They made their way up the stairs together while Chelsea and Ben went to get ready, and Natalie ran home to change her clothes. Willow couldn't stop smiling.

It was great having other women around to have fun with. Back home, she had Nikki, but it was different. They never did anything together without Shane and Kyle.

With a shake of her head, she pulled her thoughts away from her problems back home and focused on having fun.

• • • • ● • ● • • • •

Willow walked through the crowded restaurant behind a hostess and slid into a booth, careful to keep her short skirt down. When Natalie said she had the perfect dress, she should have mentioned that it was really half a dress, and more revealing than anything Willow had ever worn in her life.

Still, the attention she got as she passed by tables made her feel pretty good. She mentally slapped herself for thinking that. It was demeaning, and she was engaged.

But she still smiled when she looked up and found a dude two tables over that nodded at her and mouthed, "Hey."

She looked away from him, down at her menu, and scanned the drinks.

"All right," Chelsea said as she unpacked some crayons for Ben and he got to work colouring his menu. "Spill it."

Cara took a deep breath, then unloaded.

She told them how a mutual friend introduced her to Cooper, and he quickly became a part of their tight-knit group. And how they moved in together so quickly because her lease was up and he insisted she move in with him. And how they'd only been together a few months before he told her he was moving in with a friend who was looking for a room-mate instead, so she had nowhere else to go and moved back in with Max.

After finishing, she chugged down half of the fish-bowl of margarita she had ordered and fought back tears.

"So, did he break up with you?" Willow asked.

Cara shrugged as she sucked on the straw. She made a huge swallow, then blew out a breath. "Not technically. I told him I was upset that he was leav-ing, and it felt like his friend was more important to him than I was. Then he called me crazy and said that maybe he didn't want to be with me at all. So I said fine and broke up with him and left."

"Ugh!" Natalie said. "What a f—" She stopped, glanced at Ben, who was staring at her, wide eyed. "Crumb bum."

Chelsea nodded. "The crumbiest bum," she said, as Ben giggled.

Cara gave Ben a smile, but after a moment, it dropped. "I don't know. He probably has a point. It all happened so fast, and he'd known his friend since they were kids. He only knew me for eighty-three days. I think I made a mistake."

Willow cocked a brow at Cara knowing the exact number of days but shook it off. "He didn't treat you well enough."

"I know, but I still love him. He was my first everything," she said, heartbreak etched on her features.

Willow's shoulders drooped. She wanted to say more, but anything she'd say at that point would be far too hypocritical.

"You're young," Natalie said. "And you're beautiful, and brilliant, and fun to be around. You'll find someone better."

Cara lifted one shoulder, then turned to Willow. "Tell me why you said you understand."

Willow gulped at her own margarita before speaking. "I took back my fiancé after I caught him sort of cheating on me," she said, glancing at Ben and wondering whether he understood what that meant, but he was far too engrossed with his colouring to be paying attention.

"Wait a minute," Cara said. "You're engaged?!"

"Yeah, his name is Shane. I lied to him about coming here," she said, dropping her head in her hands.

"Damn," Natalie said, as she sat back and sipped her drink.

"What's he like?" Chelsea asked.

"He's a typical northern guy, you know."

They all looked at each other, then back at her. "No," Natalie said.

Willow shrugged. "He's tough, into hunting, doesn't bat an eyelash when he comes face to face with a polar bear, stuffs the things he kills, and hangs them on our walls."

Chelsea pulled back, shocked. "Wow. Sounds kinda hot," she said, whispering the last word with a grin.

"He's like Gaston."

Willow's face snapped over to Ben, who was looking at her with a smile, his crayon suspended in the air.

"I didn't think you were listening, small one."

Ben giggled.

"He's always listening," Chelsea said.

"He uses antlers in his decorating, like the song," Ben said.

"We watch a lot of movies, as you can tell," Chelsea said with a flourish to her son.

Willow considered the Gaston thing, then nodded to the cute little guy. "Yeah, I guess he's like Gaston. But unlike Belle, I said yes to marrying him."

Ben's jaw dropped, and she cringed, realizing that Gaston was the villain in the story.

Natalie cleared her throat, drawing Willow's attention. "Now you're jonesing for the beast?" she asked with a smirk and a raised brow.

"Oh, God," Cara said, picking up her glass and chugging the rest of the drink as Chelsea laughed.

And then Willow finally realized what she meant. "Max?"

Natalie nodded.

"No," she said with a laugh, shaking her head. "Absolutely not."

She got three looks, all indicating her new friends thought she was full of shit.

She had to admit that Max was incredibly good looking. He had the widest shoulders she'd ever seen, and those eyes that saw so much more than anyone else. And if she was being honest, she actually kind of admired the guy. He was smart and determined, and he'd stepped up and been an amazing constant in Cara's life. She would've killed to have an older brother to look after her when her mom overdosed. She'd had her dad, but he wasn't all that present. For the most part, she had been alone.

Until she'd found Shane.

"How did he propose?" Cara asked.

Willow's eyelids dropped closed for a moment as she took a breath. "We'd broken up after I found hidden messages on his phone that were . . . you know . . ." she said, glancing at Ben.

"Not okay?" Natalie asked.

"Exactly." Willow nodded. "I was staying with a friend, and he came over, said he wanted to get back together and that we could get married, which was what I had always wanted. So I said yes, and I moved back in with him that night."

"How long ago was that?"

"Six months."

Cara placed a hand on hers. "Well, that's great, right? That's what you wanted?"

Willow looked at Cara and breathed out a deep sigh. "Yeah," she said. "That's what I wanted."

The waiter came over, dropped off their food, and they dug in while Chelsea told them about Adam getting tickets to a Leafs game for that weekend, and Natalie told them all about the tour company she worked for and tried to convince Cara and Willow to go on a tour with her.

It was great hanging out with them, but Willow couldn't shake all the feelings that it brought up. Had she been living in her little cocoon so long that she hadn't even realized that other people's relationships were way more normal than hers?

When they finished eating, Natalie and Chelsea took their bills, paid, and left, and she and Cara stayed and ordered one more round.

Which turned into two more rounds.

Then three.

Then four.

Then they lost count altogether.

FOURTEEN

"How's the pub coming along?"

Max took the beer from Ethan's outstretched hand and sat down at the patio table on Adam's back deck. There was a cool breeze coming off the dark, moonlit lake that chilled his still-sweaty skin. They'd played a late hockey game that went into overtime, and he really should have said no to a beer and got some extra work in, but he had to admit, he needed the downtime. And there was nothing better than a cold beer with his friends after a game.

"Surprisingly, everything is going well," he said, sitting back and taking a drink. "Luis's menu is great. He hired the kitchen staff, and he's been training them. We have a lead for the dining room, and I have interviews this week with the wait staff. We'll see how the soft opening goes in a couple of weeks, but I think it should be good."

"And the brewmaster? How's she doing?"

Max pushed his anger down and suppressed a grunt. "She just hired an incompetent weirdo who's starting tomorrow, but at least she finally made some fucking beer."

Antonio's eyebrows shot up. "You two aren't getting along?"

"She's a pain in the ass."

He smirked. "Are you a pain in hers?"

Max shrugged and drank again to hide the smile forming on his lips. He knew he was being a pain in her ass, too.

It was 100 percent up to her whether she hired Jer, and if the roles were reversed, he wouldn't have hesitated to tell her to go to hell and would have hired who he wanted. Honestly, he was happy she had enough gumption to stand up for herself.

He just wished she'd done that with the joker she was engaged to.

And that, he realized, was the crux of his problem with Willow.

If she wasn't as pretty or funny or talented or, most of all, easy to talk to, he wouldn't have any problem with her at all. But something about her drew him in, as if she were the perfect lure on the end of a line and he was all too happy to get hooked. In fact, he'd been ready to bite right before she told him she had a fiancé.

He took another chug from his beer.

"Chelsea and Ben love her," Adam said, sitting back.

"I love her," Ethan said, then smiled when everyone looked at him as if he'd committed a felony. "She's making a peach ice cream milkshake IPA. If it tastes even half as good as her other beer, I'll shit myself."

Max laughed at his friend with a roll of his eyes. Hopefully everyone else in town jumped on the bandwagon and fell in love with Willow's beer. Then they'd have a shot at turning a profit in a couple of years, even with the massive debt hanging over the place.

"Have Chelsea and Ben even spent any time with her?" he asked Adam. "She was sleeping when I moved Cara's stuff in."

"No. You worked her too hard," Adam said with a smirk.

Oh, if only. He'd love to work her hard. In more ways than one.

"It'll be great once you're open and we can go there for her beer after our games," Antonio said. "Not that it isn't great here. But it's getting cold."

Max nodded. "It won't be long. We're opening on time, come hell or high water."

He really had no choice. Every day they spent closed, they were losing money.

"Hey, look," Adam said, holding out his phone. "The girls went out for dinner earlier."

Max leaned forward and looked at the photo on Natalie's Instagram. His gaze immediately landed on Willow. She stood out among them with her bright hair and pale skin. Actually, there was a lot of skin. Way more skin than he normally saw. She usually wore thick flannel and denim from head to toe.

He resisted the urge to grab the phone and zoom in.

"Damn," Antonio said. "Who's that?"

Max sat back, annoyed. She was gorgeous. Obviously, she would get a lot of attention.

"She looks like Mia Wallace."

"Mia Wallace?" Max asked, looking over at Antonio.

"Yeah, from *Pulp Fiction*."

Max racked his brain. "Yeah, I know, but Uma Thurman has black hair in that movie, not red—"

Then it clicked.

He wasn't talking about Willow. He was talking about Cara.

"That is my little sister," Max said, ready to smash his bottle over Antonio's head.

"Oh," Antonio said, recoiling from Max's boiling rage. "Sorry."

Ethan and Adam snickered.

"Don't say *damn* when referring to her," he said, trying to control himself. "And stay far away."

Ethan's brows drew together. "Why?" he asked. "Antonio is better than that kid with the mullet that you hate, right?"

Max met Antonio's eye.

"Relax," Antonio said, defusing. "I wouldn't dream of going anywhere near your sister and I'm never dating again, anyway."

"Why?" Adam asked.

Antonio gave a shrug. "My divorce has completely fucked me. It's just not worth it."

Max had heard all about Antonio's fucked-up relationship when he'd first moved to Mapleton and they'd reconnected. He hoped Antonio would move on and be happy, just not with his little sister. He'd wanted to apologize for being too direct, but his phone rang in his pocket. He pulled it out and saw that Cara was calling.

"Hey—"

"Maaaaaaaaxx . . ."

He waited for Cara to continue but couldn't hear anything except distant giggling in the background. "Are you okay?"

"I'm greeaaaaate."

Max rolled his eyes. "Are you drunk?"

"I just kot picked, I pot gicked . . ."

"You got kicked?"

"YES!!"

Max pulled the phone from his ear to save his hearing from Cara's outburst.

"Who is it?" Antonio asked.

Max glared at him. "It's Cara," he said, before turning his attention back to his sister. "Where are you?"

"Misty Moose."

"In Lakewood?"

"Mmmm-hmmmmmm," she said.

"You need a ride?"

"We," she said. "We need a ride."

Max paused. "Who's *we*?" he asked, wondering whether they were all out still or whether she'd called up that fucking Cooper and gone out afterward with him. If she had, he'd leave Cooper in the gutter, where he belonged.

"Me and Willow."

Max's skin buzzed. "Stay where you are. Don't leave with anyone. I'll come get you."

"Us. Come get us."

Cara hung up, and Max rolled his eyes and stood. Then remembered he hadn't driven. Antonio had.

"Can I get a ride out to Lakewood? I have to pick up Cara."

"And Willow," Antonio said with a smile.

"You could hear her?"

"I'm pretty sure the neighbours could hear her."

Adam laughed. "At least she's not with mullet boy, right?"

"Who's mullet boy?" Antonio asked.

"This fucking guy that sort of dumped Cara. She's not taking it well."

Antonio let out a whistle as he stood. "Why haven't you killed him yet? Are you planning to do it slowly? Make it look like an accident?"

Adam and Ethan laughed, then said goodbye, and he and Antonio went to his car.

It only took them ten minutes to drive to the Misty Moose, and another minute before they spotted them. Willow was sitting on the wooden bench outside of the bar with Cara's head on her shoulder.

Max rolled down his window. "Cara!"

Willow glanced up toward the car, then shook Cara until she opened her eyes and lifted her head.

"Holy shit," Antonio said with a laugh. "They're loaded."

Willow stood and tugged down the short dress she wore that barely covered her ass, then grabbed Cara's hands and pulled her up off the bench, throwing her arm around her back and trying to walk to the car.

Max unbuckled his seatbelt. There was no way Willow could hold Cara up. Cara had at least six inches on her.

Just as he was about to open his door and help them, Cara started losing her balance and tipping to the side.

"They're going down," Antonio said, unbuckling his own belt.

Together, they started tipping, with Cara flailing around. Willow spun and grabbed her arm, but clearly didn't have the strength to pull her back, and they both fell sideways, disappearing into the bushes.

Antonio jumped out of the car, trying to contain his laughter as they jogged across the path. They arrived just as Willow was laughing and crawling out of the bushes.

She looked up at him, her eyes widening for a moment before she burst into laughter again.

"Are you hurt?" Max asked.

"No," she said, turning and pulling Cara's hand without enough strength to really help. "Your sister's a lightweight."

Max reached under Willow and pulled her up to her feet, where she swayed for a minute before righting herself. "Can you get to the car?"

Willow nodded. "Oh yeah," she said, full of bravado. "No problem." She took a single step before tipping again.

Max rolled his eyes and put a hand on her back to stop her from falling.

"Which one should I grab?" Antonio asked.

Max squeezed his eyes shut, annoyed. "Don't say *grab.*"

Antonio snorted.

He was already holding Willow up, so he put one arm around her back, the other behind her legs, and picked her up. He expected her to resist him, but she did the exact opposite. Her whole body relaxed, and she snuggled into his chest as a peaceful look took over her face.

"I'll get Cara," Antonio said, but Max barely heard him.

The shadow of Willow's lashes resting against her pretty freckled cheeks made him lost.

"So warm," she said, rubbing her cheek against his chest. "I miss Barley."

It was as if she'd just slapped him back into reality. He shook off the feeling of her in his arms.

"Barley?" he asked, letting all his feelings loose. She was too drunk to realize how annoyed and jealous he was. "Your fiancé's name is *Barley*?"

She let out a way-too-pleasant-sounding giggle. "No, Barley is my dog. My fiancé's name is—"

"Stop," he said, his words coloured with disgust. "I don't want to know."

Willow lifted her head, stared at him. "Why?"

Max shook it off. Maybe she wasn't as drunk as he thought.

"Why didn't you bring Barley with you?" he asked, trying to get the conversation on a more comfortable track.

It worked. She dropped her head back down to his chest and let her eyelids flutter closed.

"Nana's allergic."

Max raised an eyebrow. "You've spun quite a web of lies. Do you miss your fiancé?"

Willow's eyes stayed closed, but a line formed between her pretty red eyebrows. "I should, shouldn't I?"

"Yes," he said, wanting to lecture her again about how shitty her fiancé seemed, but his sister's scream grabbed his attention.

"Get away from me!"

Max swung around with Willow in his arms to find Antonio still standing next to the bushes, his hands up like a gun was pointing at him.

"People are going to think I'm trying to abduct her."

Max couldn't help the laugh that bubbled up. He would have continued enjoying the show, but Willow's eyes shot open as her head came off his chest, pulling his attention away.

"You laughed," she said, shocked.

Max rolled his eyes. "Cara!" he yelled.

"Max?" Cara said from inside the bush.

"Yeah, that's my friend. Let him help you."

He turned and started walking to the car, smiling and shaking his head. "I told her to draw attention to herself if anyone ever grabbed her."

Willow didn't respond, so he looked down at her. She was still staring at him, wide eyed.

"I've never heard you laugh before."

Max shrugged. "You're too drunk to remember it."

Willow's head moved from side to side. "I'm not that drunk," she said, then closed her eyes and dropped her cheek back down onto his chest.

He raised an eyebrow. She was obviously drunk enough to have the poor sense to cuddle into his chest, but would she remember any of this?

He decided not to read into it too much as he arrived at the car and pulled open the back door. He tried to place Willow on her feet, but she wasn't moving, so he squatted down without disturbing her and placed her gently in the back seat.

He closed the door just as Antonio arrived on the other side of the car, with Cara slung over his shoulder like a firefighter.

"You should have taught her how to drink," Antonio said as they got in the front seat and he turned on the car.

"I tried to teach her not to drink at all."

Antonio smirked. "Abstinence. Same route my overprotective parents took. Look where it got me."

Max reflected on where he'd gone wrong with Cara as Antonio drove them back to Monroe Manor. He pulled up in front, and they each picked up the girls again.

"Which room is yours?" he asked as he climbed the giant staircase.

"Fourth door on the right, across the hall from Cara," she said.

He pushed open the door, brought her to the bed, and laid her down. She rolled over until her butt was facing him, and he looked away, trying to give her some privacy. But he took off her shoes and pulled the blanket up to cover her.

He was just about to leave when a picture on the bedside table grabbed his attention. He knew he should ignore it but couldn't help himself. Bending over, he looked.

It was an old photo of her, but she looked exactly the same, just a little younger, and she was sitting on a guy's lap. Must've been the asshole fiancé. They were both smiling widely. One of his hands was on her waist, the other on her inner thigh.

That annoying jealousy started rearing its ugly head once more. It mixed with the newfound affection he had for her now that he knew how she felt in his arms and caused a rage to brew in his chest.

He opened a new mental box, labelled it Willow, and shoved all the feelings inside, then sealed it up and put it on a shelf, way, way in the back of his mind. Once it was gone, he immediately felt better about the whole thing.

But it didn't stop him from turning the photo down.

He shook his head and left the room, telling himself to get a fucking grip.

FIFTEEN

Willow gently knocked on the outside of the metal fermentation tank that Jer had been working under for the last hour. He slid from under it and glanced up at her.

"Time for a lunch break, Jer," she said. "You're working too hard."

He glanced at the colourful watch on his wrist. "It's already noon?" he asked, then rubbed his stomach. "I guess I am pretty hungry."

Willow reached out her hand to Jer, then helped pull him up from the floor. "I can't say the same," Willow said, her stomach still iffy from the hangover she'd woken up with.

They sat together at a table in the corner and Willow took a sip from her water bottle. Across from her, Jer pulled a tuna salad sandwich from his lunch pail and took a giant bite, making her stomach roll.

She couldn't remember the last time she'd been so hungover.

"I'm just going to step outside for a minute," she said, deciding that some distance between her and the smell of fish and onions would be best for everyone.

"Sounds good, boss," Jer said with a salute.

She smiled as she walked out the back door of the brewery and into the parking lot. Jer had proven to be a great worker. He'd shown up on time that morning, ready to work. And although at his last job he'd been more of an assistant, he had great taste, and she knew he was ready to take on more. Plus, he was strong enough to lift big sacks of grain while also being small enough to fit into the tanks.

But even if he wasn't, she'd still have hired him. Something about him made her feel at peace. Probably because he wore his heart on his sleeve. One glance at his face and she knew exactly how he felt.

Unlike the other men in her life.

She took a few steps before sitting down on a curb and pulling her phone out. She'd missed a call from Shane early that morning, and she'd called him back but never heard from him again. When she realized she might have paid with their credit card at the bar while being extremely drunk, she had a moment of panic, thinking that maybe he knew about her being in Mapleton. But when she checked her statement, there weren't any charges, so she assumed she'd paid cash and he still believed her lie.

She would have kicked herself had she done something so careless, but she couldn't be mad at herself for going out. Cara was so much fun. After Natalie, Chelsea, and Ben had left, Cara decided they needed a shot, then another.

Her memories after the third shot were fuzzy.

Except for when Max showed up.

Maybe she'd sobered up a little on that bench while they'd been waiting for him, or maybe he was just unforgettable, but she could clearly remember everything. How he didn't want to know Shane's name, how jealous he'd sounded, and how pleasant his chest was when a deep laugh rumbled through.

She'd passed out before he left, but she knew he was responsible for her photo being flipped down.

Unlike Jer, Max seemed to be a master at managing his emotions. But he hadn't even tried to hide them last night with her. He probably thought she was too drunk to remember and it wasn't worth the effort.

But she remembered. And worst of all, she liked it.

Like, a lot.

There was something about him being open after being so guarded. As if she'd finally broken the lock on a treasure chest and glimpsed what was inside.

She sighed, dropped her head in her hands. She knew she shouldn't be thinking about what was behind Max's firewall protection, which was why she'd avoided seeing him all day. But then she wondered whether he was doing the same.

There seemed to be a deeper connection between them. At least, there was for her. But it was probably because they were business partners now and had a vested interest in each other's success. Which automatically put them on the same team, rooting for each other. And with no one in her real life, besides Nana, even knowing about her new business, it was nice to have someone—even a grumpy someone—in her corner.

Maybe that was why she felt good when she was with him. Because they were in this together. Not because he was impossibly attractive.

She shook her head, ridding her mind of the image of him.

It would probably be a lot easier to ignore Max if she and Shane had been on the same side. But he'd somehow become more like an opponent to her than a teammate. Someone who she had to dance around because she was uncertain how he would react to things.

Max was easier to be around. She already knew how he would respond to her. Grumpily. Or sarcastically. But at least not in a mean way. She always believed actions spoke louder than words, and Max's actions were admirable. How many twelve-year-old boys would take care of their four-year-old sister?

And do such a good job of it?

Would Shane have?

She shook her head and walked back to the door, silently yelling at herself to stop comparing Max and Shane. She was engaged to Shane. She loved Shane.

Max was just some guy.

A hot-as-fuck guy, but nobody of any consequence in her life. The world was filled with attractive men, but she'd already chosen her husband, and she was content with that choice.

She pulled open the door and walked back in, and found Cara sitting with Jer, laughing and eating a chip out of the bag in front of him.

"Hey," she said.

"Hey!" Cara said, swallowing the chip. "How are you feeling?"

Willow put out a hand and tipped it from one side to the other.

Cara nodded. "Same," she said. "I would still be in bed, but I had to talk to you. And Max."

Willow raised a brow. She had to talk to both of them? Why?

She was about to ask when Max walked through the door. His eyes immediately grabbed Willow's and held. She struggled to look away until he smirked and asked, "How are you feeling?"

Willow rolled her eyes. "Excellent," she said, refusing to show weakness. "Never better."

No one bought it.

"I feel like a truck hit me," Cara said. "Why do I have all these scratches on my arms?" she asked, holding her arms out and lifting the sleeves of her jacket. Tiny red slashes covered her skin.

Willow snorted a laugh. "Rose bushes."

Cara's eyes went wide. "I was in rose bushes?"

"You remember that?" Max asked.

Willow nodded, and Max shook it off.

"You dragged Willow in with you," he said to Cara as he crossed his arms and a smile tugged the corner of his lips.

Jesus, he looked incredible with a smile. His eyes looked brighter, kinder, and his mouth looked softer.

He narrowed his eyes at her, and she realized she was staring, so she blinked back toward Cara.

"I landed on top of you, so you spared me."

"Antonio said to monitor the scratches," Max said. "Make sure they don't get infected."

Cara's eyebrows drew together. "Who's Antonio?"

Max rolled his eyes. "My friend who carried you and put you in bed. He's a doctor. You screamed at him."

"Oh God," Cara said with a cringe as she dropped her head into her hands.

"Why are you here instead of in bed, Cara?" Max asked.

"Right," she said, sitting up straight. "I got an email this morning with ticket confirmations for a comedy show tonight. Apparently, we booked tickets while we were drunk."

"Oh yeah," Willow said with a laugh, remembering Cara throwing back a shot, then declaring that she was buying tickets. Willow hadn't given it much thought, since Cara was too drunk to see clearly. She'd been peering at her screen with one eye to stop the double vision as she entered her credit card number, and Willow figured it wouldn't have gone through.

"So, what's the problem?" Max asked.

"Well, I forgot about plans I'd already made, and I can't break them," Cara said. "I was hoping you could go with Willow instead."

Max spared Willow the tiniest of glances before turning back to Cara. "What plans?"

"None of your business," she said. "Don't make Willow go alone."

Willow shook her head. "It's okay," she said, feeling like an awkward charity case. "We don't have to go."

"But you really wanted to," Cara said. "And Max never gets out. All he does is work and play hockey. He could use a laugh or two."

Max stood silent, his expression completely un-readable, leaving her wondering whether he was an-noyed with Cara for asking, considering going with her out of obligation, or genuinely wanting to go. It was impossible to tell.

It didn't really matter, but she didn't want him to go with her if he didn't want to. She looked over at Jer, who'd been silent since Max walked through the door.

"Are you busy tonight, Jer?"

She kept her eyes on Jer but could see Max's eye-brow rise out of the corner of her eye.

"Sorry, boss," he said. "I have sound bowl therapy tonight. It grounds me."

What the fuck was that?

"I'll go," Max said.

All eyes swivelled to Max, but he didn't change his expression. She was pretty sure her expression was a mix of excitement and horror.

It felt wrong. As if going to a comedy show with him was akin to cheating on Shane. She knew it wasn't. But why did it feel like that?

"Is that okay?" he asked.

Willow looked up; her eyes connected with his. He was blank, except for a slight roundness of his dark eyes that looked like concern. God, she really wanted to go with him. Which probably meant that she shouldn't, but instead of saying no, she nodded.

"Great!" Cara said. "I'll forward you the tickets. Show starts at seven."

Max gave one nod. "I'll drive. We're leaving at six."

Willow snapped out of the trance. "An hour before?"

"Six," he said, then turned and walked out the door.

Jer waited for the door to close behind Max before letting out a low whistle. "You just scored a hot date with Max," he said, waggling his eyebrows.

Willow's eyes doubled. "It's not a date."

Jer ignored her. "The way he commanded you like that," he said, fanning himself.

Willow looked away with an eye roll, her gaze landing on Cara, who was looking at her with renewed interest.

Willow shook it off. "What are your plans tonight?" she asked.

Cara looked over her shoulder at the door Max had just left through, then back. "Promise you won't tell?"

Willow and Jer nodded.

"I called Cooper last night. I really shouldn't have a phone when I'm drunk," she said, rolling her eyes. "Anyway, he wants to hang out."

Willow raised her brows. "Hang out?"

Cara smiled and nodded. "I'm hoping we can get back together. I think your story about getting engaged to Shane after breaking up inspired me to call him."

Willow's face froze. She really didn't know how to feel about that.

"Wait a minute," Jer said, shocked. "You're engaged?!"

Willow nodded. "Is it not obvious?"

"No," Jer said, a look of astonishment on his face. "I thought you were trying to reel in Max."

"Oh God," Willow said as she dropped her head in her hands. "What am I doing?"

"It's not that big a deal," Cara said. "You're just going out to a show with your business partner. You're not doing anything wrong."

"Shane would definitely disagree," Willow said in a muffled voice, her head still down.

"Well, Shane can go to hell!" Cara said.

Willow looked up at her, shocked at first, before a small smile took over. "Sometimes, it's incredibly obvious that Max raised you."

Cara smiled. "I'll take that as a compliment," she said. "I gotta go, but I'll drop some clothes off for you to wear tonight. Please don't tell Max about Cooper."

Willow nodded, and Cara headed for the door.

Jer stood, tossed out his garbage, and gave her a pat on the back. "Don't sweat it, boss. Going out with Max isn't cheating. Just because he's huge, and built, and hot, and has this sexy, scary intensity that really—"

"Jer?"

His eyes snapped out of the daze they were in. "Yeah?"

"Where are you going with this?"

"Sorry, I lost my train of thought," he said, shaking his head. "Just don't touch his dick, and you're good."

Willow smacked the sides of her face, trying to remove the image of Max taking over her brain.

"I don't think that's how cheating works," she said.

Jer shrugged. "Everyone's definition of cheating is different."

He turned to the storage area and left Willow standing alone, wondering whether Shane's definition of cheating was as loose as Jer's.

Probably.

He'd brushed off the sexting as if it were no big deal and never even truly apologized for it. He might still have been doing it, for all she knew.

Maybe she was overthinking this. It was just a show.

She shook her head, got back to work. Even if it was cheating, it wasn't nearly as bad as what Shane had done. And she desperately wanted to go to see a comedy show. She'd done nothing like that before.

She exhaled a deep breath, let it all go, and decided she deserved to have a bit of fun. Besides, she had asked Shane to move there with her and go do things together, and he said no. Did that mean *she* shouldn't allow herself to have fun?

No.

She gave a nod and decided that she *was* going to go to the show with Max. And she was going to have a great time.

And she *definitely* wouldn't go anywhere near his dick.

Sixteen

Max stepped into the comedy club and swore under his breath.

The place was fucking packed. And the only seats left were two chairs at a small round table, front and centre. They couldn't get any closer to the stage if they tried.

"Wow," Willow said, walking to the empty table. "These are great seats."

Max shook his head. "Not if you want to disappear."

She bunched her eyebrows at him. "What?"

"The best seats in the house are back there," he said, jerking a thumb over his shoulder. "We're gonna get called out by the comedian."

She laughed as she removed her jacket, and every thought in Max's brain fell away. As if the short black skirt wasn't bad enough, she was wearing a stunning red top that was tightly fitted against her body and scooped low in the front, showing off her cleavage.

She draped the jacket on the back of her chair and sat down, and he had to literally force his eyes off her as he did the same. Not staring at her all night was going to take all his strength.

He caught the eye of the waiter and waved them over, thankful when they came right away. He needed food and a good stiff drink.

"We'll take the nachos, fried pickles, a cheeseburger, and a chicken burger, and I'll have a Canadian Club on the rocks," he said, hoping the waiter was getting it all. He glanced at Willow. "What do you want to drink?"

Willow's pretty little mouth lifted into a smirk. "Just a Diet Coke for me."

The waiter left, but Willow continued staring.

"What?"

"Hungry?"

"Naw," he said with a smile. He'd worked through lunch and only had some fries from Luis about an hour before they left. He was ready to eat his fucking arm off. "They have a limited menu, so I ordered everything. We can share."

"I could have ordered for myself," she said.

He rolled his eyes. "No. I know how you operate. I'd be here all night waiting for you to decide, and I'm already starving."

She let out that little *ugh* that he liked so much just as the lights went down and the MC came onto the stage.

"Hey, everybody, how are you all doing ton— Whoa," he said, stopping on stage as his eyes landed on Max. "Can everyone see me, or have I disappeared behind this guy?" he asked, pointing at him.

Max dropped all expression from his face as the crowd, and Willow, laughed. He wanted to be more annoyed, but when he caught the sound of Willow's laughter and the way her nose crinkled a little when she smiled, he stopped caring that there was anyone else in the room. Or that they were making fun of him.

The comedian moved on as the waiter came and dropped off their drinks. Max immediately asked for another drink. A double this time.

It took a few minutes for the MC to get through warming up the crowd before the first comedian, a weirdo with a suitcase full of props, came out and began.

Willow seemed to love the guy, but he knew she had an affinity for the ridiculous, if her hiring Jer was any sign. Luckily, their food came after that, and Max ate the burger Willow didn't want in three bites. He felt a lot better and realized that the weird suitcase guy actually wasn't that bad. He'd just been too hungry to laugh.

He wrapped up his set to a roar of applause and left the stage, and the MC came out to introduce the next comedian. Max was feeling pretty good after his whisky and burger until the MC announced that the next comedian was known for his crowd work.

"Great," Max muttered under his breath.

"What's wrong?" Willow asked.

"I hate crowd work."

"What's that?"

"When the comedian makes fun of people in the crowd."

Willow pushed his arm in a friendly "Get outta here" gesture, but the contact felt good.

"You didn't like being called out for blocking everyone's view?" she asked with a smile.

Max raised an eyebrow. "No. Maybe all the short people should have sat up here."

She rolled her eyes, but before she could make her next snarky little comment, a new comedian came out onto the stage.

He spoke for a while and told jokes and stories that Max had to admit were hilarious. But once his bit was done, he started calling out people in the crowd, including a newly divorced woman with thirteen cats, and a drunk twentysomething guy who showed everyone in the crowd his favourite tattoo—a Pokémon on his ass cheek.

Max checked his watch; the show was almost over. He wouldn't be called on. He actually started relaxing, but that quickly passed.

"What about you, darling? You have a great laugh, by the way," the comedian said to Willow.

"Oh," she said, surprised. "Thanks."

"What do you do for a living?" he asked.

Willow glanced at Max, then back at the comedian. "I'm a brewmaster. I'm opening a brewery here in town."

The comedian's eyebrows shot up. "Marry me?" he said, and the crowd laughed.

Willow laughed along but shook her head. "I'm engaged."

That's when the comedian's eyes swerved to Max, and shit got incredibly awkward. "You're a lucky guy to be marrying a hot brewmaster."

Max swallowed. "Not me."

"Oh . . ." the comedian said, looking at the crowd with his eyebrows raised. "So you two are . . . ?"

Max wanted to tell the guy to fuck off, so he said nothing. But Willow locked eyes with him for a moment, then smirked before saying, "We're business partners and pains in each other's asses."

The comedian's eyebrows shot up, and he laughed. "You seem pretty close. How does your fiancé feel about the two of you hanging out?"

Willow shook her head. "Uh . . ."

She glanced over at Max, and he gave her a shrug. He was just about to lie to get them out of the awkwardness, but the comedian spoke before he could.

"You two seem to have some secret language."

"No," she said.

"Have you fucked?"

The audience roared with laughter as Max's fists bunched.

Willow shook her head, trying to keep her expression light. "No."

"But you've thought about it . . ." the comedian said, leaning in toward her, his ear moving closer as if he was waiting for her to confess.

Willow spared Max a tiny glance before she gave a shrug. "Um, maybe a little."

Max turned to look at her, to see whether she was just saying that to get the guy to back off or whether she actually meant it.

When she met his eyes, she cringed a little, then mouthed, "Sorry."

Max stared at her for a moment, trying to process the idea that she might think of him the way he'd been thinking about her. He wasn't sure whether he should be happy that she was into him or horribly disappointed that she would think of a different guy when she was engaged.

The lying to her fiancé was one thing. He could justify it, given the circumstances. But cheating? No.

"Oh, come on, buddy," the comedian said to him. "You're not really surprised, are you? I've been out here for three minutes, and I've thought about fucking you."

Max rolled his eyes as the crowd howled once again.

"They all have, too," he said.

"I have!"

"Me too!"

Max shook his head, refusing to look at the female voices coming from behind him. Mercifully, the comedian stopped, said something that Max was too distracted to process, and thanked the crowd for being so great. He walked off the stage just as the lights in the place came on, and people started filing back out of the room.

He pulled some bills from his wallet, placed them on the table, and stood.

"Sorry, Max," Willow said, putting her coat on.

Max shook his head. "Nothing to be sorry about."

They silently, awkwardly walked out the door, up the stairs, through the parking lot, and into the car. It wasn't until they were halfway back to the pub that the silence finally got to him, and he broke it.

"Were you being honest?" he asked.

She looked at him. "When?"

He rolled his eyes. "You know when."

She held onto her answer for a couple minutes before her soft voice came. "Yes."

Max's grip on the steering wheel tightened. "Why are you thinking about me like that when you're engaged to someone else?"

Willow blew out a breath. "Well, you're . . ." She gestured at him with her hand, and he couldn't help but want to stop the car and drag her into the back seat.

He'd never really felt a sexual attraction to random women. Honestly, the attention he got from the women in the crowd in there had made his skin crawl. But knowing Willow wanted him was completely different. Attention from her made him hot as fuck. Which was a total nightmare, because that meant that he liked her.

"And . . ." she added quietly, "things between Shane and me aren't really the best."

Shane.

Max tamped down the jealousy. He'd fucking hate the name Shane as long as he lived. "How so?"

She shrank down in on herself in the passenger seat, looking small, and he resisted the urge to reach over and tip her chin up, force her to feel about herself the way he felt about her.

"He kind of cheated on me."

Max's grip on the steering wheel tightened even further. "How do you 'kind of' cheat on someone?"

She huffed out a sigh. "He was having an affair with someone online. But only online. They were texting back and forth. It was pretty . . . explicit. But it was only with some random woman through text."

Max's anger built, and his head began shaking on its own from the anger.

"Why did you stay with him?"

"I left him when I first found out. But he wanted to get back together, and then he proposed."

Max stayed quiet. He knew that if he opened his mouth, he'd start yelling.

"Well, *proposed* is a strong word," she continued. "What actually happened was, he said, 'We can get married,' and I said okay."

They sat in silence for a while, Willow becoming smaller and smaller in the seat while he tried desperately to see this from her point of view. How could she agree to marry him after that?

"I'm just confused," she said, twisting to face him. It seemed as if, now that she had started opening up, there was no closing her.

"He's hard to talk to. I never know how he's going to react to things. And it's been months since we've had sex. And we never talk about it and it's so awkward and I don't know how to fix it. And you're so . . ."

Max glanced at her, still shocked about the six months thing.

"I'm so what?" he asked, refusing to let her leave him hanging like that.

"So . . . easy to talk to," she said, releasing a breath.

Max thought for a second, then gave a nod. He felt that way about her, too. "Maybe it's because we're alike."

She looked up at him as if he'd lost his mind.

"Well, okay, maybe not *alike*," he said. "But we have similar backgrounds and similar goals."

He turned into their parking lot in silence and pulled up next to her rental car, but she didn't move to leave.

"What about you, Max? Why aren't you in a relationship?" she asked.

His initial reaction was to tell her to get out, but when he looked at her, his shoulders relaxed for the first time since they'd walked into that club.

Why wasn't he in a long-term relationship? Probably because every time he got close, it always fell apart.

"I just can't seem to make it work," he said. "One thing or another goes wrong, and it all falls apart."

She nodded as if she understood what he was saying. It was likely that she did. She'd just stuck it out longer than he ever had.

"I think relationships are just really hard work," she said. "Nothing's ever perfect."

"Yeah, maybe. I just hoped that when the right person came along, things would feel easier."

Like they do with you.

He shook the thoughts from his head. He was so fucking screwed.

"Can I ask you something?" she said.

He wanted to say something sarcastic but couldn't summon it, so he nodded.

"What's your definition of cheating?"

Max thought for a moment, then shrugged. "I think it's more of a feeling than a hard definition. But if you think what you're doing is cheating, and you want to do it anyway, then you should just break up with the person you're with."

She turned contemplatively, looked out the window.

"Did you feel like coming out with me tonight was cheating?"

She stayed still for a long moment, then finally nodded.

"But you wanted to come, anyway?"

Her face turned toward him, her pretty green eyes taking on a sad look, and she gave another nod.

He stared at her, wondering why the hell she was still with that guy. He knew she was wishy-washy, but he hadn't realized it was this bad.

Willow unbuckled her seat belt, opened the door, and stepped out, then awkwardly bent back down to talk to him through the door.

"Thanks for coming with me," she said with a smile. "I had a lot of fun, except for, you know, the whole thinking-about-fucking-you thing."

Her entire face turned pink as he let out a laugh that snapped away all the tension that had grown between them.

She shook her head. "I can't believe I just said that. I'm just gonna . . . okay."

She closed the car door, turned, and walked to her car.

Max watched her leave, tortured with the jealousy and sadness that she wasn't available and probably never would be.

She obviously wanted to make it work with *Shane*, and there was no way he was going to be some guy she cheated on her fiancé with.

He swept all his feelings back up and shoved them into the box where they belonged. Now he just needed to keep them there.

SEVENTEEN

Willow thanked the mobile canning team and waited for them to leave before breaking the professional face she'd been wearing all morning with an excited scream.

"Happy?" Jer asked with a wry smile.

"You have no idea," she said, fighting back tears as she held a can in each hand as if they were her children.

The art that she and Jer had chosen from the canners was incredible, and they'd done a great job filling the cans that morning. Probably better than she could have done herself.

She grabbed the first box from the floor, went to the cooler behind the bar, and filled it with neat rows of cans.

"I can't wait for the soft opening," she said as Jer worked away mopping the floors.

"Same. Is it okay if I invite some friends?"

Willow nodded. "Of course," she said, pushing away the guilt that she didn't care that Shane wouldn't be there. She should want him there, maybe even feel sad about it. But she kind of wanted to be surrounded by people who were excited about the brewery, not naysayers who would try to find reasons why it was a stupid idea.

"Cool," Jer said. "I already told them about the peach ice cream beer we brewed. They can't wait to try it."

Willow smiled, knowing she'd be celebrating the opening with supporters. She was just as happy keeping her personal life and business life separate.

She'd just finished filling the coolers when the invoice from the canning company came through her email and killed her mood.

It wasn't because she couldn't pay but because the accounting software Max had given her was confusing as hell. She'd gone through it, watched tutorials, contacted support, but she hadn't figured it out, and she could no longer ignore it.

She'd have to either ask Max for help or buy new software that actually made sense.

She'd been avoiding him since her horribly embarrassing admission that she thought about having sex with him, so buying new software didn't seem that wild to her. She'd even priced it out. But it was way too expensive, so she resigned herself to the fact that she would need to go talk to Max.

She sucked in a deep, cleansing breath and pushed it back out. "I gotta go to the office for a while," she told Jer as she picked up her laptop and unplugged it from the wall.

He looked up from the mop with a raised brow. "Isn't Max in there?"

Willow nodded. "I won't be long."

"Good luck," he said with a shake of his head. "I went by there earlier to go to the washroom, and he was yelling at Luis."

Willow's brows shot up. "He was yelling?"

Jer nodded. "To be fair, Luis was yelling back," he said with a shrug, "so it's hard to tell what was going on."

Willow sighed. "I'm glad we don't yell," she said.

"Same. Good luck."

Jer went back to mopping as Willow braced herself to see Max for the first time in a week. She made her way to the office but found the door closed tight, so she balanced her laptop on one hand, raised her fist, and knocked on the door.

"Come in," Max said, his deep voice loud and commanding.

Ugh, he shouldn't be allowed to sound that good when he was being a dick.

She pushed open the door and stepped in as he raised his eyebrows.

"You knock now?" he asked in a hard tone, but the corner of his full mouth rose with a smirk. "I thought this was *our* office."

She shrugged, tried to look away. "Door was closed," she said.

Max sat back in his chair, rolled his neck. "I was trying to keep Luis out. He's been in here five times, raving about your wheat ale and wanting to adjust his recipe for the cabbage roll sandwich to a more expensive bun."

Willow's shoulders relaxed as she realized they were just having a heated discussion, not actually yelling at each other. "He's pretty passionate, eh?"

"He said the flavours would dance on the tongue," he said with an eye roll. "I'm guessing you're all set for the soft opening?"

Willow nodded. "Yeah, the canners already came and left. They did a great job. I just need to hook up the kegs and sort out the samples. You?"

Max nodded. "We'll be ready. Just a billion things to do between now and then," he said, raising his hands to lift off his hat and run his hands through his dark hair before putting his hat back.

She'd seen him make that move before, when he'd been stressed. It made his biceps look huge.

She glanced down at her computer. "So . . . is this a bad time?" she asked.

Max shook his head. "What do you need?"

"I can't seem to figure out this accounting software you installed. I got the invoice from the canners, but I'm stumped."

Max nodded. "I know it's complicated, but once you get the hang of it, it makes everything easier. Come here," he said, standing and pulling a chair around the desk for her to sit next to him.

She walked over, sat down, and placed her computer on the desk in front of them, watching as he clicked away on the keyboard with his long fingers.

Even his fingers looked hot. And his giant hands with the tattoos from his arms peeking out from under his long sleeves.

"You see this folder?"

She blinked up away from his hands to the screen. "Yup."

"This is where you enter accounts payable. Do you have your other invoices from the suppliers yet?"

She turned to look him in the eye. He was so close. Closer than he had been in the car, even.

She shook her head. "They haven't sent them yet."

He blinked hard and shifted his gaze back to the screen. "Uh, right," he said with a swallow. "When you get them, add them in here. Do you want me to walk you through everything else?"

"Do you have time?"

He nodded.

With an exhale, she slumped in her chair a little. "Yes please. I was afraid to ask."

He raised an eyebrow and shook his head. "You can ask me anything. And you can walk in here without knocking."

She couldn't believe how different he was from Shane. If she asked Shane even a simple question that only needed a one-word answer, he'd huff and roll his eyes and make her feel dumb.

She'd never have pegged Max as the patient type, but now that she knew him better, she realized he was incredibly patient. And kind. And caring. Just not on the surface.

She really needed to stop comparing him with Shane. No good came of that.

Just as she realized she was staring at him, not breaking eye contact, her phone rang in her pocket.

She startled, then pulled it out, sparing a glance at Max, who was now wearing a deep frown.

Nikki.

"Sorry, can this wait a minute?" she asked.

Max gave a single curt nod.

"It's my friend NikkiR," she said, feeling the need to explain that she wasn't about to take a call from her fiancé while she was with him.

God, how fucked up was that?

She shook her head and answered as she walked out of the office. "Hello?"

"Willow!" Nikki said in a burst. "Thank God you answered. I need your help."

Fine, thanks. How are you?

"Uh, what's up?"

"I need you to make a seating chart for me."

Willow froze. A seating chart? She glanced at the brewery door, then back at the office door. There was no fucking way she had time for that.

"I'll email you the list," she said, not even noticing that Willow hadn't said yes. "You know all our families and friends. You can just put people who know each other together and send it back to me."

Willow rolled her eyes.

"Um, are you sure you don't want to do that yourself?" she asked, not wanting to sound like a jerk but knowing she couldn't possibly find time in her schedule to deal with that. Guilt flooded as she thought about what she'd just said. She *was* maid of honour, which meant she should probably do these things without question.

"I can't!" Nikki yelled. "Everyone is telling me what to do with the seating plan, and it's making my head spin. I can't make everyone happy. If you do it, then I can say to my stepmom, 'Sorry, Willow is doing it, not me,' and I don't have to worry about it."

Ah, she needed a scapegoat.

"I'm actually pretty busy right now. Can't you do it and just tell them it was me?"

"No, Willow, I need . . ." She paused, as if realizing something. "Wait, what are you so busy with? You said your Nana is sick in bed and sleeps all the time."

Uh oh.

Willow swore silently to herself. Anything she said now would just be going deeper into the lie unless she came clean.

She squeezed her face together, unsure. The truth would come out eventually, and if she lied now, she'd be even deeper in this mess. She couldn't do that.

She took a deep breath, blew it out. "Um, actually, I'm not in Ottawa with Nana."

Silence.

"Where are you?"

Willow sighed, braced herself for the scream. "I'm in Mapleton."

"What!?" Nikki screamed.

"I'm so sorry, Nikki. But please, you can't tell anyone, especially not Shane and Kyle."

"Oh my God, Willow. Why are you there?"

"I bought a brewery. I'm just getting it set up, and I'm really crunched for time."

"Are you coming back?"

"Yes, of course," she said.

"Will you be back for my wedding?"

After suppressing an exasperated huff, Willow said, "yes, I'll be there for your wedding. I just don't have the time for the seating plan right now. But you can blame it all on me. I'll take your stepmom's wrath."

"Holy shit . . . Shane is going to lose it."

Willow's stomach rolled at the thought of telling Shane. "Promise me you won't tell anyone. I'm going to tell Shane soon."

"Of course I promise. I won't tell him."

An awkward silence settled on them.

"Are you mad at me?" Willow asked. "For not telling you the truth?"

"No," she said, but it was clear she was.

Willow sagged, defeated. She hated knowing that her friend was mad at her. Hated that she'd lied. She closed her eyes and dropped her chin. "I'll do your seating plan. Just email me the list."

"Really?"

Willow cringed, wondering whether there was ever a time when she'd told Nikki no. She shook off the thought and put on a fake smile. "Of course."

"Okay, thanks. I gotta go," Nikki said.

Willow's eyebrows went up. She shouldn't have been surprised that Nikki hadn't asked about the brewery, or how it was going, or anything, but it still hurt. It felt like Nikki didn't care at all.

Hell, Jer's friends seemed more excited that hers did.

"Okay," Willow said, resigned. "Bye."

"Bye," Nikki said and hung up.

Did she have any right to be upset by Nikki when she was the one who'd lied? Besides, maybe Nikki was just overwhelmed by her wedding or shocked by Willow's news and would ask her about her new business once everything calmed down.

She put her phone in her pocket and joined Max at their desk, hoping that Nikki wouldn't tell Shane before she had time to, then feeling guilty for even thinking she would. Whatever Nikki was, she wasn't untrustworthy.

She would keep Willow's secret for sure.

Eighteen

Max walked into the kitchen to find Luis barking orders at the kitchen staff as they scurried about, trying to please their boss. It was the night of the soft opening, and Luis was obviously on edge.

The dining room was filling up with all the friends and family of the staff, and thankfully, everything seemed to be going smoothly.

At least it was now.

They'd had a few glitches earlier on in the day that they had easily fixed. But that was exactly why they were having a soft opening. To find all the problems that could arise at the grand opening and deal with them.

"Luis?" he asked, approaching slowly. "Are we good?"

Luis looked up at Max and blinked, as if he hadn't seen him walk in. "Fine," he said. "Go away."

Max hesitated. Even though the kitchen was in utter chaos, he believed Luis when he said it was fine. He just didn't want to leave yet.

"Stop avoiding people," Luis said, taking a container of chopped onion from one of his cooks before shooing her away.

Max frowned.

"That's why you're in here, no? Because you don't like the crowd?"

"I didn't realize I'd hired a therapist," Max muttered.

"Out of my kitchen!"

Max headed for the door. He wasn't avoiding *people*. More like, *person*. But it was a fool's errand, because as soon as he stepped out of the kitchen, he spotted her.

She was standing at the bar with Cara and Ethan, her head tipped back in a laugh.

She always stood out in a crowd with all that shining red hair, but even more so now in the tight black dress and high heels she was wearing.

Cara had told him they were going shopping, so he'd already braced himself to see her out of her jeans and flannel again, but the sight of her still stopped his heart. They'd been avoiding each other since the comedy show. But the more he tried to stay away, the more he wanted her.

It was super fucked up.

"Max!"

He pulled his eyes off Willow's mouth and forced them onto Ethan standing next to her. He waved Max over with a look of jubilation on his face.

"Have you tried this?" he asked, handing Max a sample glass of beer as he got to the table.

"No. Is this the peach one?"

Willow smiled and nodded at him. "A peach ice cream milkshake IPA. We've named it Fuzzy Milkshake."

Max smiled at her. "Clever."

"Jer named it. He's brilliant."

Max rolled his eyes, put the glass to his lips, and drank down the hazy orange-coloured beer in one shot. His eyebrows shot up. It tasted exactly like peach ice cream.

"Wow," he said. "This is delicious."

Her pretty skin flushed a little. "Thanks."

He tried to ignore her pink cheeks and focus on how amazing her beer was. Thank God she'd taken a chance and bought the brewery. They wouldn't be able to keep this in stock.

"I'm gonna go sit with Natalie," Ethan said, excusing himself.

Willow waved to Natalie, then turned to Max. "I really like your friends."

Max nodded as he took a drink from the next sample, a dark lager that usually wasn't his favourite type of beer, but honestly, this he could drink by the keg.

"He's your biggest fan," he said with a swallow. "This one's great, too."

She chuckled, then looked around at the room full of guests. "I know. I can't believe I ever considered not doing this."

He took another sample glass of a juicy IPA, drank it down, shook his head. It was unbelievable how talented she was. "You're meant to do this."

He meant for it to come across light and complimentary. But it came out serious. Too intense.

She stared back at him for a moment, then turned her pretty head away to look at the crowd. "Are you ready for this?"

"No."

She laughed, and it hit him how happy he was that he didn't have to do this alone.

He wanted to pull out everything he'd been cramming into his mental box of feelings and unleash it. What would be so wrong about admitting he liked her? And that he thought she was great? If she was single, he wouldn't have thought twice about asking her out.

But she wasn't single. And not only that, she planned to marry the fucking guy.

Still, he had this burning need to tell her. It was weighing on him too much. He was just about to let it out when the door opened behind them.

"Boss!"

They both turned to find Jer coming from the back of the brewery.

"I need you for a minute."

"Sure," Willow said. She flashed him a smile before walking past him and following Jer.

He shook it off, looked away. Maybe this was the universe's way of telling him to fuck off and leave the beautiful engaged woman—that he was tripping all over himself for—alone. He scanned the room before his eyes found Adam's, then Chelsea's. They were staring at him from across the room, mouths agape.

Had they noticed him staring at Willow?

As his eyes narrowed, they quickly averted their gaze. He scanned the rest of the crowd, wishing he could just retreat to his office until the entire night was over. Being in crowds of people was something he truly despised.

"Max?"

"Yes?"

He spun to find Luis out of the kitchen, smiling and waving at his wife and kids, who were sitting in a booth in the corner of the dining room.

"We're all set. I'm going to send out the wait-staff—what's going on over there?"

Max turned, expecting the worst, but calmed immediately when he saw Adam on one knee in front of Chelsea.

Fuck, he hoped she'd say yes. An eternity passed before she started nodding emphatically and Adam finally stood, pulling the ring from the box and sliding it on her finger.

Luis let out a low whistle. "I can see that diamond from here."

"I bet a Martian just said the same thing," he said, getting a laugh from Luis. "Go ahead with the wait-staff."

He moved his way through the throng of people, finally giving Adam and Chelsea a hug and congratulating them, but a flash of red caught his eye. He turned to find Willow standing in the room's corner, looking a lot less jubilant than everyone else. Maybe Jer had run into some problem?

He made his way back to her, bracing himself for bad news. "Everything okay?"

She gave a solemn nod. "They seem thrilled."

He glanced across the room, then back. "I've never seen Adam happier. And I've never seen you look so down."

Willow shrugged. "I'm just in my head, I guess."

"What is it?"

Willow glanced back at everyone surrounding Chelsea and admiring her ring as she held out her hand. "I just wish . . ."

She trailed off, then her voice dropped to a whisper.

"I wish Shane had given me a ring."

Anger surged through Max's veins. That fucker had treated Willow so shitty. She deserved a ring. She deserved the entire world.

"Why did you say yes?"

She looked up at him with those sad eyes. "I wanted to say yes. I just wish he'd act like he actually wants to marry me. He never wants to set a date. He brushes me off when I try to talk about our wedding. Adam seems like he'd rearrange mountains to marry Chelsea, and I can't even get a ring."

"Are you really gonna marry that guy?"

She looked up at him, met his stare, shrugged.

"It's okay to have standards, Willow," he said. "Just because you love him doesn't mean he should stop trying. It's okay to demand more."

She gave a little smirk. "You think I should demand a ring from him?"

He shook his head. "I don't think you should demand a single thing from *him*. I think you should tell him to take a fucking hike. But from someone else, someone who treats you right, yes. Expecting a ring is pretty standard."

Her eyes went sad, and he felt like shit. He hated she was sad, but he couldn't stop the words from coming out anymore. She needed to know that she deserved more than to be let down repeatedly.

He took a deep breath and cracked open the mental box, and out poured all the emotions he'd been stopping himself from feeling.

"Willow?"

She turned to him with a shake of her head, as if she was shaking off all the disappointment she'd dealt with from her fiancé. "I don't want to talk about Shane anymore."

Max nodded. "Okay," he said, shifting his thoughts. Maybe now wasn't the best time. He'd tell her later.

"Luis is sending the food out. Do you want to eat with me?"

She smiled. "Sure. I was going to sit with Cara, but I think she's leaving soon."

Max pulled back. "Why?"

Willow rolled her eyes. "She doesn't like when you're in her business."

"Because she's up to no good?"

Willow laughed. "Come on," she said, walking to the table where Cara sat with Jer's weird friends.

He let it go, vowing to get to the bottom of it later. In the meantime, he'd try to enjoy the night, and after everyone left, and they were all alone, he would finally let Willow in on the feelings he'd been boxing up inside since their first conversation.

Nineteen

"Everyone's gone."

Willow looked up from the ballots she'd been counting to find Max strolling into the office and making the whole place close in around them. Her body reacted to the energy from him, the smell of his cologne, the sound of his voice. He sat in the chair across from her, took a swig from his beer, then nodded toward the piles of ballots on the desk.

"Any winners?"

She nodded. "Fuzzy Milkshake in a landslide. I'm going to brew a batch tomorrow."

Max smiled. "We'll push it on influencer night, get the whole town talking about it. It'll do great."

Her eyebrows rose. She wasn't used to all this praise. For the last few hours, she'd had person after person shaking her hand and telling her how great she was.

If this kept up, her ego would grow out of control.

"Thanks," she said, collecting the ballots. "It literally couldn't have gone better."

Well, besides her whole meltdown in front of Max after Adam's proposal about how messy her own engagement was. She hated how selfish she'd felt after that. She was happy for them. But no matter how hard she tried, she couldn't seem to let go of the jealousy. What would it be like to be engaged to a man who couldn't wait to marry her?

She sighed and opened her old notebook, slipped in the ballots, and wrote Fuzzy Milkshake on the blank line in her brew schedule. At least her professional life was going well.

She closed her notebook, rolled her shoulders, and found Max staring at her. "Everything okay?"

He nodded, braced his elbows on his thighs, and rested his chin on his steepled hands. "I was hoping to talk to you about us."

Her eyes widened. "Us?"

He blew out a breath, straightened in his seat. "The night we went to the comedy show, and you said you thought about me . . ."

"Yeah," she said, feeling her cheeks flame, knowing her face had gone all pink.

"I think about you that way, too," he said. His voice was deep and calm, and her stomach dropped out.

She couldn't tell whether it was nerves, or terror, or guilt. All she knew was that her body had ignited, and she'd never felt that strong a reaction to anything. Maybe ever.

"Max—"

"It's not just that," he continued. "I like being with you. I think we really click together. And, honestly, it's killing me to think you aren't getting everything you want from—"

He stopped awkwardly, midsentence, and turned his head toward the door. "Did you hear something?"

She swallowed, trying desperately to rein in the feelings swirling deep in her belly. "I feel the same, but I'm engaged, Max. And I know its—"

"Willow?"

She froze, then slowly turned toward the door.

Was that . . . No.

"Willow!"

All the blood drained from her face as she finally accepted who the familiar voice yelling her name from the dining room was.

Shane.

She snapped out of her shock and jumped from her chair, trying desperately to pull in a breath, but couldn't make her lungs work.

"That isn't . . ." Max trailed off, staring at her.

She forced air in and out while trying to smooth her dress and pull the sweater she'd bought to go with it tighter around her. God, what would he think about her in these clothes?

Not to mention the fact that she was alone there with Max.

Fuck.

She met Max's eyes for the first time, found him watching her in abject horror.

"Stay here," she said, then turned and left the office before he could insert an opinion. She closed the door behind her and forced her feet to take steps until she reached the dining room and saw him.

"Shane," she said on a shaky breath. "Hi."

He turned toward her with a shocked look on his face. She didn't know what to do or how to act. Maybe she should hug him? She hadn't seen him in weeks. She took a few steps toward him, but he put up his hand, stopping her.

"Are you fucking kidding me, Willow?"

She planted her feet, told herself to breathe. Told herself to ignore the fact that Max could hear every word.

At least he was still in their office, out of sight.

"I'm sorry, Shane. I'm so sorry."

He shook his head as his face started turning red. She'd seen him angry before, but this was next level.

"I just really felt like I had to—"

"I can not believe you did this. When Nikki told me—"

"Nikki told you?"

Her own anger blinded Willow for a moment. Nikki had promised she wouldn't tell. That was two days ago. It would have taken Shane approximately the same amount of time to buy a plane ticket and travel all this way.

"Yeah," he said, his voice terrifying. "She had a hard time lying to my fucking face, but apparently you had no problem with that."

The anger drained from her body, and she hung her head as the guilt swarmed. She was in the wrong here. Not Nikki.

"I hate that I lied to you. But maybe if you could see what I've been working on—"

Shane cut her off with a shake of his head. "This is truly the dumbest fucking thing you've ever done. How much debt did you go into for all this?"

Shit.

Willow steadied herself and shook her head. "I didn't take on any debt. I had money."

"How?"

"Please don't be mad at me," she said, squeezing her eyes shut.

"How, Willow?"

"My mom had a life insurance policy."

He took a step backwards, as if she'd slapped him.

"I got a payout when she died."

"You've been lying to me for ten years?"

She steadied herself. "Well, it's a good thing, though. Right? Because I invested—"

"Invested?"

"Yes. I had it invested with Nana's financial adviser. It grew a lot over the years."

"Until now. How much did you spend of it on this brewery?"

"All of it."

Shane started pacing the room. He was so mad now that he couldn't even stand still. "This is stupid, Willow. Really fucking stupid—"

He stopped midsentence and looked over her head. "Who the hell are you?"

Willow whipped around, found Max taking up all the space of the doorway. He had his arms crossed and a murderous glare in his eye.

Willow sighed, dropped her head. She hadn't even heard him open the door.

"Who the hell are you?" Shane repeated.

"Max."

Willow took hold of Shane's arm. "Please, just come with me to the brewery so you can see it. It's really incredible. We just had an opening, and everyone loved—"

"No," he said, shaking her off.

"Can you please just listen—"

"No. We're going home. Get your shit."

Willow stared at him in shock. She knew he had a nasty temper, but she honestly hadn't seen that coming. Did he really think that she was just going to abandon her business like that?

She glanced at Max, who was staring a hole through Shane, and remembered how he would've handled the situation but shook it off. She couldn't tell Shane to go fuck himself.

She loved him.

And she could still fix this. He'd calm down in a few days and then think more clearly about how great this could be for them.

"Shane, I can't leave right now. There's only a couple of weeks left to get everything ready to open."

Shane rapidly blinked a few times. "Come with me now, or we're done."

Her heart stopped beating. "Why?"

Shane spared a glance at Max, narrowed his eyes. "You're really asking me why?"

"Yeah, why?"

Shane glared at her. "Because you're not supposed to be here at all. You're supposed to be in Ottawa, and you lied. And who the fuck is this guy?"

How the hell was she going to explain Max, her incredibly hot business partner, to her incredibly jealous fiancé? She couldn't, so she ignored the question and tried to explain to Shane that she needed to stay there but didn't want to lose him.

"I just need more time to get this off the ground. I already have a flight booked in two weeks."

Shane gave a curt nod. "I guess this"—he gestured around the room, notably landing on Max—"is more important to you than I am. Don't bother coming home in two weeks."

"Shane, you don't mean that—"

"I mean it," he said, cutting her off. "We're finished. This is over. I could never marry someone so . . . untrustworthy."

His face fell from sadness to anger right before he turned and walked out the door, letting it slam closed behind him.

Willow stared at the door for a solid two minutes before her eyes started filling with tears. Shane was here. Now he was gone. And he felt as if she'd chosen a brewery over him.

Had she? And more importantly, had she just made the right choice, or the worst mistake of her life?

Her eyes overflowed as a wave of nausea took over. She literally had no clue.

What if he was right, and she'd just wasted all her money on a business that would never work, leaving her with no money, no brewery, and no fiancé?

Max walked past her, clicked the locks on the door into place, then turned to her. She couldn't face him, hated that he'd heard all that. It was more embarrassing than she could stand. She dropped her eyes down to the floor and covered her face with her hands as her tears soaked her palms.

TWENTY

M ax locked the deadbolt on the door, then turned to find Willow standing in the middle of the dining room, just where she had been. Her head was bent low, her face in her hands, and her body shook as tears slid down her cheeks, escaping her hands and forming little drops on the floor.

He closed the distance between them and gently placed his hands on her shoulders. "Are you okay?"

She shook her head softly and rubbed her eyes as if she could erase the scene that had just played out in front of them.

He couldn't believe anyone would speak to her like that without getting slapped across the face. He knew her only as a sharp-witted, funny, sarcastic, capable, creative woman. And he loved that woman. But that hadn't sounded like her at all.

If he'd read a transcript of that conversation instead of witnessing it with his own eyes, he'd never have believed it was Willow.

He'd wanted so badly to step between them and shield her from that, but he couldn't. It wasn't his place. He'd already pushed it enough when he'd stepped out of the office. But the tone of that fucker's voice was so abusive, he couldn't stop himself.

She should be happy he hadn't dragged Shane out of there and tossed him into the parking lot where he belonged.

Max reached under her chin, tipped her face up. It made him sick to see her like that, head hung low as if she'd done something wrong, when she'd done *nothing* wrong. It was her fucking money, and she could spend it however she wanted.

He'd known from the first word out of Shane's mouth that his anger had nothing to do with her and everything to do with his own insecurities. He was a toxic narcissist. And apparently, a master at it, if Willow's shift in demeanour was any sign.

As if on cue, her head dipped back down, even lower than before, and he couldn't stand it anymore. He pulled her against his chest, wrapped his arms around her shoulders. He wanted to offer her some comfort, but he also wanted to hide her tears so he didn't have to see them.

It was more than he could take. He knew his feelings for her were growing, but seeing her like this made him realize how much.

She tensed for a second, then melted against him, pressing her face into his chest. He tightened his arms and stayed like that for a few minutes to give her a chance to process what had happened before he asked the question that was burning inside him.

"Does he always talk to you like that?"

His voice came out garbled and tight, exposing how strangled with anger he was.

"Not always . . ." she said, her voice muffled by his shirt. "I'm so embarrassed that you saw that."

"You have nothing to be embarrassed of," he said. "All of my anger and judgment is on that guy. He's fucking horrible."

She started shaking her head. "I lied to him. This is my fault. He came all the way here. He hates flying, won't even go on vacation because he hates it so much, and he came here and found out that I lied to him."

It was extremely telling that she was worried about *his* feelings at a time like this. Not to mention the fact that he would get on a plane to come yell at her but not to go have fun with her.

Was his definition of *fun* bringing people down?

"Don't make excuses for him. He's a manipulative asshole."

She pulled away from his chest and glanced up at him with those pale eyes, looking even more green against the bloodshot red of her sclera.

He wanted to chase the guy down and break all his fingers.

"Come sit down," he said, turning and guiding her toward their office.

Once he'd settled her into the chair, he leaned back against the desk and crossed his arms. He'd almost hoped her fiancé would come back and apologize just so she could stop hating herself, but there was no sign of him. He hadn't even stuck around to make sure she was okay.

He was just gone.

Max shook his head. He probably got away with treating people so badly because he'd been doing it for so long to the same people that they were used to it.

"I'm sorry," she said, her head still down. "I didn't know he was going to come here and freak out. I thought I'd be able to go home and tell him when the timing was better."

His heart rate sped up at the thought of her going back there, and he realized in that moment how badly he wanted to protect her, shelter her, keep her there with him where she wouldn't have to feel bad about being herself.

"Don't let anyone talk to you like that, ever again," he said, going into "lecture mode," as Cara called it. But there was no controlling that, now. He was fucking livid. "If you don't have it in you to tell them to go fuck themselves, then you need to ignore them until they talk right."

"He wouldn't even listen to me."

"Exactly. So you don't fucking talk to him."

She looked up at him as if he were deranged. "I should just sit there in silence, staring at him?"

Max glared at her silently.

Her pretty eyes doubled. "I can't do that," she said, shaking her head. "I can't let silence just hang there all awkwardly."

"Yeah, because you're trying too hard to make him happy. You have no fucking problem giving me shit, so I know you have it in you."

"It's different with you," she said with a head shake.

"Why?"

"Because I don't . . . need you . . ." She trailed off, losing all gumption, dropped her face back down to her lap.

Max stared in shock. "You don't need him, either. In fact, you'd be way better off without him."

She shook her head. "He's my—"

"Anchor," he said, cutting her off before he had to hear the word *fiancé* again.

Her brows drew together. "What?"

"It's like he's got you tethered down at his level, drowning, and he makes you feel bad that you're better than him so he can keep you from going after what you want. People like that are fucking awful."

She stared at him for a long moment as her expression softened back into the pretty, confident look he'd grown accustomed to.

"You keep saying nice things to me."

Max's shoulders relaxed a little, and he rolled the anger out of his neck. "I'm not that nice."

"You are," she said, matching his smile, and he couldn't believe the relief he felt now that she was looking like the woman he knew.

It was as if she'd lifted a three-hundred-pound barbell from his chest.

"You hide it well, but you are nice, Max."

She stood from her chair, and this time, her head stayed up. "Thanks for the pep talk. I'm gonna go home now and cry myself to sleep."

She leaned toward him, rose to her tiptoes, and put her arms around his neck in a hug.

He immediately relaxed into the hug and brought his arms around her, his chin down lightly on her head. He hated the idea of her going home alone, crying into her pillow over that fucker. Maybe he'd call Cara, give her a heads up, tell her that Willow was on her way home and was upset.

A few moments passed before he realized she hadn't pulled away. She'd stayed in his arms, pressed against him on the desk for a long moment.

Finally, she loosened her hands as if she was going to pull away, and his heart began aching again.

It was torture.

He didn't want her to leave his arms.

She leaned her head back slightly and looked up at him with her beautiful eyes. She was so close. And he wanted her so bad.

"Max?"

"Yeah."

He was just about to admit defeat, loosen his hold of her, when her eyes dropped to his lips, and she swayed slightly in his arms, moving incrementally closer to him. He did the same, matching her movement.

His brain was telling him to stop, but his hand moved on its own, up to her cheek where some strands of hair had fallen near her eye. He gently brushed them away and tucked them behind her ear so he could get a better look at her beautiful face.

With her eyes fixed on his mouth, she slowly closed the remaining distance between them, then gently pressed her lips against his.

A jolt shot through him as if he'd shoved a knife in an electrical socket. All he could think was, *Fucking finally!*

He put his hands in her hair, then grabbed her gently and tilted her head to the side so he could deepen the kiss. She melted into him, using her hips to wedge herself closer, settling between his legs. Pleasure flooded his body.

He had an overwhelming desire to rip off their clothes so they could be even closer, but his brain wouldn't allow it. He liked her way too much to just go for it without a second thought and have it blow up in his face, so he forced himself to grasp for some kind of order.

Why were they doing this now, right after she'd been dumped? Was he the world's fastest rebound, or had this been as inevitable for her as it was for him?

Most of all, how would he feel if she got back together with that fucker? She'd done it before.

The nagging voice in the back of his mind screamed, *You'd be crushed!* But he could shut that voice up if he needed to, as long as he went into this knowing what to expect.

He brought his hands to her cheeks, broke the kiss, then immediately regretted it when he saw her swollen lips and heavily lidded gaze. She was staring at his mouth, lustful, desperate.

He wanted more. But he needed some self-preservation first.

"Are you using me?"

As if being snapped out of a dream, she blinked hard twice, then looked down. "Uh," she said, looking everywhere but at him before dropping her eyes and squeezing them shut. "I'm sorry. I shouldn't have . . ."

She straightened abruptly, shaking her head, about to push away from him, but he put his hands on her hips to stop her.

"It's not a deal breaker for me, Willow," he said. "I just need to know what's happening here."

He trailed his hands up her back, through her hair, exploring her as she tipped her head back and exposed her beautiful neck. He never wanted to stop touching her.

She let out a dreamy sigh, and her mouth relaxed into a little smirk. "You need order for your hookups?"

"Evidently," he said, shaking off the annoyance he immediately felt at the word *hookup*. "Is that what this is for you? Just a one-time thing?"

She gazed into his eyes for a long moment before her brow furrowed. "I really don't know, Max. I just don't want to think about everything that just happened."

Max schooled his features, refusing to let his face show the disappointment. He'd already known logically that he was a rebound. Having sex with someone minutes after getting broken up with wasn't normal. But holding her against his lap, her soft breath on his chest, felt way too good. Not to mention it had been way too fucking long since he'd last had sex, and he'd been way too fucking stressed over the last few weeks.

Maybe a hookup wasn't the worst idea ever.

He'd wanted nothing more than to bend her over their desk and fuck all the tension from both of them. So why shouldn't he? She wanted it; he wanted it. As long as he kept it all ordered in his mind, it would be fine.

"Okay," he said, doing the millionth cleanup of his emotions that day. This time, he put a lock on his mental Willow box and threw a blanket over it.

She searched his eyes back and forth. "You really want to?"

Was that a serious question? He was certain she could feel how badly he wanted to. The evidence was currently straining in his pants, pressing against her stomach.

He smirked. "Yeah, obviously," he said with a pointed look down.

She unleashed a smile and huffed out a pretty laugh and moved even closer to him, and his ridiculous fucking heart seized again.

Ugh.

He ignored it, grabbed the backs of her thighs, pulled her up until she wrapped her legs around his waist, then he sat down on the top of their desk, settling her onto his lap.

She rocked against him, her dress up around her hips, her hands on his shoulders. He kissed her as she reached for the bottom of his shirt and lifted it up, pulling it off his head and tossing it on his chair. She then placed her palms against his heart pounding in his chest.

He closed his eyes against the shivers that racked his body from her touch, then leaned forward, kissed her throat, down her chest, along her cleavage, all while reaching for the zipper on her back. He grew harder and harder as the zipper descended. Once it was low enough, he grabbed the bottom of the skirt and pulled it up and off, dropping it behind her on top of his shirt. Then he kissed her collarbone as he unclasped her black lacy bra and slid it down her arms.

Her body shuddered once she was exposed, and he gently ran his hands up the sides of her body, caressing her breasts with his palms.

"So soft," he said, more to himself than to her. He'd dreamed about what she'd feel like in his hands. Reality was better.

She sighed and rolled her hips against his lap, as if searching for some relief.

"Max," she said, her hands gliding up his bare back, up his neck until her fingertips raked through his hair.

A deep grunt escaped. He'd wanted to take it slow, take his time. He'd been dreaming about this for a while now. But she started rolling her hips against his erection in a slow, calculated rhythm, and he thought he might die if he didn't get his jeans off.

He stood, picking her up with him, then turned around and sat her on the desk where he'd just been. She reached for the button on his jeans and undid them, then quickly slid down the zipper and tugged them down his hips.

"Good," he said with a smile as he watched her eagerly tugging at his pants.

His jeans dropped. Then she watched, wide eyed, as he slid his boxers down and let them drop at his ankles with his jeans. He didn't even bother stepping out of them. His mind was on one thing and one thing only: getting her little black panties off.

He hooked his fingers around the waistband, and when she lifted her hips off the desk, he slid them off her soft, pale legs.

He wanted desperately to drop to his knees and taste her, but before he could, she grabbed his shoulders and pulled him to her.

"Now, Max," she said, bringing her mouth to his ear and sucking.

God. Why did he love it so much when she ordered him around?

His gaze dropped back down to her, and he huffed out a breath. He wanted to give her what she needed, but fuck, he was dying to take it slow, too.

"We're doing this again," he said, his voice harsh, "at my pace."

Her mouth dropped open as her eyes widened, then she nodded. "Yes," she said.

"Good."

He bent down and grabbed his wallet from his jeans pocket and pulled out a condom, then ripped it open and slid it down his length. As she watched, her pretty little mouth formed a surprised o.

Yeah, they would *definitely* take this slower next time.

He took hold of himself and slowly slid into her, and she let out a soft moan that made his whole body shudder with relief.

He put his hand on her back and guided her down, bending with her until they were both laid back on the desk. She brought her legs around his waist, squeezing as he slid in and out of her, falling further and further into the pleasure.

She urged him on by tugging his hips with her legs, but he resisted, forcing her to go at his pace. He wanted more from her. Had to feel every part of her.

He leaned forward, pressed his lips against her breasts, kissing and gently sucking. She writhed under him, her breath becoming erratic. He reached between them and made soft, slow circles with his thumb until her whole body went still and she came calling out his name.

When her orgasm waned, she pulled him close to her into a hug, and he buried himself deeper, grabbing the edge of the desk with one hand and her neck with the other.

He slid into her once, twice before pleasure spread through his whole body and he emptied himself deep inside her. He collapsed against her chest, letting out a whole-body shiver as she brought her hands up and dragged her nails against his back.

They held each other close for what seemed like an eternity. But before he could stop them, all the feelings he'd been burying came flooding in.

You like her. Too much. You want to keep her. Forever.

He threw up a mental wall, blocking the intrusive thoughts and forcing them back down. This was just a hookup to her, and so it was just a hookup for him, too. Nothing more.

"Max?"

He lifted himself just enough to see her eyes, but not enough to lose the feeling of her warm skin against his. "Yeah?"

"Do you want to come sleep over at my place?" she asked, an irresistible smile playing at her lips. "Maybe we can do it again?"

He put up a second wall, just to be safe, then pulled back from her body and took her in, glistening and spread out in front of him on their desk.

"Absolutely."

TWENTY-ONE

Willow woke up to the sight of Max fast asleep beside her and felt her eyes widen. The shock waned as she watched his giant sleeping form bathed in the morning sunlight streaming through her window and landing directly on his face.

Closing the blinds hadn't even been on her radar when they'd got back to her room and tumbled into bed together.

She stared at him for a long while, taking in the peacefulness of his features as he slept, and could not contain the stirring deep in her belly that couldn't seem to be satisfied. His bare chest, smattered in dark hair and dark tattoos, rose and fell which each deep breath, and his huge hand rested against his hard stomach. He'd pulled the sheet over them in the middle of the night, and it was now pooled around his waist, but the thin fabric was leaving little to the imagination.

He looked unbelievable.

She wanted to ever so quietly crawl out of bed, tiptoe across the room, and close the blackout curtains before he woke up. That way, they could stay like this for longer, without the reality of the situation setting in.

She stared at his thick dark eyelashes fanned out on his cheeks, waiting for the guilt to come rushing in, but instead of regretting sleeping with him, all she felt was slightly lightheaded from the warmth radiating off his body and infusing hers. She was deep in the sexy, euphoric little bubble they'd created, and she never wanted to leave.

Carefully, she peeled the sheet back from herself, tiptoed to the window, and pulled the curtains tight, then glanced at the door, then back at Max. Should she get back in bed, or go pee so she would be ready for round three?

Or was it four?

Five?

Shrugging, she tiptoed to the door.

She grabbed a sleep shirt from the dresser and pulled it on, then silently stepped through the door. After gently closing the door behind her, she turned around to see Cara emerging from her room, closing the door in the same hushed manner as Willow.

Cara turned toward her, then jumped, her hand going to her throat as if she was trying to stop herself from screaming.

Willow's eyebrows shot up. "Hi," she whispered.

Cara gave her a sheepish grin. "Hi," she said, glancing over her shoulder. "Cooper slept over last night."

Willow's mouth fell open.

"I know. It just sort of happened," Cara whispered, her brows drawn together. "He messaged me when I was at the pub earlier and asked if I wanted to hook up. Please don't tell Max."

Willow grimaced, then glanced over her shoulder at her own door. "Uh, I won't."

Cara's eyes went wider than Willow thought possible as her whole body recoiled.

"Is Max in there?"

Willow nodded.

Cara stared at her, speechless, and Willow racked her brain, trying to find something to say and coming up short.

She suddenly realized how fucked up it all was.

The door behind Cara swung open, and a shirtless guy emerged and leaned against the door frame. All Willow could see were abs and a ton of hair.

"Car—"

He stopped when he caught sight of Willow, then looked her up and down and plastered on a douchey grin. "Nice. I'm Cooper."

"Ugh," Willow said, crossing her arms to cover herself as much as possible.

"Everyone shhh!!" Cara hissed, pushing Cooper backwards into her room. "Max is in there," she said, tipping her head to Willow's door.

Cooper's body froze midmovement. "What?"

"I didn't know."

He slowly shook his head as if he couldn't believe it, before finding some words. "I guess today's the day I die."

"No one's dying," Cara said with a roll of her eyes.

"I just hooked up with his precious baby sister. He's going to throw me off the fucking roof."

Willow smiled as she imagined herself yelling *Max!* and watching that mullet careen off the highest pitch of the house.

Cara shoved Cooper the rest of the way back. "Just go back in there and stay quiet," she said.

She closed the door, but Willow heard one last mutter about hiding under the bed before the hallway was silent again.

Cara took hold of Willow's arm and dragged her to the end of the hall. "You and Max?" she asked, biting her lip.

Willow blew a breath out, not sure what to say. "Are you mad?"

Cara's frown deepened. "Mad isn't the right word. I guess I'm . . . concerned."

Concerned?

Cara glanced across the hall to their doors, then back. "What about Shane?"

"Yeah," Willow said, her eyes downcast as the guilt came. It rolled in like a mudslide, burying her.

"He showed up last night after everyone left."

"Oh shit," Cara said. "What happened?"

"He was angry that I lied, and he wanted me to leave with him, but I told him I couldn't, so he broke up with me and left."

"He broke up with you?" she asked, rubbing her face with both hands. "Are you okay?"

That was a loaded question. She had no clue. She hadn't even given herself a second to process the whole mess before jumping Max.

He'd been protective of her, as if he actually cared how she was feeling, and he'd said kind things to her, and all the inappropriate thoughts she'd had of him since the day they first met came flooding in. But this time, there was no reason to stop them, and her brain just poof! Disappeared.

"I don't know if I'm okay," she said.

They stared at each other for a long moment before Cara broke the silence.

"So, was this just, like, a one-night stand?"

She nodded. "Yeah."

Cara blew out a breath, her brows drawing together. "I know everyone always assumes Max is so tough, because he's constantly in control and barking orders, and he's huge, and he has a scary look to him, but he's actually very—"

The sound of a door opening down the hall killed her words. They both jumped and turned to see which door would open.

Finally, Willow's door pushed in, and Max stepped into the hallway in black boxers. His eyes zeroed in on hers before dropping to her naked legs, then back up. Her knees literally wobbled.

He looked so incredibly hot she couldn't take it. Where Cooper had been showy and pretty, as if he spent hours flexing in front of his bathroom mirror, Max looked as if he spent his days crushing skulls.

He stared at her for a long while before sparing Cara a quick glance. But his eyes landed back on her. "What are you doing?"

"Uh," Willow said, not sure how to answer. She wanted to drag him back into her bed and never leave.

There was something seriously wrong with her.

Guilt and lust had locked into a battle in her body, but lust just got the upper hand.

She stared at him, knowing full well she was eye fucking the crap out of him, trying to figure out what to say, until Cara elbowed her in the ribs.

She glanced over, saw a pleading look in Cara's eyes. Right. She should probably do something about the Cooper situation, but what?

Maybe bring Max back into her room and "distract" him? He wouldn't even know Cooper existed once his dick was in her mouth. She glanced one more time at Cara, caught the terrified look in her eyes, and knew she should get Max to leave, as painful as that was.

She shook her head, determined to be a good friend.

Focus.

"Morning," she said, leaving the corner she'd been in with Cara and closing the distance between her and Max. She took his hand and pulled him into her bedroom.

"Everything okay?" he asked after the door was closed.

"Yeah, great. Um, I'm just kind of tired, and I'm going to take a shower, and I need to get into work, and . . . uh . . ."

And what?

And nothing. None of those things were important. Her eyes landed on the bed behind him, and she sighed.

"Are you trying to get rid of me?" he asked with a smirk.

God, his smirk was so irresistible. Especially now that she knew he made that same smirk right before he dropped to his knees and put her legs over his shoulders.

She shook her head, then realized she was supposed to say yes, so she nodded instead. She was all confused.

His face transformed into a full smile, and he stepped closer before running his long fingers through her hair. "You sure that's what you want?"

She melted into his big hand, but her eye caught the door, and she remembered her mission. "Yes, I'm sure," she said with a sigh.

He narrowed his eyes. "There's something you're not telling me."

His hands felt incredible. Almost as incredible as his dick. She wanted to put his fingers back between her legs again.

"There are a *lot* of things I'm not telling you."

He stared at her for another minute before giving her a kiss on the cheek and turning toward his pants.

"Fine," he said, pulling them on and collecting his things off her dresser. "I'll see you at work later."

He pulled his shirt over his head, his torso stretching, and she wanted so badly to drop to her knees and lick his stomach. She fixed her face as his head came through the shirt, but he seemed to know what she'd been thinking, anyway.

He bent down and kissed her lips. "Bye," he said, then left.

She listened as his footsteps retreated down the hall, then at his quick, muffled conversation with Cara before she heard the front door close.

She went down the stairs to the kitchen and found Cara at the counter, filling the coffeepot with water. "Hey, sorry I put you in a weird position," she said.

Willow shook her head, dropped onto a stool at the island. "That's okay. I'm sorry everything is so . . . awkward."

Cara glanced at her, then back to the coffeepot. "So, are you guys going to . . . continue whatever this is?"

Willow cringed. "I don't know," she said.

"Are you going to go back to Churchill in two weeks?"

Fuck. She hadn't even thought about that. Shane had told her not to bother coming home. But Barley was there, and she had Nikki's wedding that she'd already committed to, so she nodded. "Yeah, I have to go back."

Cara pressed a few buttons on the coffeemaker, then leaned against the counter. "Do you think you'll stay, though?"

"I . . ." Willow looked down. She had no clue. Churchill was her home, with or without Shane. Wasn't it? Her job was there, her friends, her family. She'd never intended to uproot her entire life forever. "I don't know."

Cara nodded. "Does Max know you're going back?"

Willow shook her head. "I don't know, but I don't think it matters. We made it very clear last night that this is just a hookup," she said.

She sensed Cara wanted to press further, but Cooper came down the stairs, and she met him at the front door to say goodbye.

When she was finally alone, all the feelings came. The guilt for lying to Shane, the guilt for using Max to forget about Shane, the comfort she felt in Max's arms, the difference between how Shane made her feel and how Max made her feel.

Ugh.

How had she fucked her life up so badly? A couple of weeks ago, everything was fine. Now she was single, homeless, and had slept with her business partner. Worst of all, she didn't know what to do next.

She dropped her head onto her arms on the counter in front of her and tried to wipe her mind of all the rash things she'd done in the last fifteen days. If she'd stayed in Churchill, none of this would have happened.

"Can you just promise me something?" Cara asked.

Willow looked up, nodded.

"Please, just be honest with Max about what your plans are."

She took in the concern etched all over her friend's face, then nodded. "I will," she said. "I'll talk to him later today."

Cara smiled. "Thanks."

TWENTY-TWO

Max checked his watch as he slammed the car door behind him and made his way into work, hoping his lateness had gone unnoticed. He hated showing up hours after everyone else, but he'd exhausted himself with Willow all night and ended up sleeping like a fucking baby.

He was only a few steps in the door when Luis bolted from the kitchen, concern all over his face as if he were a father waiting up all night for his child to come home, ready to dial 9-1-1 and report a missing person.

"Why didn't you call?" he demanded, fists on his hips.

A smile came to Max's face. "Were you worried about me?"

"It's noon," he said, throwing his arms in the air. "And your office is a mess. We thought someone kidnapped you!"

Max glanced at the office, then back, wiping the guilt off his face. "Who's gonna kidnap me, Luis? The Hulk?"

"They could have had weapons," he said, his eyes widening. "Large weapons."

Max rolled his eyes. "Everything's fine."

Luis steadied himself, took a few breaths. "What happened in there?"

Max fought to keep off the smirk. "Go back to work, Luis," he said, turning and marching into the office.

He and Willow had left in a bit of a hurry the night before. They were both far more concerned with getting into her bed than fixing the mess they'd made. But when he walked through the door, he could see why Luis was all worked up.

Papers and pens were scattered all over the floor; the chairs were knocked backward, and his coat was still hanging on the hook in the corner. He shook his head, remembering the desperation they both had felt that first time. He couldn't think of anything but Willow when she was straddling his waist with her skirt hiked up around her hips.

He dropped his bag on his chair and went to work tidying the space back up before Willow got there. She had no poker face whatsoever. If someone asked her what had happened in that room, her expression would give it away in an instant.

Not to mention her pretty blush.

God, he was thankful Shane showed up and cut her loose. Now she was available. And all the roadblocks to him pursuing Willow had cleared.

The only problem was that she'd said it was just a hookup. And she clearly wasn't ready to jump into another relationship just yet. But that didn't mean it couldn't become something more in the future, right?

He sat in his chair and pulled out his laptop. Probably best to focus on work, instead.

He'd been working for about an hour when the office door opened and Willow popped her pretty head in. His whole body simultaneously relaxed and tensed as his heart foolishly prepared for the best-case scenario, while his brain tried to force him to be realistic.

He pushed it all down and away.

"Hey," she said, stepping in and closing the door behind her.

"Hey," he said, trying and failing to stop his face from breaking into a smile. "You should have seen this place this morning. It was a disaster."

She gave a little laugh and sank down into the chair across from the desk. "Last night was fun."

Max nodded. "Yeah."

She looked down, picked up the bottom corner of her flannel shirt, and started fiddling. "So, are we okay, then?"

Max smiled. Flashes of the night before played through his mind. He'd never look at that desk the same way again. "All good. Are you okay?"

Willow nodded. "Yeah, I'm okay. I just feel awkward, I guess. I've never done *this* before," she said, gesturing between them.

Max tensed. "*This*?" he asked, mirroring her.

"Like, hooked up. I've only ever been with Shane."

Max's smile dropped. He wasn't sure what triggered it. Her calling it a hookup again or saying that fucker's name. He wanted to move on, move forward. Together.

"Sorry," she said, going on, incapable of leaving silence hanging in the air. "I just figured you'd know what to do in this situation better than me."

Every muscle in his neck tensed. "Why is that?"

She dropped her head to one side and gave him an impatient look. "I'm sure this isn't your first time doing something like this."

Max wondered how honest he wanted to be at that moment. Tell her the truth, that he'd only ever been with a handful of women himself, or not say anything and leave her to her assumptions? In the end, she spoke before he had time to say anything.

"I just don't want things to be awkward," she said.

"Then stop making things awkward," he said, rolling his neck and trying for a smirk.

She laughed, her pretty smile taking over her face, and he never wanted to look away.

"Do you want to have dinner with me tonight?" he asked.

"Oh," she said, glancing around. "Um, I don't think I can. Jer and I are brewing the first big batch of Fuzzy Milkshake this afternoon. It's going to take a while."

Max nodded. "I'm sure your fans will be thrilled."

"Yeah, I'm happy they chose that one," she said with a smile. "It turned out great. I think I'll bring some cans with me when I go home."

Max's chest tightened. He blinked up, meeting her eye. "Home?"

Willow's eyes rounded before she gave a tiny shrug. "Yeah."

"You're going back?"

She nodded. "Well, Barley's there, and I'm Nikki's maid of honour."

Max's head shook as he tried to rein in his temper. "You're gonna go to Nikki's wedding, after she ratted you out?"

Willow broke eye contact and started fidgeting with the bottom of her shirt once more. "Well, I promised her I would be there. Besides, it wasn't fair of me to ask her to lie to him. She's his friend just as much as she's mine."

Why the hell was she making excuses for these fucking people? He'd had the question answered in his mind before he could silently get it out. The root of his anger wasn't just that she was acting like a doormat. It was that he didn't want her to leave. If he hadn't already fallen for her, he wouldn't care whether she stayed or left.

He needed to get his feelings in check. She'd basically told him he was a rebound, and he'd said he was fine with it. Now he'd have to live with it.

He mentally shoved his feelings away, wishing there was a way to incinerate them and remove them from his mind forever so they wouldn't come creeping back up again.

"Okay," he said with a nod once he knew his voice wouldn't betray his real thoughts.

Her eyes tightened. "So, we're okay? You and me?"

He matched her pinched look, trying to decode her decoding. Was she relieved? Disappointed? It was impossible to tell.

"We're great," he said.

Her features smoothed.

"Go make your beer. I'm going to send out a bunch of exclusive invitations for our influencer night, bragging about your Fuzzy Milkshake."

"No pressure," she said with a forced laugh, then stood and left the room.

He waited for her to leave before he allowed the tension to leave his body. The thought of her leaving made him want to punch a hole in the wall. He knew he couldn't stop her from leaving, but he hoped that she'd see the light before then and decide on her own to stay.

With him.

Forever.

Or at the very least, he hoped that whatever happened, her relationship with Shane was well and truly over.

TWENTY-THREE

W illow walked from the office to the brewery, trying to process Max's shift in tone that had thrown her off balance. She hadn't expected him to give a shit about her going back home, but he'd seemed downright annoyed when she'd mentioned going back for Nikki's wedding.

Maybe it was because he'd been there comforting her after Shane had left. Or maybe it was because he had actual feelings for her.

God, she hoped that was the case.

Didn't she?

Ugh . . . maybe not. If Max had feelings for her, beyond just friend/business partner/pain in the ass/hookup feelings, then things would be even more complicated than they already were.

She walked through the taproom and into the brewery, where Jer was busy moving bags of grain to the grinder.

"Hey, I'm glad you're here—"

Jer stopped midsentence as he took her in from head to toe. "What happened to your heart chakra?"

"My what what?" she asked, mostly ignoring him and flipping open her notebook.

Maybe trying to smooth things over with Max had been a bad idea. She should have just left things unsaid, treated him as a one-night stand, and avoided all talk of the future. That would certainly have made things less complicated.

Jer came close, held his hands up a few inches from her face, and swirled them around with his eyes closed. "Your energy is slow and several vibrations lower than it usually is."

"What does that mean?"

He opened his eyes and stared at her for a long moment, his gaze flitting between her two eyeballs before his face transformed as if he'd had an epiphany. "You had sex with Max."

Her eyes flew open, and she could feel her flush taking over her face. She took a cautionary step back.

"Uh, how did you do that?"

Jer's face split in two. "I knew as soon as I saw the office this morning. But your vibration *is* way off. I expected you to skip on in here, feeling like a million bucks. Wasn't he good?"

Good? She could almost still feel his giant hand splayed across her back and his soft, full lips sucking on her neck.

She sighed. "He was perfect."

Jer laid his hand gently on hers. "Are you feeling off because of Shane? Because you didn't technically do anything wrong."

"No," she said with a shake of her head. "I know I didn't— Wait. How did you know about Shane?"

"Cara told me," he said. "Her energy was off this morning, too."

Willow's brows rose. She hadn't realized Jer and Cara had become friends. It was kind of nice that they were getting close. Cara had lost a lot of her friend group when Cooper had broken up with her, but now that they were back together, maybe she was okay. She could just imagine what Max would say if he found out that Cara was back with Cooper because of her.

She shook her head, trying to stay on track. "I know I didn't technically do anything wrong, but it still feels like I did. I climbed into Max's lap literally minutes after Shane left. And the worse part is, I've been wanting to do that since I met him."

Jer snorted. "*Everyone* wants to climb into Max's lap when they meet him."

Willow cocked a brow. "Even you?"

Jer gave a solemn nod. "Yes, even me."

Willow sighed. He was probably right. Max exuded this energy that just made you want to rip off your clothes. It wasn't her fault she thought those thoughts.

"Yeah, I guess."

"So what's the problem?" he asked. "You're both single and consenting."

She looked down at her feet. "He sort of shut down when I mentioned going back to Churchill."

Jer's eyebrows knitted. "He wants you to stay."

"I can't really tell."

"Well . . . what do you want?"

That was the question, wasn't it? Unfortunately, she had no clue. What she'd wanted—to open her brewery and marry Shane—wasn't really on the table anymore. Everything was moving too fast.

"I just want to feel normal again. Between the lying and the travelling and the tension with Max and the guilt about Shane and the duty I feel to Nikki, I'm so . . ." She trailed off, not sure how to articulate it.

"Uncomfy?" Jer asked.

"Exactly. I'm very uncomfy," she said, turning her attention to the recipe section of her notebook. "I need to focus on something else. We're brewing Fuzzy Milkshake today, so we need to get the mash going."

She closed the book and turned toward the mash tun, but Jer's hands came to her shoulders, stopping her.

"I know you're my boss, but can I give you some advice?" he asked, staring deep into her eyes.

She wanted to say no, but he seemed incredibly adamant. "Okay."

"Honour your inner light, and allow it to guide your soul's purpose."

She stared at him. "My soul's purpose?"

He smiled and nodded.

She didn't know what the fuck her soul's purpose was or what that even meant. But she also didn't have the heart to tell him he was confusing her, so she just smiled.

He smiled back, and a wash of calm suddenly soothed its way over her. She'd never really bought into all the new age stuff, but something about him made her incredibly calm. Maybe it was his voice, or the serene look on his face, or his unflappable positivity.

She was pretty sure hiring him was one of the best decisions she'd ever made.

"Thank you, Jer."

He grinned and gave a nod before grabbing his bag of grain and continuing with his task.

Willow turned toward the mash tun, feeling better than she had all morning. She made it two steps before her phone started ringing in her pocket. She pulled it out, and just like that, all the calm energy Jer had somehow transferred to her vanished.

Nikki.

She sucked in a deep breath, then accepted the call. "Hi Ra—"

"Oh my God, Willow. Is everything okay?"

Nothing was okay, but the last thing she wanted to do was talk to Nikki about it. "Yeah, I'm okay."

"Shane just got back home. He said you guys broke up."

The sting of guilt pierced her as she remembered the anger and betrayal in his eyes. "Yeah, he told me not to bother coming back home."

Nikki let out a long breath. "I don't think he's angry anymore."

"What?"

"He was just here with me and Kyle," she said. "And he was devastated."

Willow's jaw dropped. *Devastated?* "Oh."

"He said that he made a mistake and that he shouldn't have been so angry with you. He's really beating himself up over this."

Willow didn't know what to say, so she just stood there, silently confused.

"He wants to get back together, Willow," Nikki said. "So don't worry about the lying and everything. It's going to be fine."

She almost laughed.

Fine? No. Absolutely nothing was fine.

She didn't even know where to start.

Part of her wanted Nikki to be right so she could go back to her home and be with Shane. That would be easy. Comfortable, even. But the thought of Shane touching her made her want to vomit. And the guilt that followed that thought was really weighing on her. She'd told Shane she'd marry him, and she didn't take her promises lightly.

If he would forgive her for lying to him about the whole thing, what kind of person would she be to not take him back?

What a fucking mess.

She wanted to scream. Wanted to cry. Wanted a fucking time machine.

She also wanted desperately to get off the phone and think about work instead of talking about her fucked-up personal life.

"Sorry, Nik," she said, not touching on the whole devastated–ex-fiancé thing. "I gotta go."

"Wait! You're still coming back for my wedding, right?"

Willow nodded. "Yes, of course," she said. "I'll be there in a couple of weeks."

"Okay," she said, hesitating. "I hope it won't be too awkward between you guys."

"I'll be fine."

"No, I know. I mean, I don't want to feel awkward on my wedding day."

Willow sighed at the selfishness, then shook her head. Maybe she was being selfish for thinking Nikki was being selfish. It was her wedding day, after all.

"Your wedding is going to be great," she said. "I have to go."

"Okay, bye."

Willow couldn't match Nikki's energetic send-off, so she silently hung up the phone and forced her mind off the shitty mess she'd created and onto something she could control: the delicious beer she was going to make for her grand opening.

TWENTY-FOUR

Max avoided Willow for three entire days following their awkward morning-after talk. He would have liked to pretend that it hadn't been torturous, but who was he kidding? Whenever he'd see her walk through the dining room, or talk to Luis in the kitchen, or hear her laugh from the brewery, his heart would race, and he'd have to go into an internal battle to stop himself from going to her, throwing her over his shoulder, and dragging her home with him.

Or better yet, laying her back down on their desk.

Now, after all that work to keep her out of sight and out of mind, he was making his way to her brewery to find out what the hell was taking her so long.

It was influencer night, their last trial run before the grand opening, and all the food and beer bloggers and Instagrammers and TikTokers were outside with their selfie sticks waiting to be let in.

And where was Willow? Nowhere in sight.

He swung open the door and found her sitting at a table with her eyes closed and her hands out, holding a shiny grey rock in each palm as Jer danced around her with weird, jerky movements.

He let loose an annoyed grunt. "What the hell are you two doing?"

Willow's eyes flew open. As soon as they found his, a brilliant smile broke out on her face, making his heart lodge in his throat.

"Jer's grounding me with these," she said, holding his eyes for a long moment before clearing her throat and turning to Jer. "What are they called again?"

"Hematite crystals," Jer said, waving his hands around her face. "They reduce nervous energy."

A pounding headache began forming behind his eyes, and he rubbed at his temples.

"You're up next, big guy," Jer said with a snap of his fingers that he turned into a finger gun.

Annnd the headache reached its full intensity. He needed to find a painkiller.

"Absolutely not," Max said, blinking down at his watch. They didn't have time for all this crap.

"The influencers are here. I'm telling the host to open the doors."

Willow hopped up, handed the stones to Jer, and joined Max as he turned back to the dining room. She was wearing a short green dress, and her hair was long and loose in pretty waves that went down her back. He tried not to crane his neck too obviously as she fell in step with him, but he'd clearly failed when she turned and caught him checking her out.

"What?" she said.

Max let his eyes drop along her body and back up. "You look pretty in green."

Willow's eyes went wide, and she gave the little smile she made whenever she got a compliment. Her soft pink lips stretched a little but didn't part, giving an overall look of discomfort.

"Jer says this is my power colour."

"Jer is really something," Max said, pushing open the door and nodding to the host.

She rolled her eyes. "He's great. You don't give him enough credit."

He glanced at her as the host opened the door. "Don't worry. I won't be a dick to Jer-bear after you go back home."

He watched for a moment as the influencers came through the door, showing their invitations to the host and being led to the centre of the room to meet

Luis. A moment passed before he realized Willow had fallen silent beside him. When he chanced a look at her, she was staring expressionless at the crowd.

"What's wrong?" he asked.

"Nothing," she said, shaking it off. "What's the plan here?"

Luis will guide the influencers through the menus, then Jer will take them to the brewery to explain the beers and give samples, and finally, they will all be seated while the waitstaff distributes the food, and they select their favourite beer.

Willow nodded. "Good."

"It will be," he said. "It'll build some buzz for the grand opening, and we'll get an idea of which dishes and beers we can expect to be the crowd pleasers."

Luis led the influencers to the kitchen, where he passionately discussed local ingredients of the highest quality, and then to the brewery to introduce them all to Jer. Max held his breath, watching, but he relaxed as the crowd started eating out of Jer's hand. Apparently, his over-the-top, ridiculous personality was a hit with the influencer crowd.

He must have been vibrating at the right frequency or whatever.

The influencers cleared out of the brewery, and the host led them to the main dining room. As soon as they were gone, Willow elbowed Max in the ribs with a big grin.

"I told you Jer was the guy. They loved him."

Max raised his eyebrows. "Maybe the shiny rocks actually did something?"

Willow laughed. "You're so closed minded."

"And you're a better brewer than you are a hirer."

Willow laughed while mocking offence. "I think I'm pretty good at both."

Max smiled, his shoulders relaxing as he stared at her. "I heard a guy with a beer blog call Fuzzy Milkshake 'inspired' before telling his followers to get down here opening day for a pint."

She turned to him with her jaw down. "Really?"

Max nodded, taken aback by her surprise. "I can't believe how much you doubt yourself. You're exceptionally good at this. It's unthinkable that you even *considered* not pursuing it."

She did her uncomfortable little smile again before her gaze dropped to her feet.

"You know," he said, trying to keep his tone even so it wouldn't betray how much he felt at that moment. "It says a lot about your ex, and your old boss, and your shitty-ass friends, that you're not used to hearing compliments."

Her smile dropped into a frown. She opened her mouth to say something, then closed it, then opened it, and closed it again.

He rolled his eyes. "What?"

Another moment of hemming and hawing went by before she finally spoke.

"Thank you for saying nice things to me, even if you deliver them in your grumpy Max way."

He looked away from her pretty eyes with a shrug. "Would it make you feel better if I smile the next time I criticize the assholes you surround yourself with?"

She laughed. "I think that'll have a more serial killer effect than a good friend effect."

"Good friend?" he said with a laugh. "We're not friends, remember?"

She smiled. "Good pain in the ass?"

His eyelids dropped closed as the weight settled back on his chest. He was about to ask her what the hell they were doing when a blond woman walked back into the brewery. She was pretty, tall, wearing a tight dress, and had those overly filled lips that made her look as if she'd been in a boxing match with Mike Tyson.

"Hi," she said, marching toward him. "I'm Paige."

"Max."

He shook her hand, expecting her to say hi to Willow, but she acted as if there were only the two of them in the room.

"Are you the owner?" she asked.

He glanced to the side at Willow but saw only her back as she retreated past the taps and into the back of the brewery. He frowned at her, mostly because he wanted to be close to her, but also because he needed saving from this woman.

"I'm one of them," he said, loud enough for Willow to hear.

She ignored him.

"I just wanted to say that this place is amazing, and I'd love to stick around for a while after everyone leaves. Maybe you can give me a private tour?"

"No."

He said it so fast he knew it came across asshole-ish, but there was only one person on earth he wanted to stick around with after everyone left. And she was entirely too far away from him at that moment.

Her eyebrows shot up. "Oh," she said.

"Sorry," he said, wondering whether he'd been way too rude. "I'm too busy."

There.

That was as nice as it was going to get.

"Well, I don't mind waiting," she said with a smile, batting her caterpillar eyelashes. "I have a hotel room here in town."

Max glared at her. "No."

She flinched back, apparently in shock for a moment, then rolled her eyes. "Whatever," she said, then walked away.

Finally.

He waited for her to leave, then followed Willow's steps to the brewery and found her sitting at a table, looking through her notebook.

"Why did you do that?"

She looked up. "Do what?"

"Leave me alone with that woman?"

Willow laughed. "You really don't like people, do you?"

"Only a very select few."

Her smile retreated. "She was pretty. And interested in you. Why didn't you say yes?"

He closed the distance between them. "Because I know what I want," he said, brushing a lock of her hair off her face, tucking it behind her ear.

She melted into his hand, and all the feelings he had for her came loose.

"Come home with me."

She smiled, her eyes soft until she saw the seriousness in his expression. "Like, now?"

Max nodded. "Yeah. Luis and Jer can lock up."

A moment of hesitation passed where she seemed at war with herself. Eventually, she stood, closed the distance between them, and pressed her body against his with a deep sigh.

"Okay."

TWENTY-FIVE

*C**ome home with me.*

Max's soft, commanding words were still raking down Willow's spine five minutes later. She'd been so confused since the morning she'd spoken to him in their office that she'd convinced herself the whole thing had been a bad idea. But when he leaned in close and brushed her hair from her ear and his deep voice rumbled those words, she changed her mind.

Hooking up with Max was the only thing she was absolutely certain she wanted to do.

Next thing she knew, she was asking Jer to lock up for her so she could go home with Max. She'd worried about how Jer was going to react, given he seemed to hate Max, but he'd just smirked and said, "You got it, Boss."

"Are you okay?"

Willow turned in the passenger seat of Max's car and took in his sharp features with a smile and a nod. She couldn't believe how far they'd come from their first encounter. She'd thought he was the biggest dick on earth back then. But now? She felt comfortable with him. And safe.

He pulled into the driveway of a duplex and put his car in park. "Are you having second thoughts?"

She glanced over at him and started rolling her eyes, but the look on his face stopped her in her tracks. His brows were drawn together, and his shoulders seemed too stiff, as if he was . . . nervous? She'd never seen that look from him before.

"No," she said. "I'm excited to see your place."

He relaxed fractionally as he unbuckled. "Don't get too excited. It's not much."

She got out of the car and met him in the driveway in front of his car. "Which side is yours?"

"I own both sides, but I live here," he said, pointing to the door on the left. "There's a family renting that side."

"Oh," Willow said, impressed at first, but then her mind started racing. She took in his face and finally formed a complete picture of who Max was in her mind. She hadn't realized until that moment how he'd set up his whole life to be completely self-reliant.

"What?" he asked.

"You really like to own everything, eh?"

He shrugged and walked to the front door. "I don't want my livelihood to depend on the whims of someone less reliable than me," he said, unlocking the door. "And I don't want my home to be owned by someone who can kick me out at any time."

She followed him inside. "Is that independence or paranoia?"

He paused and stared at her, one eyebrow cocked, and she was worried he was going to tell her to stop asking personal questions again.

"Probably both," he finally said, then smirked. "I enjoy being in control."

She snorted. "The understatement of the century," she said, looking around at the simple builder-basic decor and sparse furniture. "How long have you been here?"

"Three years. I bought it after paying off the first laundromat. The rental covers the mortgage, so my business income stays in my corporation to finance new acquisitions."

She stared at him for a moment, shocked he was giving her so much personal information.

"What?"

"I'm just surprised you're telling me these things."

He smiled and shook his head. "I know now that you won't let it go, so I might as well make it easy. Drink?"

She nodded and followed him down the hall to the kitchen.

"So, I can ask you anything?"

"Sure," he said, pulling a couple cans of beer from the fridge and handing her one.

Hmm . . . better make it good.

She took the beer from his hand, then looked around the room. He was so organized; she wondered whether he ever did anything on a whim. He probably had his clothes for the week laid out on his dresser and a fridge full of prepped meals. Maybe even a plan for next week. And the week after.

There was no telling how far in advance he made plans.

She smiled as her mind screamed a brilliant question at her. "Do you have a five-year plan?"

He opened the beer and took a drink, then stared at her for a moment before answering. "That's what you want to know?"

She rolled her eyes. "I want to know what it is," she said. "I already know you have one. You probably have a ten-year plan."

He laughed and shrugged. "Fine," he said. "I'm going to get the pub established and hire a manager to take it off my hands so I can focus on adding a few more businesses as opportunities arise. And when I'm ready to stop, I'll—"

"Ready to stop?"

He stared at her for a long moment. "Yeah, I don't want to work really long hours when I have kids."

Her eyebrows shot up. "You want kids?"

"Of course I do," he said, almost surprised she would ask.

She laughed, then took a drink. "You're more 'daddy' than 'dad,' don't you think?"

He laughed and shook his head. "I think I'm both."

She smiled and shrugged. That tracked. He was responsible and kind. Maybe if he could work on the controlling part, he'd be a good parent.

"How many kids do you want?"

"No less than four."

She nearly spit out her beer. "Four?!"

"No less than four. Could be five. Maybe six."

She stared at him in shock. "Six? How are you going to find a woman willing to birth six of your gigantic babies?"

"I can be persuasive," he said with a smirk. "Once she's pregnant, I'll buy us a house with a big yard in a good school district and rent out this unit to cover the costs."

"Wow," she said, trying to stop herself from being scared for his future wife. And also a little jealous of her, too.

Six was aggressive, but it was admirable that he knew what he wanted. She couldn't even figure out where she wanted to be living in two weeks. "You've got it all figured out."

He nodded, and his face took on a more serious look. "I like having a plan."

Ugh, she felt the same. Maybe that's why she'd been so out of sorts. Because her one and only plan—to marry Shane—had completely fallen apart.

She took another drink and leaned against the cold granite counter behind her, forcing her mind off her problems and onto the here and now.

"What about . . . this?" she asked, gesturing between them.

He stared at her as if he was carefully considering what she'd asked. "What do you mean?"

"You sure you want to do this again?"

"Willow," he said, injecting more patience into his voice than she'd ever heard before. "This is all I wanna fucking do. I haven't stopped thinking about it."

Every nerve in her body fired at once. "You're okay with a second one-night stand?"

He huffed out a breath that she now knew was his annoyance returning. "Is that what this is?"

She blew out her cheeks, then released them. She literally had no idea what the hell they were doing at this point. All she knew was that she wanted to be there with him.

He stepped toward her, closing the distance between them, and put his hands on the counter on either side of her hips. "I'm okay with a thousand one-night stands if you are," he said, leaning down and kissing her neck.

Tingles raced over her scalp as she dropped her head to the side and let him work his way down to her collarbone. She set down her drink and put her arms around his neck, running her fingers through his hair. God, it felt so good to be with him, pressed up against his warm chest. The world could end outside, and she'd still be perfectly safe and happy in this bubble with Max.

"A thousand?" she said, her eyes fluttering closed as her brain slowly powered down, letting her body take over. "That's like, three years of one-night stands."

"Mmm," he said, making his way back up to her ear. "Better make it ten thousand, then."

She pulled back, looking at him as if he'd lost his mind, but he stared back, looking genuinely serious. He reached for her face, traced his thumb along her cheek.

"Wait, are you serious?"

With no hesitation, he nodded. "You can't be surprised that I want you."

"Uh, yeah, I can," she said, pulling back slightly. "You're always so . . . distant."

He gave a pointed look down at their bodies pressed together with absolutely no space between them.

She rolled her eyes. "I don't mean physically."

He shook his head and ran his hands up her back to her neck before moving his fingertips in slow circles, massaging her traps. She relaxed into his touch.

"I'm trying to give you space because you just got out of a relationship, but I obviously really like you, Willow. I admire you for negotiating the deal on the brewery and taking it in your own direction and not letting anyone stand in your way."

She pulled back, looked into his eyes. "I thought you hated me taking over your brewery."

He smiled. "I did at first, but not anymore. You're brilliant at this, and you're a great partner."

She'd never been so flattered in her life. She honestly didn't know what to say. He bent toward her, his warm lips on her ear and his hands on her neck. She tried to say something back to him, but she found herself completely lost for words.

She went up on her tiptoes and took his lips with hers in a deep kiss that made her chest flutter. When Max pulled back, his eyes were half-lidded and his lips were red. Her lips ached for more.

"Bed or couch?" he asked.

She sagged in relief. "Whichever is closest," she said, kissing up his neck to his earlobe. He smelled so good.

He reached under her thighs, lifted her into his arms, took the few steps to the living room, then sat on the couch, resting her on his lap.

She put her lips on him, down his jaw as she unbuttoned his shirt and slid it down his arms. His hands brushed aside her hair as he unzipped her dress, and every bit of her skin went on high alert.

His hands drew up her bare back to her shoulders and gently slid the straps of her dress down her arms, freeing her breasts and making everything shiver and tighten. The tips of his fingers slowly skated up her back and into her hair as Max dropped his face to her chest. He trailed kisses across her collarbone, then down between her breasts.

Her head fell back as her hips rocked forward, needing more.

He groaned and hardened under her, and she got the friction she desperately needed, but it wasn't enough.

"Max?"

He lifted his face from her cleavage and held her gaze. "Willow?"

His deep voice caused a fresh wave of shivers across her skin. She relaxed into the sensation as she reached between their bodies for the bottom of his shirt.

"I want to feel you," she said, grabbing hold of the fabric and dragging it up. She pulled it over his head, tossed it backwards onto the floor, and pressed her bare chest against his as she kissed along his ear and down his neck.

He groaned again as his hands explored her thighs, back, and every other part of her body, except where her dress still clung to her waist.

She needed to get the rest off.

She gave him one more kiss on the lips and stood. He watched closely as she let her dress hit the floor. Slowly, she tucked her thumbs under the elastic of her panties and pulled them down and stepped out.

It took him a few seconds, but eventually, he seemed to snap out of the trance he was in. He stood and turned her around, then gently pressed her shoulders down, guiding her to lie on the couch.

She lay back as he unbuttoned his jeans and slid them, along with his boxers, down and off. He made an impressive sight with his giant tattooed shoulders and muscled stomach. She couldn't look away or keep her mouth closed.

He reached for his wallet, grabbed a condom, and slid it down his length, then moved toward her. She spread her legs apart, making room between them for him to rest.

He pressed up against her as he leaned forward and kissed her, teasing and pushing and increasing the tension instead of relieving it.

But she really didn't mind. As badly as she needed that release, feeling his weight on her, his warmth engulfing her, gave her a satisfaction she couldn't really understand. She wrapped her legs around his waist, her arms around his neck as he finally pressed himself into her, and she let out a moan.

He pressed further and further, slowly, until he couldn't go any deeper. He paused, dropping his head forward on a moan.

She almost came on the spot.

He slid his arms under her, cradling her against his chest before sliding out, then pressing back in, this time much faster and harder.

"Oh, God," she breathed, not knowing what else to say.

He groaned and did it again. And again. And again, before she squeezed against him, unable to fight it any longer.

"Willow," he said against her ear, licking her earlobe and making her even closer to release. "You feel incredible. I can't hold back."

"Don't hold back," she said, knowing she was so close.

He tightened his hug, dropped his head, and started pumping in and out of her, twice as fast as he had been.

She rose steadily, unable to process the fact that she was being held as if she was something precious to him while being fucked so hard. Her orgasm came on strong, spurring him on as he groaned and emptied himself inside her. He dropped his face onto her chest, trying to catch his breath.

She squeezed her legs tighter around him, pulling an almost painful-sounding groan from his chest, then rubbed his shoulders and back, basking in the warmth she felt lying under his weight.

A long while passed before he pushed himself up and stood, holding out his hand.

"Come to my bed."

She took his hand and let him help her up. Once she was on her feet, he bent down, putting one arm behind her back and the other behind her legs, then lifted her off the floor and carried her to his room.

He lowered her down on his bed, then lay down next to her and pulled the covers over them. When he reached out, she instinctively gravitated to him, snuggling into the comfort of his muscular arms.

She sighed, never having felt so content in her life, and never wanted to stop feeling that way as long as she lived.

The last thing she felt was Max's lips dropping a sweet kiss on her head before she fell into a deep, peaceful sleep.

TWENTY-SIX

"Don't forget about the drive-through."

Max shuddered at Willow's reminder as he turned the key in his ignition and pulled out of the driveway, but the sound of her soft chuckle had his smile quickly returning.

His alarm had gone off at five a.m., and on any other day, he'd have jumped out of bed, got in a gruelling workout, and eaten eggs before going into work early. But just before he was about to get up, she'd rolled over to his side of the bed and pressed her soft body against his.

Then she'd kissed his neck.

They had spent the rest of the morning in bed together until their stomachs had growled so loudly that they were forced to get up. He'd offered to make her breakfast after his shower, but she'd followed him into the bathroom, stepped into the shower, and asked him to get her breakfast on the way to work, instead.

As if he were ever going to say no to that.

He shook his head, astonished that he had already allowed himself to get wrapped around her little finger. It made him uncomfortable to care about her as much as he did, but it also felt right. It was hard to explain.

"You're a bad influence."

She smiled as she flipped down the visor and braided her still-damp hair. "I really want to try one of those egg sandwiches everyone talks about."

His nose wrinkled. "They're gross."

She laughed and rolled her beautiful eyes. "You're way too stuck in your routine."

He wanted to disagree, but she was mostly right. He couldn't remember the last time he'd broken it. Maybe last year when he'd had the stomach flu and couldn't get out of bed. But he'd never wanted to break it. He did it because he liked it.

"I've refined my routine to perfection. There's no reason to unstick myself."

"Hmm . . ." she said with a smug smile. "If it's so perfect, then why did you stay in bed with me all morning?"

Vivid images of her in his bed flitted through his mind. Her bright hair against his white sheets; the soft, pale skin of her back under his hands, not to mention the sensation of her fingers lightly tracing up and down his back.

How the fuck was he supposed to care about a five a.m. workout and a balanced diet after that?

"That's what I thought," she said, finishing her braid and flipping the mirror closed with a smile.

He rolled his eyes and turned into the drive-through lane. "Fine. You might be right."

"I'm definitely right."

The employee's muffled voice came through the intercom, and Max ordered their food. They were just about to pull back onto the road when Willow's phone pinged with a text.

She pulled out her phone, clicked a couple times, then laughed. "It's Cara," she said. "She's asking if I'm dead. I probably should have told her I wasn't coming home last night."

Max slowly nodded, controlling his expression. He was still working through how to feel about Willow and Cara being roommates and becoming friends. It was probably a good thing that his sister liked his . . . What the hell was she? He'd told her how he felt, but she'd never told him what she wanted, and he'd been far too distracted to ask her about her plans and what she thought about their multiple-night stands.

"Is it okay if I tell her I was with you?"

Max's brow furrowed as he glanced over at Willow. "Of course," he said, wondering why she thought it wouldn't be.

Willow smiled. "Okay."

She clicked away on her phone for a few seconds before dropping it in her lap and opening the wrapper on her egg sandwich. "Do you want to—"

She stopped when a message came through, and he wanted to scream. Did he want to what?

Have lunch together?

Meet up for an afternooner in the office?

Sleep over again tonight?

Be her boyfriend?

He glanced over at her and rolled his eyes. He wanted to hear the end of her question so badly he was ready to pull her phone from her hands and throw it out the fucking window.

"Tell Cara to fuck off," he said, but she just sat there, staring at the screen.

"It's not Cara," she said, her voice coming out heavy with worry.

His spine went rigid. "Is it Jer?"

"No," she said with a deep exhale. "It's Shane."

Now he really wanted to throw the fucking phone.

They could stop by the store before getting to work and get her a new one with a new phone number so he couldn't contact her again. She'd want that, right?

Right?

He swallowed his aggravation and sucked in a breath. "You've been talking to him again?"

"This is the first time since he broke up with me."

"What does he want?"

She looked over, giving him an assessing look with her pretty green eyes, and he turned his attention back to the road and tried to control his face.

"I ordered a gift for Nikki's wedding, and it came in," she said. "He needs the email to pick it up."

His shoulders relaxed incrementally, but the tension was still there. He really fucking hated this. Hated that he had no clue what he meant to her. And hated thinking that she still had feelings for her ex.

But he had only broken up with her a week ago, and she'd been left devastated. She probably wasn't over that. And yet, he was so much further along in his feelings already.

He just wished she'd see that asshole for what he was and move on. With him.

"What's wrong?"

Max shook his head. "Nothing."

She gave a slow blink and tipped her head. She knew he was full of shit.

He shrugged. "I'm just . . . worried, I guess."

"You don't look worried. You look angry."

He shook his head, braced himself to speak.

"I'm not angry. I'm . . ."

Jealous.

Scared.

Frustrated.

He knew it, but there was a 0 percent chance he was going to fucking admit it.

"You're . . ." she drew out, waiting for him to finish.

"Annoyed."

It was true. He was very annoyed.

Annoyed that he couldn't ask her to tell that guy to never call again. Annoyed that she didn't seem to know what she wanted. Annoyed that he'd let himself feel all the feelings.

Annoyed that he was just a hookup to her. A rebound. A way to distract herself from the guy she actually wanted who'd dumped her.

He let out a heavy sigh.

It had been impossible to contain his feelings for her. She was like a magnet, drawing him in. Every word, look, laugh, sucked him deeper and deeper, no matter how hard he fought to control it.

He pulled out his mental broom and started sweeping it all away. But the little Willow box in his mind was severely overflowing, so he visualized an entire wall of shelving full of totes and filled them all up with his wayward feelings, then sealed them and backed out of the room.

"So . . . you don't think I should talk to him?"

He gave a casual shrug as he pulled into the parking lot of the pub. "That's your call."

She frowned at the shift in his tone. "What if he wants to get back together?"

"Then you'll have to decide if that's what you want," he said. He grabbed his coffee and stepped out of the car, headed for the door.

She fumbled with her stuff, but made it out of the car, and fell in step beside him. "But you think it's a bad idea?"

He stopped and turned to her. What the hell did she want from him? He'd told her how he felt about her, and she was talking to him about texting and getting back together with her ex.

"Since when do you care what I think, Willow?"

"I guess it's a recent development," she said, shuffling her feet.

He took in the tortured expression on her face and wished he hadn't fallen in love with someone so indecisive. If she would just tell him she was into him, or tell him to fuck off, then he could move on instead of being left in this torturous limbo.

"Fine," he said, his voice betraying his frustration. "I think it would be a terrible decision."

The door from the back of the kitchen burst open, and Luis came stepping toward them. "Max, thank God you're here."

Max pushed all that out of his brain and switched gears again for the billionth time that morning. "What's wrong?"

"We just received the delivery from the supplier, and it's all wrong. All wrong."

"Okay," he said. "I'll sort it all out."

"And the lead host just came to me. We're having problems with the point-of-sale equipment."

"Okay," he said again, this time slower. He sensed Luis might have been having a meltdown.

"And I think the thermostat in the cooler isn't working properly. My tomatoes froze."

"Everything is going to be fine, Luis," he said, making mental notes of all the issues he'd just run through. "Let me worry about all of this. You worry about the menu and kitchen staff."

Luis started shaking his head. "We might not open on time."

Max closed the distance between them and put a hand on Luis's shoulder. "I don't care if a fucking tornado rips the roof off the place. We're opening on time. There's no way around that."

"But I don't know—"

"You don't need to know anything. Just do your job. I'll deal with it."

Luis took a few deep breaths, then turned without another word and disappeared back into the kitchen.

"Do you need me for anything?"

When he turned to Willow, he noticed that she'd shrunk back, nervously twisting her hands.

"No," he said. "I'll deal with all of this. Just make sure we have beer."

She nodded, then awkwardly closed the distance between them. He wasn't sure what to expect, but she rose on her tiptoes and kissed his cheek before walking off. He stared at her back as she walked away, the feel of her lips still on his cheek, and couldn't believe how calm her touch made him feel.

Just as his mind created a vision of a future where they commuted into work together every day, he forcefully rejected it with a violent shake of his head.

God, what a fucking mess.

He needed to give himself some space from Willow to pull himself together, so he resolved to stay away from her for a couple of days and put a moratorium on the multiple-night stands.

He shifted his focus to work, walked into the office, and opened his laptop, then began putting out all the fires so they could open on time.

TWENTY-SEVEN

"Guess what!?"

Jer's voice startled Willow awake as he rushed into the brewery. She'd arrived at work that morning super early to balance the books on the accounting software before getting to work brewing that day.

The last thing she remembered was deciding to rest her eyes for a moment.

She rubbed her eyes and looked up to find Jer directly across from her, staring at her with a dazzling, excited smile.

"Uh, what?" she asked.

He sucked in a dramatic breath, sat down on the stool across from her, and put his phone on the table.

"Fuzzy Milkshake is already getting reviews," he said, doing a little happy dance in his seat.

Her heart seized.

"Reviews?" she asked, bracing herself and praying they would be positive. "Are they good?"

"See for yourself."

He opened the beer review app on his phone and spun it toward her. When she looked down, she found five little yellow stars all filled in and immediately sagged.

Oh, thank God.

At least something was going right.

"Want me to read my favourite review?" Jer asked, vibrating with energy.

She let out a long exhale. "Sure."

Jer clicked a couple times, then cleared his throat.

"Fuzzy Milkshake is an absolute dream. This may be the most delicious and unique beer I have ever tasted! It's hazy, thick, and sweet with a bright peach flavour, sure to be a crowd pleaser. Literally impossible to dislike!"

Willow stared at Jer, astonished, as she tried to fight back the happy tears that began filling her eyes. "It really says all that?"

Jer nodded, his smile doubling. "You can cry," he said, standing from his seat and slinging an arm over her shoulders. "You did it."

"We did it," she said, blinking and wiping the tears from her cheeks. "This is as much you as it is me."

Jer smiled before squeezing her tighter. "I disagree. But thank you for saying that."

"It's true," she said, turning to look at him. "It's not just developing the recipes. Execution is ninety percent of it. You're a very talented brewer, Jer."

His eyes went misty, and he blinked the tears away. "I'm gonna miss you," he said. "If . . . I mean, *when* you leave next week."

Willow sighed. "I'm gonna miss you, too."

When Jer finally broke the hug, he lifted a questioning brow at her.

"What about Max? Will you miss him?"

Willow glanced over her shoulder at the door that led to the dining room. It had been a few days since they'd driven into work together and he'd shut down when she'd told him Shane texted. She'd expected him to not be happy about it, but she hadn't expected him to be so . . . distant. He'd clearly been upset, but instead of talking about it, he just went cold and shut down.

She hadn't spoken to him since, even though she'd really wanted to. But she'd heard through the grapevine that he was working round the clock dealing with endless supplier issues and other problems that kept cropping up, so she gave him some space.

Not to mention that he hadn't come to see her, either. Maybe he hadn't wanted to. Or maybe he had wanted to, but he was "annoyed" again. Every time she thought she had him figured out, he'd flip a switch and go from burning hot to icy cold in the blink of an eye, leaving her more confused than ever.

"I'll take your silence as a yes."

Willow slumped forward and let out a sigh. "I think he's hard not to miss. He's a big presence."

Jer snorted. "I, for one, would not miss his moody energy-vampire ass."

"Energy vampire?" Willow asked, genuinely shocked. "I don't get that vibe from him at all."

In fact, she felt very energetic around him. A little too energetic.

"Yeah, we know," Jer said, pulling a face.

"Uh, *we*?"

He looked at the door, then back at Willow. "Everyone's been talking about you two. In the break room, on the floor. They all suspect you're banging."

"Oh my God," Willow said, looking down at her feet. "How embar—"

Her phone blared in her pocket, saving her from materializing that thought. Should she really feel embarrassed?

Ugh, probably.

She pulled her phone out and checked the screen as her heart stopped.

Shane.

"Fuck," she said, not knowing what the hell to do.

"I better get to work," Jer said, clearly having seen she just received a call from her ex. "The vanilla's not going to add itself to the Fuzzy Milkshake."

He promptly turned on his heel and made his way to the tank across the room, while Willow retreated to the opposite corner of the brewery, hoping for some privacy from the rest of the gossipy staff that might overhear.

She considered screening the call to see what the hell he wanted but figured it was likely about Nikki's wedding gift.

"Hello?"

"Willow, hi," Shane said. "How are you?"

His voice was smooth, calm, without a trace of his usual annoyance or shortness. It took her a moment to process it. Then another moment to figure out how to answer him.

She'd just had a huge win with that review, and the last person she wanted to share that with was him. He'd probably find some way to piss on it, as if it wasn't that big a deal.

"Fine, how are you?"

Shane let out a long sigh. "I miss you."

She reared back, then held the phone out and silently screamed at it. Why did he always treat her the nicest when they were broken up? Why couldn't he have said that to her when they'd spoken before he came there?

She put the phone back to her ear, shook off the anger. "How's Barley?"

A moment of silence met her before he finally answered.

"He's good. I gave him a bath."

Willow almost fell over. "You did?"

"Yeah, I had to. He stank."

She imagined her sweet little doggo in the tub, getting washed by Shane instead of her for the first time in his six years, and realized she missed her dog far more than she missed her ex-fiancé. But could you really compare a dog to a human man?

If the worst thing Shane had ever done was poop on the floor, she'd probably still marry him.

"I can't wait to see you."

Ugh.

Willow's lip curled, and her nose wrinkled. She closed her eyes and dropped her forehead against the wall with a thud. "Did you need something?"

"No," he said. "I just called to talk."

Her skin crawled. "I'm pretty busy here . . . so, uh, I'm going to get back to work."

He remained silent for so long that she had to look at the phone to see whether they were still connected.

"Okay," he finally said. "I love you."

She scrunched her face up and shook her head, rolling her face against the hard wall. Maybe she should just tell him she didn't have feelings for him anymore. But what if that was just the anger talking? She'd been with him far too long to have all her love for him evaporate in a week.

Right?

She let out one more silent scream, then said, "'Kay, bye," and hung up before he could reply.

Ugh, what a fucking nightmare.

"That looked painful."

She lifted her head and spun around to find Max standing behind her, his arms crossed over his barrel chest, one dark eyebrow lifted.

Fuck, he looked good.

She gaped at him for a moment, at a total loss for words.

"Who was it?"

She sighed, dropped her head as her shoulders tensed even further. "You know who it was."

Max shifted his weight between his feet, his face expressionless. "What did he want?"

How the fuck was she supposed to answer that? She glanced up at the ceiling, across the room, down at her feet. Anywhere but his eyes. She hoped he'd move on, but he stood there, staring at her, waiting.

"He told me he misses me and loves me."

Max's face stayed completely unreadable. No nod, no eyebrow raise, nothing. He could've passed as a fucking wax figure.

She stared back for a moment, hoping he'd budge and give her something, but when their stand-off reached an uncomfortable amount of time, she broke.

"Why are you here?"

He cleared his throat, probably because it had been too long since he last spoke.

"I wanted to congratulate you," he said with a nod to the phone in her hand. "On the reviews. And to let you know I ironed out all the supplier problems. We're ready for the grand opening next week."

Willow's shoulders relaxed. "Thank you," she said. "We'll be ready, too."

She looked around the room awkwardly, searching for the words to say to smooth things over between them, when she noticed Jer at the Fuzzy Milkshake tank reaching for the sample valve.

Oh no.

"Jer, wait!" she shouted. "You need to release the—"

A loud popping sound echoed through the brewery, drowning out her voice right before a torrent of beer exploded from the tank. It hit Jer in the face with so much force that it launched him backwards, clear across the room.

Willow took off running and made it to Jer just as he was clambering to his feet in an enormous pool of beer. He flipped over to stand, then cringed in pain.

"Willow, close the valve."

She dashed to the tank and grabbed the handle on the valve, but it was no use. She couldn't turn it under all the pressure. Finally, Max appeared beside her, pushed her hand aside, and jerked it closed. But by the time he'd sealed it, there was hardly any Fuzzy Milkshake left.

She stared at the floor, wanting to look away, but the shock of the last sixty seconds kept her frozen in place. Had that really just happened? Was all their beer gone?

"Willow," Jer said, making his way to his feet, his hand over the deep gash on his arm. "I'm so, so sorry."

Finally, she snapped out of it and blinked away.

"It's my fault," she said. "I should've shown you how the valve works on this tank." She looked at his arm, and her eyes bulged. "That looks deep."

Jer looked down at his arm, then closed his eyes, swaying a little on his feet and looking as if he was going to pass out. "I must've hit the corner of that tank," he said, gesturing across the room to where he'd landed.

"I'm taking you to the hospital. You might have a concussion. And you're definitely going to need stitches," she said, putting her hand on his shoulder and leading him to the door.

Max silently flanked Jer's other side and followed them to the door, held it open and did the same with the car. They got Jer in the front seat buckled in, then closed the door.

"Was that your Fuzzy Milkshake?" Max asked.

Her heart shrunk. "Yeah."

"It's all gone?"

She nodded, and he swore under his breath. She wanted to be angry, sad, throw something, yell at someone, but she only felt . . . defeat.

She was to blame for this. If she hadn't been so distracted by all the Shane and Max nonsense, she'd have been paying closer attention.

She sucked in a breath and forced her focus on what was most important. Jer.

"I have to go," she said, brushing past Max and dropping into the driver's seat. She turned on the car, reversed out of her spot, and headed for the road before realizing she didn't know where the hospital was.

"Willow, I feel awful about the beer—"

"Let's worry about that later. Which way to the hospital?"

Jer sighed. "Go left."

She nodded, then pulled out.

TWENTY-EIGHT

Max stared at the clock on the wall and impatiently tapped his pen on the desk. It had been six hours since Willow and Jer had left to go to the hospital, and he'd been seething ever since. The more he attempted to control his anger and frustration at the situation, the more it seemed to consume him.

He shook his head as he replayed the scene in the brewery over and over in his mind and couldn't help but think that everything would have gone smoothly had he still been the owner.

He never would've hired Jer, and they would've had the beer they needed for the grand opening.

He stood from his chair and paced the room. It was hard to put into words how incredibly frustrating it was that he'd been grinding nonstop for days, negotiating with suppliers, taking phone calls at all hours, doing everything he could to make sure they could open on time, and then that fool stepped in and fucked it all up.

And it wasn't only him. The rest of the staff had also been working around the clock.

He pulled his phone from his pocket and checked the social accounts for the pub and brewery. The latest post had over a hundred comments from people expressing their excitement for the opening. And that was nothing compared to the comments on the post announcing Fuzzy Milkshake.

Their marketing efforts had worked almost too well. And now they couldn't deliver on the promises they'd made.

He caught himself grinding his teeth and gave his head a shake as he shoved his phone back in his pocket. He needed a plan.

If Willow brewed another batch right away, it would take two weeks for it to be ready, but they were only one week out from the grand opening. So they were going to have to make a choice between two equally shitty options: either open on time without the beer that everyone wanted, or open one week late with it.

He hated both.

Every day they spent not open, they were bleeding money. But opening without the beer was just inexcusable at this point. The only other option would be to have separate grand openings, but he hated that idea, so he refused to entertain it.

He paced the floor before letting out a heavy sigh.

The best thing to do would probably be to bump the grand opening back one week and open together with the beer everyone was excited for.

He hated it, but there was no changing what had been done.

Just then, the office door swung open, and in walked Willow. She was in the same clothes from before, but her hair was pulled back and her eyes were all red.

The anger and frustration that had been bubbling over waned as she closed the door behind her and sat in the chair at their desk.

"Are you okay?"

She lifted one shoulder and let it fall.

"How's Jer?"

"He needed ten stitches, and he has a mild concussion, but overall, he's okay."

Max winced, hating the defeated look on her face. He wanted to pick her up, take her home, and hold her all night. Honestly, he probably needed the same thing.

"I just dropped him off at home so he could shower and rest," she said, rolling her shoulders. "He'll be in tomorrow."

He stood from his chair and made his way behind her, then gently took her shoulders in his hands and massaged her. "I think we should do the same," he said. "You can come to my place, and I'll order us dinner."

Willow shook her head. "I want to get the brewery cleaned up and start the batch over again. There won't be enough Fuzzy Milkshake to open."

Max nodded, shifting his plan in his head to carrying her out of there after she'd done what she wanted to do. "I know. We're going to have to open a week late."

Willow shook her head, then twisted in her seat to look at him. "We can't."

"I know it sucks," he said. "But we don't have a choice. Opening on time without that beer is a bad idea."

She squeezed her eyes shut as if she had just received horrible news.

Max cocked a brow and wondered why she'd reacted that way. She'd had the same problem to mull over for the last six hours as he had. It shouldn't have been a surprise that they'd move it back a week.

"Willow, it's going to be fine. Jesus, you're taking this worse than me. It's only one week—"

"Two weeks."

Max stared at her, trying to make it make sense. One week to the opening, two weeks to brew, so it would be one week late. What wasn't he understanding?

"You said it takes two weeks to brew. We'll open as soon as it's ready. The canners can come back the day before. It'll be fine."

She shook her head. "Nikki's wedding day is in two weeks. I have to be in Churchill."

Max stared at her, shell-shocked. Was she actually considering putting off their opening for an extra week over a friend's wedding?

And a terrible fucking friend at that?

There was a nagging voice in the back of his mind telling him it wasn't just that she didn't seem to care about their business but also that she was going back there, where that fucking guy was, and the whole thing made him feel nauseous.

His control slipped as the frustration flooded in, and he'd just opened his mouth to let out his exasperation when the office door swung open and Luis popped his head inside.

"Max are you— Willow, you're back!" he said, stepping in. "How is Jer? Is he okay?"

Willow managed a smile in his direction. "He's okay, thanks."

"But the beer," Luis said, his face falling. "It's all gone."

She nodded and sighed. "I know. We're—"

"We're in a meeting," Max said, cutting her off with a hard tone and a pointed look directed at Luis.

He nodded and backed out, then Willow turned on him.

"That was very rude."

He clenched and unclenched his jaw. "I don't care, Willow," he said as his entire body overheated. "Are you seriously suggesting we delay our opening because of a fucking wedding?"

"It's my best friend's wedding, and I promised her I'd be there," she said, her eyes hard and cold.

Max seethed. "And didn't she promise you she'd keep her mouth shut about you being here?"

Willow rolled her eyes. "That was my fault. All of this was my fault. And I won't leave her without a maid of honour. She means too much to me."

His heart cracked, but he forced his mind off it and let the anger flood in instead. "So all of this means nothing to you?"

"Of course this means something to me," she said, her eyes searching his.

He looked away and shook his head.

She let out a heavy sigh. "Churchill's my home. All of my friends are there. I never really wanted to be without—"

"Shane."

She dropped her face in her hands. "This is too much."

Max knew he shouldn't say anything more, but he was just so fucking sick of this back and forth, not knowing how she felt or what she was planning to do. He hated being so uncertain about everything.

"Are you getting back together with him?"

Willow met his eye, held his stare for a moment, but her expression gave nothing away. Just when she opened her mouth, the office door opened again.

"Max, I was just going over the . . ."

The lead host took one look at his raging face, then mumbled an apology and scurried away.

The next person to touch that fucking door was getting stabbed through the eye with a pen.

"Answer my question," he said.

Willow's eyes snapped to his and narrowed. "I don't know."

Max shook his head and let out a humourless laugh.

They both knew she was getting back together with that prick. She'd never wanted her relationship with him to end. He'd ended it, and she was devastated. Max had been foolish enough to get involved with her and hope that she felt the same way.

But clearly, she didn't.

"Are you angry about the opening date or about Shane?" she asked.

He stared at her, unable to contain his feelings. It was all too much. She was taking up way too much real estate in his heart and mind.

And she was leaving.

"Both," he said, not able to meet her eye.

All the mental boxes he'd been carefully tucking away, tried desperately to keep closed, exploded off the shelves and filled up his mind. He tried to find a shovel, a broom, anything, but it was impossible. He could only manage to shut down completely.

He dropped all expression from his face, stood, closed his laptop, put it into his backpack and slung it over his shoulder. He had to get out of there.

He walked to the door, opened it, and stepped through.

"Wait."

He shook his head. "Good luck," he said, walking out the door and closing it behind him. "You're going to need it."

Twenty-Nine

Willow waited until she knew Max had left the building before she left the office. Her body felt heavy and her mind foggy as she finally arrived in the brewery.

She rubbed at the ache in her chest as she filled a bucket with soapy water. Once the bucket was filled, she began cleaning up all her ruined beer from the floor.

The day had gone so badly that she almost couldn't even believe it. Over the past three weeks, she'd gone from engaged and starting a business to single and homeless. The worst part of it all was that she couldn't shake the feeling that no matter what she did or how hard she tried, she was constantly disappointing someone.

She hadn't imagined things would go so wrong so fast. She'd truly believed she could pull this whole thing off, but she'd failed miserably.

Maybe Shane had been right.

Maybe this was a bad idea, and she should have just left well enough alone. She'd been happy enough with him in Churchill. Just because things weren't perfect didn't mean they weren't good, or weren't worth trying to save at least.

She fought back tears as she moved around the room, mopping. It didn't take long for her mind to land on Max.

His reaction hadn't surprised her, but the sudden change in his expression had sent a chill down her spine. She'd never seen him as angry before.

But how could he expect her to miss her best friend's wedding?

She suspected Shane was the underlying reason for his frustration, but it was unreasonable for him to expect her to just abandon her whole life in Churchill. Especially when she'd only known Max for three weeks and he was so hard to read.

Granted, she had much stronger feelings for Max than she'd ever imagined she could have in only a few weeks. And the thought of leaving him made her feel sick.

He was supportive and encouraging.

Until he wasn't.

She fought back tears. This was a hard decision to make. The only thing she was certain of was that she couldn't miss her best friend's wedding.

It took her a couple of hours to mop the floor, clean and sanitize the tank, and start the mash for a fresh batch of Fuzzy Milkshake. She let her mind pour over her predicament the whole time. She still didn't know what she wanted, but she'd figured out some key things.

One, it wasn't right to delay the opening more than a week. Max, Luis, and everyone else had worked hard to be ready on time, and it wasn't fair to ask them to delay for her friend's wedding in Churchill.

And two, she was far too overwhelmed and stressed to make life-altering decisions.

She pulled out her phone, opened Max's contact, and typed out a simple message: *Open one week late without me. Beer will be ready.*

She stared at it for a moment, the tears flowing again. It was going to kill her to miss the grand opening, but at least she would still be a good friend and business partner.

She hit Send, then packed up her things and drove home. When she got there, the house was empty. She wished Cara or Chelsea had been around to talk to, but she'd rather have someone without bias to talk things through with and help her.

And that's when it hit her; she should go to Nana.

She had a flight from Ottawa in a few days, anyway. And Jer was more than capable of finishing the beer. He had made one mistake—a mistake that even she had made before—and she knew it was traumatic enough that he wouldn't repeat it.

She gave a single nod, decision made, and went in the closet to pack, trying to ignore the sick feeling rising in her gut at the possibility that she might never be back.

Thirty

Max forced himself off the couch and made his way to his dining table where he'd left his laptop untouched the day before. On any other day, he'd have already dealt with a million problems, but after the text he'd received from Willow the night before telling him to open without her, he'd been having trouble finding the energy for even his usual routine.

His email had been going off all morning while he lay on the couch, ignoring it, and watching sports highlights he'd fallen behind on. It was about noon when he finally got up and dealt with it before it got out of control.

The first ten emails were mindless, about things that weren't urgent, so he skipped them and scrolled until he saw the name that he'd been seething over for the past twenty-four hours.

Fucking Jer.

He'd sent out a mass email that morning apologizing for his mistake that caused the delay. Max quickly read through the responses, all positive "we all make mistakes" bullshit, and he couldn't take it anymore. Rather than replying, he started a new email addressed to only Jer.

He could feel the tension in his shoulders and knew this was probably a bad time to be corresponding with that fool, but he couldn't take it anymore. Jer was the reason everything had gone to shit. Willow was partly to blame, since she'd hired him, but he refused any further communication with her, so he couldn't very well take his anger out on her.

He started, stopped, deleted, and rewrote the few sentences repeatedly, trying to sound as calm as possible. He wanted so badly to write "Don't fuck this up again!" but he knew that wouldn't be okay. In the end, it wasn't too mean. He'd just made it clear that, going forward, Jer would answer to him, and he expected Jer to check in twice daily, starting tomorrow, to ensure they would open on time.

A few minutes went by before he got a reply.

He opened it, read through quickly, then sat back in his chair, shocked.

Jer had quit.

And he'd done a terrible job at it. All he wrote was, "I will never work for you. Buh bye!"

Max rolled his eyes. The guy couldn't even quit properly.

He opened his spreadsheet and was sifting through the other candidates he'd gone through weeks earlier when the doorbell rang. Before he could even get up, it rang again.

Then again.

"Okay," he yelled. "I'm fucking coming."

He'd barely got the door open when Cara pushed it the rest of the way and forced herself in.

"What the hell, Max?"

He stared at the back of her head, dumbfounded. "What the hell, Cara?"

She spun on him, looked him up and down, then frowned. "Where's Willow?"

"How should I know?" he asked, slamming the door behind her. "You're her roommate."

"Yeah," she said. "I went by the pub on my way home this morning, and neither of you were there, and when I got home, she was gone, poof, vanished."

Max narrowed his eyes at her. "On your way home this morning?"

She stopped dead in her tracks, blinked twice. "I thought maybe she'd moved in with you or something. What the hell happened?"

Max shook his head and went back to the table. "Her ridiculous protégé destroyed all the beer and forced us to move the grand opening back. Willow decided she'd rather be with those toxic assholes in Churchill than with—than here, so she left."

Cara's shoulders sank. She moved to the chair opposite him as her face took on a pained expression.

"Stop," he said, looking back down at the spreadsheet.

She sagged back in the chair. "Do you know when she'll be back?"

Max shrugged. "Maybe never."

"I'm sorry, Max. You must be so—"

"I'm not so anything."

"But I thought you guys were, like, together. Weren't you?"

All the Willow memories came pouring out. The first time she'd made him laugh over the phone, her pretty flushed face every time they kissed. How she looked spread across their desk.

Fuck, even the ripped-up pen box.

He shook it off and narrowed his eyes at her, taking the focus off of himself. "Do you really want to have a heart-to-heart about our love lives, Cara?"

She schooled her features and fell silent.

"Where have you been lately?" he asked. "You haven't been coming around. I never hear from you, and you didn't even know your roommate was missing."

She shook her head a little, looked to the side out the window.

"You're back with that fucking Cooper. I know you are."

Her shoulders slumped.

Max let out a humourless laugh. "It's no wonder you and Willow got along so well."

"I know you don't like him—"

"I don't like the way he treats you. I don't like the way you let him. And I don't like his fucking mullet."

"I love him."

And that was exactly the fucking problem. Same with Willow. They were both letting their feelings guide their decisions instead of basic logic.

"So?"

"So, I can't just pretend that I don't have feelings," she said, her own temper flaring. He knew Cara well enough to know that as bad as his temper was, it was no match for hers.

"Of course you can," he said, forcing his tone to even out. "And you absolutely should."

Silence fell over them, and Max was thankful his words were sinking in. Maybe she was finally getting it now and realizing that feeling love was the most surefire way to get trampled all over.

"Is that what you did to Willow?"

Max's gaze flicked to hers. "She was engaged to someone else," he said.

"But then she wasn't, and then you fell in love with her, and you still iced her out, didn't you?"

Max opened his mouth to speak, but Cara beat him to it.

"And that's why she left, and that's going to be the reason she never comes back."

Max shook his head. "You're wrong. I told her how I felt, and I asked her to stay, and she left."

What the fuck did she expect him to do? Fall to the floor, latch onto her ankles, and beg her to never leave him?

"I don't have time for any of this," he said, turning his focus back to his spreadsheet. "I have a brewery to run, and now that Willow and Jer are gone, I can do it properly. Everything is the way it always should have been."

He had a responsibility to the other people working for him, to Luis, who'd moved his whole family for the job, and Adam, who'd invested to get the place up and running.

That was something he could control, something that he could, with enough work, make happen. Getting Willow to make a fucking decision wasn't something he could fix.

He'd banged his head off the wall enough when it came to her. It was time to move on.

Cara slowly stood from across the table.

"I don't blame Willow for leaving," she said, her eyes filling with tears that he knew were a mix of anger and sadness. But mostly anger.

Max ignored her feelings and shrugged. "It's probably for the best."

Her eyes flared, and she seethed. Literally seethed. "You can be such an asshole sometimes," she said, then marched across the room, out the front door, and slammed it behind her.

He got up immediately, followed her steps, and locked the door. He didn't want to see another person for the rest of the day.

THIRTY-ONE

"Drink this."

Willow took the pretty yellow teacup from Nana's hands, then sipped at the perfectly steeped Earl Grey tea as her nana joined her on the couch.

"Thanks," she said, feeling a little calmer now that she was in her nana's living room. It had changed a great deal since she was young and would visit with her mom, but the feeling was still the same. She absolutely loved it there.

Maybe instead of opening the brewery, she should have just come for a visit. At least then, her life would still be intact.

"What's wrong, Willow?" Nana asked, sinking into the floral couch beside her and rubbing a hand up and down her arm. "Your ruse didn't work as you'd hoped?"

Willow shook her head, wanting to laugh at the irony. She was supposedly going there to take care of Nana, but here she was, being taken care of by Nana.

"No. It all blew up in my face."

Nana's eyebrow arched above her frameless glasses and she shook back her sleek gray bob.

"It can't be that bad. At least you went after what you want. I'm proud of you for that."

Willow's eyebrows scrunched together. It wasn't that out of character for her to go after what she wanted, was it? She was constantly pushing Doug to let her make new beers at work, and she wasn't really what you'd call a pushover. Though it would be a stretch to say she was the master of her own destiny.

"Tell me what happened." Nana said, searching deep in her eyes.

Willow sighed. "I don't even know where to begin."

Nana sat back and crossed one leg over the other. "Start at the beginning."

Willow took a deep breath, then unloaded it all. She told her about the lying, about how freeing, yet scary, running her own brewery was, about Max and all the feelings he brought out in her, about how different he was from Shane, about Shane showing up and breaking up with her.

She even told her about the desk sex with Max in their office immediately afterward.

By the time she got to the end, she was in tears.

Nana nodded, thought for a moment as she passed Willow a box of tissues.

"Do you love Max?" she finally asked.

Willow blotted her eyes. "I'm supposed to be engaged to Shane."

"Answer my question, Willow."

She sagged. "Yes, I love him. Well, *loved* him. He was so horrible the last time we spoke."

Nana nodded. "Why do you love him?"

She thought for a moment. "I just feel great when I'm with him, like I could take over the world and he'd be there next to me, cheering me on and threatening to kill anyone that got in my way."

Nana's brows shot up. "And you'd do the same for him?"

Willow immediately nodded. "Absolutely. I think we're alike, in some ways."

"How are you different?"

Willow huffed out an annoyed breath. "Well, for one, he's an asshole."

Nana laughed. "I'm seventy years old, and I still haven't figured out what it is about assholes that makes them so damn appealing. My second and fourth husband was like that."

Willow laughed. "Is that why you married him twice?"

Nana nodded. "I just kept getting drawn back in to his orbit."

"Why did you divorce him?"

"Because the deeper in love he fell, the more controlling he became, and I just couldn't take it. I thought he'd changed after the first time, but obviously, I was wrong," she said with a shake of her head. "At least he's dead now, so I can't make the same mistake three times."

Willow smiled, but it was fleeting. "Do you think being with Max would be a mistake?"

Nana thought for a moment. "If he respects your boundaries and doesn't let his controlling get out of hand, then no. But you have to know what your boundaries are, Willow," she said with a pointed look.

"What about Shane?"

Nana shrugged. "What about him?"

"He wants to get back together."

Nana shook her head. "What do *you* want?"

"I told him I'd marry him."

"But that was before."

Willow's chin dropped. "Yeah, before I lied to him."

Nana sat back, her eyes narrowing. "So you're going to marry him because you lied to him?"

"Uh," Willow said, her mind running. "No."

"I can't tell whether you're people-pleasing or being manipulated."

"Neither. I'm following through on my commitments."

Nana shook her head. "It seems like you're saying yes to everything and everyone, and now all your yeses have come due, and you can't make a decision because you're going to *have* to let someone down, and that's making you uncomfortable."

Willow stared at her in shock. That seemed pretty accurate, actually. She had to admit she'd felt like a worn-out old rope in a tug-of-war match that was ready to break.

"Willow, you need to decide what you want, then stick to it. And you can't let Shane or Nikki or Max or anyone else shame you into changing your mind."

"But I—"

"Every *yes* to one person is a *no* to someone else," Nana said. Then she stood, picked up the empty teacups and left the room.

Willow sat staring at the wall, then slumped down, annoyed at how right her nana was.

Every *yes* she gave Mapleton was a *no* to Churchill, and vice versa. The *yes* to Nikki's wedding was a *no* to her brewery. So it stood to reason that any *yes* she gave Shane would be a *no* to Max.

She flopped her head down onto the soft throw pillow in the corner of the couch.

Her feelings for Shane had felt forced for a long time, like a puzzle piece that didn't quite fit. Whereas her feelings for Max had been effortless from the start. She clearly knew where her heart was, so why hadn't she just gone for it?

Because it wasn't just Shane versus Max. It was her whole life, her job, her only home, her dog, her friends; it was all of that versus a total fresh start in a new city.

A fresh start she'd never even really wanted.

And with people she'd known for only a few weeks.

She'd started this whole mess because she needed some fulfillment in her work. But once she started down that path and got some distance, it was easy to see all the flaws in her whole life. But that didn't mean she wanted to throw the baby out with the bathwater. She loved living in Churchill, despite everything else.

The whole thing was complicated.

She was certain she didn't want to give a *yes* to Shane if that meant a *no* to Max. But even though her feelings for Max had become pretty deep, he'd been so impatient and difficult and pressed her so hard that she couldn't stand it.

And what about her friends? What about Nikki?

She wanted to give a *yes* to Nikki, even if that meant a *no* to her business. She was quite certain of that. But what would she do after Nikki's wedding?

Her heart was telling her to go back and be with Max, but could she actually deal with his temper forever?

And was forever even something she wanted?

Nana came back into the room with fresh cups of tea and a plate of lavender cookies. "So, what have you decided?"

Willow huffed out a breath. There was only one thing she knew for certain.

"I want to go back to Churchill for Nikki's wedding. She's my friend, and I couldn't live with myself if I ruined her wedding day."

"Okay," she said with a nod. "And after that?"

She sagged a little, her bravado waning. "I don't know."

Nana shrugged. "That's okay, Willow. It's a huge decision, and you should take your time with it. Don't let the men in your life push you into anything. Make 'em wait," she said with a wink.

Willow laughed. "And if they both decide I'm too much trouble and leave?"

A wry smile came over Nana's face. "Don't under-estimate the peace that being single affords you. I'm the happiest I've ever been."

Willow smiled as her Nana held up her teacup, and they clinked glasses.

"Now, finish up your tea and have some cookies. We'll go out for dinner."

One good thing about saying yes to Mapleton: she'd be closer to Nana.

She stuck that as the first line in her pros and cons list, then thought about making a spreadsheet. God, a few weeks with Max and she was already making spreadsheets?

She rolled her eyes, downed her tea, and set aside the question that was now freshly burning in her mind.

Did Max belong in the pro column, or the con?

Thirty-Two

Max pulled into the pub's parking lot, grabbed his bag, and headed for the door. Although he still hadn't followed his usual morning routine, he had put on pants with a zipper and left his house. He would have argued that he was at work because he wanted to be, but that would be a lie. He'd much rather be working from his couch, but this grand opening had become a total fucking dumpster fire, so he had no choice.

At least everyone in the building, and his personal life for that matter, sensed that he was in a foul mood and avoided him as though he were a murderer wielding a machete. Which was why he was shocked when a text came through his phone.

A glimmer of hope filled his heart. Maybe it was Willow telling him she was coming back. He drew in a long breath and held it as he pushed the hope away.

Far, far away.

She wasn't coming back. He knew it, and he needed to accept it, even if the thought made a brick out of his stomach.

He ignored the text and carried on, but another text came.

Then another.

And another.

"Someone had better be dead," he muttered as he punched in his PIN on the lock screen. When he saw it was Cara, he rolled his eyes and opened the conversation. Maybe she needed rescuing from that fucking mullet guy again.

He read through all the texts and rolled his eyes again when he saw she wasn't in trouble. She was on a mission to "save" him or some fucking thing:

I figured out your problem. And since I know you HATE heart-to-hearts, I'm sending you an email.

Don't ignore it.

I'm serious.

I'm not talking to you, or seeing you, until you read it.

The last text stung a little, so he opened his email and clicked on the link, which led him to an article on a psychology website where she was diagnosing him with some ridiculous label that supposedly explained how his traumatic childhood was to blame for his current situation. He sighed and clicked on her conversation to reply.

You realize I have a lot on my plate right now.

She immediately responded. *Not talking to you.*

I don't have time for this, Cara.

If you keep being an asshole, the only person you'll have left is me.

He stared at the words as they stared back.

He begrudgingly clicked on the link she had shared and opened the article. It took him five minutes to get to the end, and although some very salient arguments had already formed against it in his mind, he had to admit the evidence was hard to deny.

Basically, she'd accused him of avoiding people he cared about to stop them from getting too close so that he could control his feelings. He wanted to argue that it was bullshit, because he'd never do that to Cara, but if he was being honest, she was the only person he never did that to.

And according to her assessment, that was because he subconsciously knew Cara could never, or would never, leave.

He shook his head, not buying it. He'd had close friendships his whole life.

But on the other hand, he kept them at arm's length. He'd even advised Adam to do the same with Chelsea, and he'd never stopped feeling guilty about that.

He just never opened up to them because when he was young, all his friends were growing up with normal families, and he'd always been too embarrassed to tell them that his life was a big steaming pile of dog shit.

It was difficult to deny that his upbringing, or lack thereof, still impacted him now. And it was impossible to deny that he craved control in order to prevent anything bad from happening again.

But that wasn't something wrong with him. That was his best quality.

If he took control, everything would be fine, and his track record proved it. He'd raised Cara, and she was brilliant. She was earning a PhD; she was a responsible adult, and everyone that met her loved her.

Not to mention all the businesses he'd started, or purchased, were thriving under his control.

And one day, when he found someone right for him, he would make certain that everything went smoothly so that if he had children, they would never experience the same struggle of fending for themselves as he and Cara had.

He shook his head, completely fucking annoyed.

What everyone else seemed to think was a flaw was actually a feature.

Then why haven't you ever had a long-term relationship?

He let his mind turn that question around and, unfortunately, came up blank. His life *was* in shambles. Willow had left. His sister was refusing to talk to him, and his new business was falling apart around him.

Was everyone else to blame but him? Obviously not. He was the only common denominator.

Was it his desperate need to control everything? He knew he'd handled the situation with Willow poorly. The hurt in her eyes when he'd shut down still haunted him.

Was she really as indecisive as he thought?

Yes.

But maybe he had been too pushy. Maybe he should have given her some space instead of trying to force her into a decision and then shutting her out when she hadn't been able to make one.

It wasn't her fault that things had gone wrong, and he supposed Jer wasn't the worst employee ever. At least he came to work on time and did what Willow told him to do.

Plus, Max had sold the brewery to her, and so it was hers to control. Not his. If she wanted to hire a team of monkeys to work there and put the opening back three months, that would be up to her.

He sighed, feeling like an asshole, and opened his spreadsheets, checked his accounts, and pulled up his calculator. The thought of having the grand opening without her felt gross and wrong.

He wanted her there, he wanted to celebrate with her, and he wanted her to experience what she'd accomplished. She needed to be there to see it all come together.

He ran some numbers, and although it would hurt his bottom line and frustrate their clientele, it wouldn't be catastrophic to push the opening back two weeks.

He stood from his—*their* chair and marched out of the office to the kitchen.

"Luis," he said as he walked through the kitchen door.

Everyone in the kitchen turned their gaze downward and scurried away as if they were bunnies and had just spotted a wolf.

"Yes, Max?" Luis said. He was the only one that wasn't scared.

"Would you be okay with us moving the opening back one more week?"

Luis blinked rapid fire a few times before his mouth fell open. "Would I be okay?"

Max cringed. "I've been a dick to you, haven't I?"

"Well, not so much to me," he said with a shrug. "But I wouldn't call our interactions *warm* by any means."

He blew out a breath, shifted his weight between his feet. "I'm sorry."

Luis gave a smirk. "Was that painful?"

"Yeah," he said with the first laugh he'd let out in days. "A little."

"It's okay, Max," Luis said, patting his arm. "It's a lot of stress, and no one's perfect. I forgive you."

"Thank you," Max said with a sigh of relief. "So you're okay if we move the opening back an extra week?"

Luis nodded. "Yes, we can perfect the systems in the meantime. Will the brewery be ready, though?"

Max suddenly remembered that Jer had quit. God, what a fucking nightmare.

"I need to figure that out still. Maybe I can apologize to Jer and talk him into coming back."

"Back?" Luis asked, a frown forming.

"Yeah," he said, the regret surging up once more. "He quit."

Luis shook his head. "Jer was here today, but he left."

Max pushed down the urge to be annoyed that it was only four o'clock and he was gone. Not his employee, not his to control. He was determined to stay in his lane from now on.

"Oh, maybe I can find him. Do you know where he lives?"

"No," Luis said. "But I know he's at sound healing tonight."

Max stared at him, trying to make it make sense. "What the fuck is sound healing?"

Luis snickered as he pulled out his phone. "I'll text you the address. You should go. He'll consider it an olive branch."

For fuck's sake.

He shook it off, determined to do whatever it took to make sure Willow could open her brewery, with the employee she loved, and be there for it. Even if that meant taking part in a bunch of hippy woo-woo crap with Jer.

He pulled in a deep breath and let it out through his clenched teeth. "I guess I'm going to sound healing, then."

Luis laughed. "You never know, Max. Maybe it'll help."

THIRTY-THREE

After two long flights and a train ride, Willow finally arrived back in Churchill the day before Nikki's wedding. She walked from the train station to Shane's house and absolutely could not contain her excitement at finally seeing Barley again.

She unlocked the door and fell to the ground, tears in her eyes as Barley jumped into her lap.

"Good boy, Barley, good boy," she said, getting way too choked up.

He looked up at her, then licked her face.

"I'm never leaving you again," she said. "Never."

Just then, a text notification came through her phone. She shifted Barley to one side and checked it. It was from Max, and he was as cold and emotionless over a text as he was in real life.

Pushing back the opening one more week.

She stared at the letters, unable to believe it. Why had he made such a big fucking deal about it before if he was just going to move it back, anyway? She rolled her eyes, shoved the phone in her bag where she couldn't see it, and latched onto Barley.

Max had taken his sweet-ass time replying to her, so she'd do the same.

"You'd hate Max," she said to Barley, and he melted into her lap and stared up at her eyes. "He's mean."

She stayed on the floor for a while longer and held Barley until she finally wondered whether she was holding him or he was holding her. Could he sense how emotionally distressed she was? Probably. Or maybe she was almost always in distress around him, so he'd just got used to it.

Finally, she stood and looked around. She knew she didn't want to stay in Shane's house, so she went to the bedroom and opened her closet door.

Should she pack everything or only what she wanted? It seemed rude to leave behind a bunch of stuff, so she took it all and figured she'd decide what to do with it later.

She was about halfway through the task when the front door creaked open. Barley lifted his head slightly at the sound, then lay back down on her pile of sweaters.

At least he wouldn't miss Shane.

A few moments later, Shane walked into the bedroom, then stopped in his tracks.

"Willow?"

She turned to face him. "Hi."

He closed the distance between them and pulled her into a hug. She let him, but didn't hug back, and couldn't shake the feeling that it was all wrong. Maybe she'd got too used to Max's enormous arms around her that made her feel so good.

Shane was shorter and bonier, and she felt uncomfortable, as if she were teetering on the edge of a cliff.

She broke off the hug and stepped away, returning to her task.

"What are you doing?"

"I'm packing my stuff," she said.

Shane's shoulders slumped. "Willow, I made a mistake. Don't go."

She stopped and turned to him. "We both made mistakes. I think it's time to call it quits."

He shook his head, took her by the shoulders. "I don't want to stop you from opening your brewery," he said, staring into her eyes. "You can run it from here, like you said, and we can still be together."

She broke eye contact Sand looked away. He was finally saying all the right things, and she felt nauseous.

"I got you something," he said.

He turned and walked across the bedroom to his tall wood dresser and pulled open the top drawer. A moment later, he returned holding a ring box. How was it even possible that this nightmare was getting worse?

"Willow," he said, taking her hand. "You mean so much to me. I can't live without you. I want to marry you, for real this time."

"For real this time?" she asked, her chest tightening. "So you didn't really mean it last time?"

He looked down at the ring, then back up. "I mean, this time I'm ready."

She couldn't even hide how annoyed she was anymore. They'd been engaged for over six months. Six! And he'd never wanted to talk about a wedding, had never given her a ring. Was he pushing this now because she'd finally had enough or because he actually wanted to marry her?

"Would you have been ready now if we hadn't broken up?" she asked.

He immediately nodded. "I just needed some time. Just please wear it for now," he said, pulling the ring from the box and shoving it onto her finger.

Her eyes widened at the sight of a ring finally on her finger. He started talking again, telling her how much he loved her, how perfect they were for each other, bringing up the good times they'd spent together, but his words weren't making an impact.

In fact, she could barely hear him. All she could feel was the ring around her finger, almost painfully, as if it were made of splinters that faced inward, digging under her skin.

She yanked the ring off, silencing his reminiscing, and held it out to him like some cursed talisman.

"I can't take this. I don't want to marry you."

An immense burden lifted from her shoulders, and she felt her forehead relax. Why had she ever thought marrying him would be a good idea?

He stared in shock, then finally took the ring and searched her eyes. "Why?"

"We're a disaster together. And we want very different things."

"What do you want?" he asked.

She blew out a breath, still uncertain. "I don't really know. I think it's much easier for me to know what I don't want. And I know I don't want to marry you. I'm sorry."

She turned and began folding the clothes twice as fast as she had been. She needed to get out of there.

"Where are you going?"

"I don't know yet," she said without looking at him. "Maybe Nikki's or the motel."

Shane huffed out a breath. "Just stay here," he said. "I'll sleep in the other room."

She shook her head. She didn't want to be in there a minute longer.

"Nikki and Kyle want the place to themselves after the wedding, and the motel is full of guests," he said.

She stopped, looked over her shoulder. She really didn't want to stay, but it seemed there wasn't really a choice.

"Okay, but just for the weekend. And *I'll* sleep in the other room."

Shane ran a hand through his hair and sighed. "Fine."

Thirty-Four

The smell was the first thing that hit Max as he walked through the door of the holistic healing centre.

It was some weird musky scent he was sure was supposed to heal him of every ailment under the sun and restore his balance or whatever. Unfortunately, Max quickly realized the smell wouldn't be the most uncomfortable thing about the place.

"Welcome, and thank you for joining us this evening," a girl said from behind the counter, steepling her hands and bowing her head.

"Uh, hi," he said.

Should he bow back?

She looked him up and down, then leaned over the counter, tipping her head to the side and batting her eyelashes. "Are you here for the ethereal frequencies sound bath meditation or the emotional release aromatherapy?"

What?

"Uh . . ."

He searched his memory for the conversation with Luis. He'd said it was something about sound, right? Fuck. It could've been a smell thing.

"I'm not really sure."

"That's okay," she said, coming from behind the counter and stalking toward him. "I can give you an overview of both, and you can see which one speaks to your quantum energy."

Okay, he was definitely out of there.

He had just started backing away, formulating a half-assed excuse, when the door chimed behind him and a fresh breeze wafted in, relieving the air of its stink for a moment.

"Max?"

He spun around and found Jer walking through the door. He never thought he'd be so happy to see the guy.

"Jer!"

Jer's expression went from shock to fright in an instant. "Uh, hi?"

The hippy girl glanced between the two of them, then seemed to have a realization. "Oh, Jer, is this your new boyfriend?"

Max smiled, then turned to Jer and wagged his eyebrows. That was one good way to stop her from speaking to his inner self or whatever the fuck.

Jer turned his nose up and placed his hand over his heart. "As fucking if."

"What the hell, Jer?" Max asked, as if he'd just slapped him.

Jer rolled his eyes. "This guy thinks he's my boss and can tell me what to do, but he's not," he said, then looked away and muttered, "and now he's here. In my happy place. Annoying me."

Max cringed. "I came to apologize."

Jer raised his eyebrows and tilted his head to the side.

"I'm serious. Can we please just talk before you"—he waved behind him in the general direction of all the woo crap of the place—"do whatever."

Jer stuck his chin in the air. "No," he said, brushing past him.

Max waited for a moment, the silence stretching between them as he desperately hoped Jer would reconsider. But as the seconds ticked by, it became painfully clear that Jer's decision was final.

He gave a defeated nod and turned to leave, but Jer's voice stopped him.

"I guess you can join me in the sound bath," he said.

Max stared slack-jawed as Jer tapped his card on the debit machine, brushed past, and sauntered through a door behind the counter.

Sound bath?

He let out a sigh and pulled out his wallet. How bad could it be?

"That'll be thirty dollars," the hippy girl said. "And it includes your yoga mat, pillow, and sleep mask."

"Sleep mask?"

Hippy girl smiled and nodded.

He tapped his card, took the armload of stuff, and followed Jer's footsteps.

The door led into a dim studio that was lit only with bunches of candles around the perimeter of the room. In the centre was a selection of weird bowls and mallets on a blanket, and fanning out from the centre were people lying on yoga mats with sleep masks on.

Max located Jer and went toward him, rolling out his mat and lying down beside him.

"I'm glad you came in," Jer said.

Max stopped and stared at the bottom half of his face. "How did you know it was me?"

"You have a very draining energy," he said in a calm, yet sarcastic, voice. "I can feel you coming from a mile away."

Max rolled his eyes. "I don't know what that means," he said as he sat down beside Jer and debated the sleep mask.

"Just put it on, and let this happen."

Max cocked an eyebrow. "That's exactly what robbers say before taking hostages."

Jer sucked in a deep breath. "See? Draining."

A man in white monk's robes walked in and took his place in the middle of the bowls. "Masks on, please."

With a suppressed eye roll, Max placed the mask on his face and lay back on the mat, adjusting the pillow under his head. As much as he hated to admit, it was relaxing to take a bit of time out to just lie there doing nothing.

The monk began tapping the bowls, and although he put up some resistance, eventually, he fell into a deeply peaceful state. So deeply peaceful that he lost track of time and forgot why he was even there.

"Okay, everyone," the monk guy said in a soft voice.

Max's trance broke with the sound of his voice, and he shook his head, pissed that it was over. That couldn't have been the forty-five minutes he'd paid for.

"We're all done for this session. Thank you for coming."

Max sat up and pulled off his sleep mask and checked his watch. He felt drugged.

"Feel better?" Jer asked.

Max shrugged. "Actually, yes," he said, rolling his neck. He probably hadn't felt that calm in . . . well, maybe never.

"Good," he said. "Let's get a green tea and talk."

Jer stood and gathered his things, and Max followed suit, keeping his mouth shut when it tried to open out of habit and suggest they go out for a *good* drink instead.

He followed Jer out of the studio to the front desk, where he poured two glasses of iced green tea from a glass drink dispenser before leading Max to a small table and chairs near a water fountain.

Jer passed him a glass, then took a drink, followed by a heavy sigh. "What do you want to talk about?"

"I'm sorry for how I treated you. And that I tried to stop Willow from hiring you."

Jer froze. "You tried to stop her from hiring me?"

Max cringed. "I thought you knew about that."

Jer visibly struggled for calm as he sipped his tea.

"I'm sorry for sending that email to you. It was a dick move. I was angry and took it out on you."

Jer shook his head and looked down. "I'm still so mad at myself over that. Willow took the blame, but it was all my fault," he said.

"Everyone makes mistakes," he said, thinking back to all the thoughtless shit he'd done over the last few weeks.

"Thanks," Jer said with a shrug. "I didn't really care that you'd acted like an asshole. Honestly, I expected it out of someone like you," he said.

Max let it show on his face how bad that stung. Normally, he wouldn't have, but what was the point in guarding his feelings now?

"Sorry," Jer said. "I know it's a high-stress situation, but you seem like the type that holds everyone to a standard of perfection."

Max swallowed against the lump in his throat.

"I just really hate that I let Willow down and made her doubt herself."

"I know how you feel," Max said, sipping from his cup and suppressing a shudder. "I was pissed about her wanting to go back for her friend's wedding instead of opening the brewery, and I feel like a huge dick about it now."

Jer glanced up at him and held his gaze for a moment. "I actually agreed with you. About her not going back there."

Max's eyebrows shot up. "You agreed with me?"

"Don't get used to it," he said with a smile. "I think she struggles with decisions because she's a textbook people pleaser. And she has some weird Stockholm Syndrome thing going on with those people. She's so used to being everything for them that she's lost sight of what she wants."

Max nodded.

"For what it's worth," Jer continued, "I think you're actually good for her, in a way. You can be a controlling asshole, but at least you don't hold her back from what she wants, like Shane."

"Thanks," he said, choosing to focus on the good in his backhanded compliment. "I think I'm good for her, too, but I can be better."

"I heard you want to move the opening back."

"You heard that from Willow?"

"Yeah."

His shoulders slumped. "So she got my text."

Jer nodded. "I wouldn't hold my breath for a reply. She's pissed."

"Yeah, I know," he said. "I just hope she comes back for the opening. She deserves to see it come together."

Jer nodded. "You're not gonna try to convince her to stay if she comes back?"

Max shook his head. "I'm going to throw the ball in her court and hope for the best."

He fucking hated feeling so . . . vulnerable. But he supposed that's what loving someone felt like.

"Sports metaphors never make sense," Jer said, shaking his head. "If you're putting the ball in her court, does that mean she's not on your team? Are you hoping she scores on you? Or are you hoping she fails? And aren't both things bad if what you want is for her to be with you?"

Max thought about it for a minute. "You're right," he said with a laugh. "That makes no sense."

They hung out for a while longer and finished the gross tea, and Max had to admit, he'd been wrong about Jer. The guy was actually cool. And his weird hippy crap was actually really pleasant.

THIRTY-FIVE

"**I**s my veil straight?"

Willow glanced up at Nikki's twisted veil and made her way to where she was standing in front of a mirror. She adjusted the plastic comb at the crown of her head until it was perfect. "Now it is."

"Thanks, Willow," Nikki said, throwing a snide look at Kyle's teen sister who was on her phone in the corner of the room in a pink satin dress that matched Willow's. If his sister had noticed the shade being thrown at her, she didn't care.

"I'm glad someone here cares about my hair," Nikki said.

Willow gave a fake smile and returned to the couch, hoping none of the guests outside the doors filling the pews had overheard that.

She watched Nikki for a moment, blotting her lipstick and reapplying, but was having a hard time stopping her mind from wandering off of Nikki's wedding and onto her brewery. She might have been in Churchill physically, as she'd promised, but her mind was squarely in Mapleton.

She wondered what Jer was up to right then, and how the batch of Fuzzy Milkshake turned out, whether the canners had already left, and whether they'd done their jobs properly. The list went on and on.

She had been too busy with Nikki to speak to Jer that morning, but she planned to call him as soon as the ceremony and pictures were done, just to check in.

"You seem distracted," Nikki said in a singsong voice she used when she was trying to soften the bluntness of her words.

Willow blinked up at Nikki and reminded herself that she was supposed to be there for her best friend, even though she had to admit that Nikki was being a bit of a nightmare. She lied to herself, said it was the stress of the wedding, but honestly, Nikki had always been a little self-centred.

It just hadn't been obvious to Willow until she got some distance from her.

"Sorry," she said, shaking out her runaway thoughts. "I guess I'm just a little distracted. I have a lot going on."

"With Shane?"

Willow cringed. The last thing on her mind was Shane. That ship had sailed. "No."

Nikki finished her lipstick and joined Willow on the couch. "I know it's hard, but I think you'd be happier if you just forgave Shane and the two of you moved on."

Willow's mouth fell open. Why the hell did she think Willow would be happier going back to that terrible relationship?

"You *really* think that would make me happy?" she asked.

"Of course I do," Nikki said, as if to think otherwise was foolish.

"Even though we don't get along, we want different things, we've lied to each other, and he cheated on me?"

Of all the people she'd told about the cheating, Nikki was the only one who didn't think it was a big deal. Except for maybe Shane himself. Nana, Jer, Cara, Chelsea, Natalie, and especially Max had all thought it was despicable.

Nikki rolled her perfectly made-up eyes. "It was just sex."

Willow narrowed her eyes at her friend. Had Nikki ever acknowledged Willow's opinion? When they first met, Nikki had been the most popular girl in grade nine, and Willow was the new girl whose mom had just died and had never had a stable home. Had she latched onto Nikki's friendship because she liked her or because she was desperate for someone in her life?

Had she done the same thing with Shane?

Willow sighed.

That was absolutely what she'd done. But she'd been young and scared back then. What was her excuse for it now?

She turned away, staring off to the other wall. What would Max think about Nikki? He'd hate her immediately. But he hated everyone, so that was no surprise. But what about Cara? If Nikki were to visit Mapleton, would Cara want to hang out with her for a girl's night?

Willow already knew the answer to that.

"Seriously, Willow," Nikki said, snapping her fingers in Willow's face. "You need to get it together. We're going to be walking down the aisle any minute now."

"Why don't you ever ask me about what I want? Or about my brewery? And why are you always pushing me to go back to Shane?"

"Ugh," Nikki said. She stood from the couch and went back to the mirror. "I hoped my maid of honour wouldn't try to make my day all about them."

Willow bowed her head. In this instance, at least, Nikki was right.

It wasn't right to bring up Nikki's lack of friendship support on her wedding day. But to be fair, she'd owned the brewery for a month, and Nikki never talked about it, asked about it, or even acknowledged it. It might as well not even exist to her best friend.

And if Nikki was her best friend, wouldn't she want what was best for Willow?

The glaring problem was that Nikki had always put herself first. And Willow always put herself last.

They were a match made in toxic friendship heaven.

Just then, the door opened, and in walked Nikki's younger sister in the same dress that Willow and Kyle's sister were wearing. Right behind her came Nikki's mom, beaming from ear to ear. They exchanged hugs and cooed over how beautiful Nikki looked before her sister passed her a big white gift bag overflowing with pale blue tissue paper.

"We got you this," her sister said. "It's just something small."

Nikki smiled and grabbed the tissue paper from the top, tossing it on the floor, then pulled out a big stuffed bunny in a bridal gown with a veil.

Nikki's face fell right before she tossed an awkward glance in Willow's direction. She shoved the bunny back into the bag and mumbled a thank you.

Her sister's face fell.

"Don't you like it? We got it for you because of your nickname," she said. "Remember how we used to call you Bunny when you were a kid?"

Bunny?

Willow shook her head, banishing the thought. There was no way. No possible way. She looked at Nikki, and her stomach sank as Nikki paled under all that makeup.

"Bunny?" Willow asked, praying Nikki would laugh it off as a coincidence.

But she didn't.

Her whole body sagged until her chin reached her chest, and Willow knew.

She knew.

"Oh my God," she said, swallowing down the sick feeling. "You're Bunny367?"

• • • • • • • • • •

"I can't believe this," Willow said, standing up off the couch. The disappointment and pent-up anger rose from her feet and filled up her head. She started pacing the room, trying to make her brain work through the overwhelm.

"Willow," Nikki said with a shaky breath. "It's not—"

"Don't you fucking say it's not a big deal," Willow said, stabbing a glare across the room. "You knew how upset I was about Shane cheating on me, and the whole time, it was you. You!"

Gasps rang out from Nikki's sister and mom as they finally clued in to what was happening. Kyle's little sister leaped out of her chair and booked it toward the door.

"Willow!" Nikki yelled, trying to stop Kyle's sister, but she slipped past her and disappeared. "I can't believe you just did that."

Willow's jaw dropped. "Are you fucking kidding me?"

"You didn't have to scream it," Nikki said, glancing at her mom and sister, who were watching on in silent shock.

"And you didn't have to tell my boyfriend you wanted him to lick your asshole!"

Nikki's eyes started filling as she let out a sob and collapsed onto the couch. "You're ruining my wedding day."

Willow shook her head, looked around the room with a disbelieving laugh. Was she the only one hearing this? "You can't be *this* self-absorbed, can you? Being a bride doesn't give you a pass for cheating."

Nikki shook her head. "I wouldn't do this to you," she said.

"You *did* do this to me, Nikki. You told Shane about me going to Mapleton," she said with a laugh. "And I actually felt bad about asking you to lie for me. This is fucking wild."

Just then, Kyle came into the room with his sister following close behind. "What's— Nik, what's wrong?" Kyle asked. "Are you crying?"

Before anyone could get another word out, Shane stepped into the room, then froze.

Willow glanced at Kyle's sister and realized she hadn't told him anything yet. She probably didn't want to be the one to break the news. They all looked at Nikki, who was in the middle of full-body sobs, then at her sister and mom, who were tight lipped in the corner.

Willow rolled her eyes.

"Willow?" Kyle asked. "What's going on?"

All the eyes in the room swivelled to her.

She looked at Kyle and finally felt an emotion other than anger. She felt pity. There was no good way to say it, and no one else was piping up, so she braced herself and let it out.

"Nikki was the woman Shane was sexting."

Kyle stared at her for a long moment before turning to Shane, who'd used the time to back away toward the door like a little fucking coward. "Is that true?"

Shane's eyes darted around the room, and he'd never looked so guilty in his life.

Kyle let out a strangled noise, then looked around the room, and Willow felt sick for him. Here he was, on his wedding day, in a rented tux and everything, having the rug pulled out from under him.

"Was it just over text?" he asked.

Willow started nodding before realizing that she'd only heard that from Shane. She looked at Nikki, whose face had melted into a mess of tears, then at Shane, who'd gone still, shell-shocked.

When neither of them answered, Kyle spun toward Shane and grabbed him by the collar. "Answer me."

He glanced at Willow for a split second, then turned back to Kyle and dropped his head. "No."

Willow's jaw dropped as chaos broke out all around her.

Kyle punched Shane. Shane crumpled to the ground. Nikki screamed as blood poured from

Shane's nose onto his rented tie. Nikki's mom started wailing, and Kyle and his sister turned and
walked out of the room.

Willow stared at all the drama unfolding and felt
nothing but regret. No sadness or anger or valida-
tion.

Just regret.

"I gave up so much to be here," she said out loud,
even though no one was listening. "I want nothing
to do with you people."

She stepped over Shane's bloody face and made
her way to the door.

"Willow, wait," he said, moving to his knees and
trying to stand.

"Absolutely not," she said. "I'm packing up my
stuff, I'm taking Barley, and I'm leaving."

"But the motel—"

"I'm leaving Churchill," she said. "And I never want
to see any of you again."

With a flip of her hair, she marched out of the
room, not stopping when Nikki yelled her name
or when the people in the church asked what was
going on. She went all the way home and did exactly
what she'd said; she gathered up whatever clothes
she wanted, a bag of dog food for the trip, put a leash
on Barley, and got herself to the train station. Once

she'd settled on the train, she pulled out her phone and booked a one-way ticket on the next flight out.

Thirty-Six

"Ah! There you are."

Max looked up from the checklist he'd printed and across the dining room to find Cara walking toward the booth he'd taken over that morning. It was two days before opening, and he was finalizing all the details to make sure everything would run smoothly.

"Have you been looking for me?"

"Yes," she said, sliding into the booth across from him.

"Does this mean you're talking to me again?"

Cara smiled. "I started talking to you again after I heard you apologized to Jer. I've just been too busy to stop by."

"Busy with who?"

Cara sighed. "Professor Tanaka," she said, then stuck her chin in the air. "You'll be happy to know that I'm going to break up with Cooper."

Max eyed her suspiciously. It felt as if she'd just laid a trap. "I'm only happy to hear that if you're happy."

"Relax, Max," she said with a laugh. "I *am* happy, and I'm ready to move on. I spent all last night downloading dating apps and setting up profiles."

There were a million things Max wanted to say at that moment, but he stopped himself. He'd lectured her enough about the merits of carrying pepper spray and only meeting up with strangers in public places, so he resigned himself to a silent nod.

She laughed as if reading his mind. "I'll be safe, and I'll call you if I need you."

His shoulders relaxed, and he tried to have a heart-to-heart instead of a lecture. "So, what are you looking for?"

Cara smiled, and it made his discomfort ease. "I want a boyfriend who isn't an asshole."

Max nodded. "That's a good start. What else?"

"I guess I don't really know," she said. "Cooper was my first boyfriend."

Max nodded, resisted the lecturing again. He hadn't realized how natural it was for him to order people around until he tried to stop.

"You're young. You'll figure it out."

She raised one eyebrow. "Twenty-four isn't *that* young, Max."

"It's not that old, either," he said, but maybe she had a point.

He might have been a tad too overprotective of her. She probably should have had more than one boyfriend by this age. There hadn't been that many boys interested in her, but the ones that were had always been afraid of him.

It hadn't been entirely his fault, though. School had consumed her entire life, and she'd seemed disinterested in dating until Cooper came around. Maybe it was good that she was opening up more.

"Fine. You're right," he said with a nod. "Just don't—"

He stopped himself and internally vowed at that moment to let Cara take the wheel of her own life. But that didn't mean he had to jump ship completely. He'd be there if ever she needed him.

"Don't what?" she asked with a smile.

He shook his head.

"It's really hard for you to not tell me what to do, isn't it?"

He sighed. "It's fucking impossible."

Cara laughed. "Well, thanks for trying. And don't worry about me. I have a plan."

Max nodded. "So, when are you going to break up with him?"

She looked down at her lap. "Next time I see him. It's going to be hard, and super awkward to run into him, but unfortunately, it's unavoidable."

He nodded. Would it be awkward between him and Willow when she came back?

If she came back.

It had been five days since he'd texted her, and she still hadn't replied.

"Still no word from Willow?" Cara asked.

He found it weird how everyone seemed to read him like a book now that he allowed his feelings to just be felt. Actually, it wasn't weird. It was more like a relief.

He didn't have to dodge questions or explain himself. How much time had he wasted trying to close himself off?

"Crickets. You?"

Cara shook her head. "Not yet, but she'll come back. I'm sure of it."

"I hope so," he said, reaching for his phone. "Would it be too pushy to text her again?"

Cara shrugged. "Probably. Just let her decide for herself what she wants."

Cara was right, obviously. But it still hurt.

Just then, the door from the brewery opened, and Jer poked his head in. "Guys, I just finished everything off. Want to come over for a pint?"

"Definitely," Max said, standing from the booth. "You in?"

Cara nodded, and they both followed Jer through the door into the taproom and leaned against one of the high bar tables.

Jer went behind the counter, grabbed three glasses, and poured from the tap. The beer came out a perfect peach colour. He passed each of them a tall cold glass.

Jer lifted his glass and said, "Here's to finally making the first real batch of Fuzzy Milkshake."

They all smiled and clinked glasses before taking a long drink. The moment the beer hit his throat, Max had to suppress a groan. He swallowed it down with a smile. "It's fucking delicious."

"Oh my God," Cara said, her eyes going wide. "How did she make it taste exactly like peach ice cream?"

"How is it even better than the sample batch?" Max asked.

"She added a touch of cinnamon to the recipe," Jer said, wiping his lip. "I knew from the moment I saw her she was a genius."

Max laughed. "The feeling was mutual. She loved you from the jump. You did great, Jer. This is fantastic."

He ignored Jer's shocked face and lifted the glass to his nose to smell it. It was no wonder everyone was still eager to get down there and try it, even with a two-week delay. She was going to fucking kill it on opening night.

He just hoped she'd be there to see it.

"This is way, way, way better than good, Max," Cara said, taking another gulp. "This might be the best beer I've ever had."

Jer reached over and patted Max's shoulder. "I'm glad you guys like it. And I'm sorry we got off on the wrong foot, Max."

"Me too," Max said, then smirked. "You're actually cool, Jer-bear. Even with all your woo-woo bullshit."

Jer tipped his head back and laughed. "You better not call it woo-woo bullshit when you come to sound bath tomorrow. And I told you not to call me Jer-bear."

Max stopped in shock, his glass halfway to his lips. "I still can't call you that?"

"No."

"But I thought we were friends."

Jer smiled as he rolled his eyes so dramatically that his head swivelled around. Halfway through the rotation, he abruptly stopped, and his jaw dropped.

"Willow?"

Max straightened from his leaned-over position and spun toward the back door to find Willow standing just inside the doorway with a little brown dog on a leash and her jaw unhinged.

"Willow!" Cara yelled, taking off at a run and pulling her into a hug. Jer ran around the table and did the same thing, hugging her from the opposite side so they smothered her.

God, he wanted to do it, too. But he also didn't want to get slapped. The last time they'd seen each other, he'd been such an asshole. He needed to fix it.

He set his glass down and crossed the distance between them. "I'm glad you're back," he said.

Her pretty eyes widened before darting between him and Jer. "Were you two . . . laughing?"

He let out a laugh as the tension dropped. He always felt good talking to her. Something about her sarcastic little comments made him oddly at ease.

"Jer-bear and I are BFFs now," he said, then felt something at his ankle.

Max looked down at a tiny brown dog who'd pressed his nose into his shin. He bent and picked the thing up. It weighed next to nothing, and before he'd even stood, the dog had rolled onto his back and stared up into Max's eyes.

"Cute dog," he said, rubbing his furry little belly. "This must be Barley."

Willow nodded, her jaw still unhinged.

He looked away from Barley's eyes and at Willow. She looked beautiful. He wanted to hold her, kiss her, tell her he loved her.

"Can we talk?" he asked before remembering Cara and Jer were still there. "In private?"

She silently nodded.

Relief washed over him. "Let's go to our office."

"Okay," she said and followed him out the door.

THIRTY-SEVEN

In a daze, Willow walked behind Max, out of the brewery and into the office, trying, and failing, to shake off the shock of having seen him laughing and joking around with Jer.

He pulled back the door and stepped to the side, gesturing her through, then followed and closed the door behind them, shutting out the rest of the world.

She rolled her eyes at Barley, who'd been staring up into Max's eyes and cuddled against his chest like a baby.

What a traitor.

He was supposed to be on her side, growling and snapping at him for being an ice-cold asshole to her, not falling in love with the guy.

She sat in Max's giant leather office chair behind the desk and crossed her legs, trying hard to hold on to her anger even though it was slipping away at the sight of him. He'd sat across, a smile tugging at the corner of his mouth as he watched her.

God, his mouth.

She'd forgotten how attractive he was.

He stared at her and sat in silence, and she stared back. Hadn't he said she should silently stare at someone until they started speaking with more respect? Not acknowledge their unacceptable behaviour?

That was actually good advice.

She cocked a brow, wondering how long the staring contest would go on for and determined not to break first.

Max finally looked away from her, down at Barley as he scratched up the little pup's outstretched neck. "This is a great dog," he said with a smile. "I had a dog when I was a kid. He died when I was fifteen, and I never cried."

Willow's face fell as her anger evaporated in an instant and all the feelings she'd felt for Max came surging forward.

What was this trickery?

"Adam cried for, like, three days," he said with a shake of his head. "I felt like crying but wouldn't let myself. Even when I was alone."

Willow desperately tried to keep being mad at him, but her face went slack as she watched the emotions work their way over his face.

"I'm sorry about how I treated you," he said. "From the first time we met until the last time I saw you."

Her eyebrows shot up, and she stared at his eyes, so open and calm. She never wanted to look away.

"I was way too pushy because I was afraid that if you went back there, you'd never return, and I'd lose you."

Her head felt too light as she pulled in a shallow breath. She'd walked into the brewery fully expecting to go into battle with Max. She hadn't expected for one second that he'd be calm and open, telling her he was sorry.

"I'm sorry, too," she said. "I didn't want to let Nikki down, but I let everyone here down instead."

Max shook his head. "You haven't let anyone down. We're all good."

The regret she'd started feeling at Nikki's wedding came rushing back, and her shoulders slumped. "I never should have gone back there."

"What happened?"

She sighed. "Nikki was the one sexting Shane."

Max's eyes grew, but he stayed quiet.

"I found out right before the wedding."

"Holy shit. Are you okay?"

She gave a half shrug, replaying the last two days in her mind. "I don't know. At first, I was kind of numb and full of regret. I was mad at myself for leaving here," she said, looking up at him. "For leaving you."

He stood and placed Barley gently on his chair, then came around the desk and pulled her to her feet into his arms.

She cuddled in, letting him hold her, and felt a thousand times better. In fact, she hadn't felt this comfortable and at home since the last time she was in his arms.

God, she loved him so much.

Why had she ever left?

"I fucking hate that they treated you like that," he said, his voice grumbling deep with anger.

He turned them and sat in the big chair, pulling her down onto his lap. She draped her legs over the armrest and put her cheek against his chest.

"If it makes you feel any better, the groom punched Shane in the face."

Max laughed. "That does make me feel better. Did he still marry her?"

"I don't know. I walked out right after that."

He nodded. "I'm sorry you had to deal with all that."

"Me too," she said with an exhale.

She sat with him like that for a long while, basking in the warmth of his hand on her knee, rising and falling with his chest. She was at peace. And it felt so fucking good.

"Max?"

"Mmm?" he said.

She took a calming breath. "I love you."

He squeezed her in tighter, wrapping his arms around her almost protectively. "I love you, too."

She pulled back and sat up, just enough to look him in the eye. "I'm staying. Here in Mapleton. At Monroe Manor."

He took her face in his hands and kissed her, softly at first, then deeper and deeper. He finally pulled back but kept her face in his hands.

"Will you be my girlfriend?"

She couldn't help the excitement that bubbled out of her throat. "Yes," she said, her face splitting into a giant grin. "I'd love to be your girlfriend."

He kissed her again, then pulled back. "That was very decisive," he said with a smirk.

She laughed. "It's easy to be decisive when you know what you want."

He smiled for a moment before his face went serious. "I'm gonna try really hard not to fuck this up."

She smiled and snuggled into his chest, then sighed out a breath of relief.

"Me too."

THE GRAND OPENING

"I'm so nervous."

Max moved behind Willow and dropped his chin to her shoulder as he wrapped her in his arms. It was five minutes to opening, and everyone in the place was buzzing with nerves.

Except him.

He was happier than he'd ever been, hanging out in the office he shared with Willow that somehow felt more like home to him than anywhere else in the world.

"Why are you nervous?"

Her body relaxed into his, and she dropped the back of her beautiful head against his shoulder.

He took the chance to trail kisses up her neck to her ear.

"I just want everything to go well."

"Mmm . . ." he said, both agreeing with her and finding inordinate pleasure in the flush that was creeping up her chest.

"Why aren't you nervous?" she asked. "I figured you'd be throwing things and threatening to fire everyone."

He laughed. "I have everything I want already."

She twirled in his arms as she made a haughty little harrumph noise. "Maybe you're calm because you're more experienced. How many grand openings have you had?"

He tried to think back, but it was a struggle. His brain only wanted to think about her. "I don't know, five. This is different, though. Better."

"Why?" she asked, tipping her head to the side to make room on her neck for his mouth.

"I have a partner this time."

She pulled away, and he resisted the urge to drag her back. "And you're happy about that?"

Max laughed. Honestly, if you'd told him two months ago that he'd be opening Keller's Pub with a partner and making out with her five minutes before the grand opening, he would have pissed himself laughing.

But after everything they'd gone through to get to this point, this felt like the most natural thing in the world.

"I'm thrilled you're my partner, Willow. I've never been happier in my life."

Her eyes went all soft. "I love you."

"I love you, too," he said, then pulled her close and took her mouth with his.

"It's ti— Oh."

Willow pulled back abruptly, and they both turned to find Cara standing in the doorway to the office.

"Sorry," she said, awkwardly turning. "I didn't mean to interrupt."

He was just about to tell her to go away when Willow pushed off from his chest. He couldn't stand the emptiness. It was great that they were finally opening, but honestly, he just wanted for it to be over so he could take Willow home and be alone with her all night.

"We're coming," Willow said, grabbing his hand in hers and dragging him from their office.

He followed her out into the dining room, where the entire staff had gathered around. Jer had passed out small glasses of beer to everyone, and when he saw them enter the room, he brought them each a glass with a smile.

"How about a toast?" he asked.

Max put his hand on Willow's back to urge her forward to speak, but she was dabbing her damp eyes and shook him off.

Max inwardly groaned, but before he spoke, Luis mercifully stepped up.

"May I?"

Max fell back. "Absolutely."

Luis cleared his throat. "Here's to the last six weeks of blood, sweat, and tears. We've taken Max and Willow's dream, and together, turned it into reality. There have been many ups and many downs, but through hard work and dedication, we've finally reached the beginning. I'm proud of every one of you. Santé!"

A chorus of cheers went up, then silence as everyone drank down Willow's incredible beer.

Everyone left in different directions. Jer collected the glasses on a tray and headed back to the brewery; Luis retreated to his kitchen with the other cooks, and the host and waitstaff went to the front door to open.

Max let Willow pull him to the corner of the room by the bar, but he was still hung up on Luis's words.

Finally reached the beginning.

He couldn't have agreed more. This night definitely felt like the beginning. Not just for the pub, but for him and Willow, too.

"What a great moment."

He glanced to the side to find Cara standing with them, nodding toward the front door as the host twisted the key in the lock, then swung it open.

"I know," Willow said on a sob.

Max smiled and put an arm around her shoulders, then dropped a kiss to her head. He couldn't put into words how proud he was of her.

She shook her head, as if trying to rid herself of her feelings, and slipped an arm around Max's waist.

"I need to talk about something else," she said, fanning her wet eyes. "How's the dating going, Cara?"

Cara shrugged a little. "I'm only in the research phase."

Max cocked a brow. "Research?"

"Yeah," she said with a nod but didn't elaborate, as if researching dating made sense to everyone.

Max shook his head and let out a laugh at his sister. She'd always had a brilliant, analytical mind. Obviously, she would approach dating the same way. Maybe it was odd, but at least she was putting thought into it, not like when she'd started dating that last fool.

"What about things with Cooper?" Willow asked.

"I'm seeing him next week," she said with an eye roll. "I keep trying to get together with him so I can dump him, but he's always too busy, apparently.

I even gathered up all his stuff from my room to throw at his face. I'm just missing one of the earrings he gave me."

Willow gave her a smile. "What about all your mutual friends?"

Cara turned sad. "I think I'm going to lose them all in the breakup. They like him more."

Max patted her shoulder. "They aren't worth it, then. Don't worry so much about what people who don't respect you think about you, Cara."

She nodded. "Easier said than done."

He was about to say more, but the front door opened, and in walked Antonio. He spotted him immediately, said something to the host that got a smile, then made his way toward them.

"Who's that?" Cara asked in a hushed tone while leaning in toward Willow.

Max scowled.

Before Willow could answer, Antonio was already across the room.

"Congratulations, guys," he said, reaching Willow first and pulling her into a hug.

Next, he extended a hand, and Max took it, but they ended up hugging as well. When he pulled back, Cara smiled at him.

Max didn't like the look on her face.

"Hi, I'm Cara," she said, holding out her hand.

Antonio smirked as he took her hand. "I know," he said, sparing a glance at Max. "You don't remember me?"

Cara's brows drew together.

"I pulled you out of a hedge of rosebushes."

"Oh God," she said, her eyes doubling before she dropped her head.

He laughed, holding her hand and shaking it. "Since you don't remember, I'm Antonio. It's a pleasure to meet you."

Cara huffed out a dramatic exhale. "Sorry about that night, and thanks for your help. I was . . . going through some things."

Antonio released her hand, then slipped his into the pockets of his dark jeans. "We've all been there," he said with an easy-looking smile.

Max knew it was a practised move. He'd seen Antonio at his worst and knew he could relate to Cara that night better than anyone.

"Hey," Cara said, looking up as if she'd just remembered something. "You haven't found a silver earring in your car, have you? I was wearing it that night, but I haven't seen it since."

"No, but I haven't been in the back seat," he said, glancing at his watch. "I'm a bit early. Do you want to go look now?"

"Yes," she said. "Thanks."

Max stared on as Cara followed Antonio out of the pub, his annoyance growing and growing until Willow tucked herself in close.

"What's wrong?" she asked.

"Antonio likes her."

Willow glanced toward the door, then back. "Is that a problem?"

"Yes."

"Why?"

Max shook his head, a list forming in his mind of all the reasons Antonio should stay the hell away from his little sister.

"For one thing, he's ten years older than her—"

Willow turned to him, slipping her arms into his jacket and around his waist, cutting off his brain.

"Let's just worry about us tonight," she said before rising and meeting his lips.

Every thought he'd had disappeared, and he pulled her with him, deeper into the corner of the room, out of sight from the people being seated. He bracketed her face with his hands and kissed her, and all of his worries and fears melted away again. When they pulled apart, she smiled up at him.

"I'm so happy we finally made it."

Max nodded, taking in her beautiful face. "Me too, but like Luis said, this is just the beginning. Not just for our business, but for us, too."

Her smile tripled. "I love you," she said. "Want to go to our office?"

Max's heart grew. "I love you, too, and yes."

· · · · ● · ● · · · ·

Bonus Scene

Author's Note: This scene is from Antonio's point of view when he leaves the pub with Cara. Hope you enjoy!

Antonio left Max gaping behind him and followed Cara out of the pub. She looked even prettier than she had in that photo he'd seen, and worlds better than when he'd pulled her from those rose bushes.

Not that she'd looked bad then.

He was pretty sure it was impossible for her to look bad.

She had short dark hair that framed her porcelain face, big brown doe-like eyes, and full red lips. Not to mention her endless legs and soft curves that he'd berated himself for loving. He had been trying hard to forget feeling her in his arms.

He forced his eyes away from hers, pulled his keys from his pocket, and pressed the button to unlock the door.

"This is your car?" Cara asked.

Antonio nodded, pulling the back driver's side door open. "You don't remember anything from that night, do you?"

She looked up at him with a small shake of her head. "Do you remember it well?"

Antonio couldn't stop the smile, and it doubled when she winced. He remembered every detail, from her screaming at him to get away from her, to the way she gave into him and let him lift her out of the bushes, to the in-depth mumblings about weight ratios, height differentials, and the physical improbabilities of Willow being able to carry her.

Her brilliant mind, functional even while heavily intoxicated, was impressive. He wanted more.

"All I remember is why I wanted to go out and how good of an idea all those tequila shots were," she said.

Antonio nodded. He knew all too well what it was like to search for answers, or at least a night of numbness, at the bottom of a bottle. But it never worked.

"Did those shots have something to do with the earring we're looking for?"

She huffed out a sigh. "Yes. My soon-to-be ex gave me the earrings," she said, twisting away from him and bending down into the backseat in one fluid motion.

His eyes dropped down her back to where her plaid skirt met the sheer black nylons colouring the backs of her thighs.

He snapped his eyes away and looked past her shoulder, trying not to think what Max would do to him if he knew he was checking out his little sister's ass.

Just the thought of Max was enough to set him straight.

Luckily, Cara didn't notice his torment as she ran her hands along the backseat in the dim light. He knew she'd be angry if she knew Max was controlling her behind her back, warning off men. But in Antonio's case, Max was one hundred percent right in telling him to stay away.

"And now I'm going to find the damn things and ceremoniously throw them in his face to symbolize the death of our shitty relationship."

He couldn't help the laugh that escaped as he turned and made his way to the back passenger side of his car. He opened the door and bent down toward her.

"Why was your relationship shitty?"

She looked up, piercing him with those beautiful eyes. The overhead light in the backseat cast a shadow of her lashes onto her cheekbones.

"He never really cared about me," she said, then blinked down and added, "I was never a priority, even after months of dating."

Antonio's brows drew together as he tossed the thought around his mind. "You deserve better," he said.

She glanced up at him and gave a smile.

He stared back for a moment longer than he should have before breaking eye contact and glancing down at the floor behind the driver's seat. A reflection caught his eye. He bent down and spotted a shiny earring halfway between them on the floor beneath the center console and reached for it.

"There it is," he said, grabbing the dangling silver earring up and holding it out to her.

She took it from him, their hands briefly making warm contact, and closed her fist around it. Before she could say anything, he backed out of the car and pushed the door closed.

"Thanks," she said, staring at him as he came around the car.

He gave a nod and shoved his hands into his pockets to warm them from the cold. "No problem."

She glanced around the parking lot, then back to him. Her skin had turned pink from the chilly night air. It was a beautiful compliment to her red lips.

He blinked away from her face and shook off his unwelcome thoughts.

"I should get back."

She gave him a smile and a nod. "I hope I didn't make you late."

"You didn't," he said. "I was early."

Cara nodded. She turned her pretty head toward the door, then back to him, piercing him with those big, beautiful eyes. "Are you meeting a date?"

"No," he said, his rapid headshake—faster than normal—made her eyebrows shoot up. "I'm not dating...or I'm sort of trying to see someone already."

Cara raised an eyebrow at his incoherent ramblings. "Who are you meeting?"

"My cousins," he said. "We're having dinner before poker."

"Poker?" Cara said, her lips stretching to a pretty grin.

Antonio nodded. "Yeah, we get together every once in a while and play."

It was one of the few fun things he had left after his marriage broke down. Well, that and his sisters and his niece. But until he'd reconnected with Max and made new friends in Mapleton, all he did was work and sit in his crappy apartment, ruminating over where he'd gone wrong.

"I love poker," Cara said with a smile. "Max taught me how to play when I was eight."

Antonio shook his head with a laughed. "If Max taught you, then you must be good. He's a shark."

Cara smiled, then looked down at the earring and back up at him. "I think it would be fun to play against you sometime."

A bit of adrenaline shot through his veins as he imagined sitting across from her playing poker. To be honest, his mind had immediately gone to strip poker. But only for a second before he came to and realized this was Cara.

Max's little sister.

Not to mention he was technically still married and had made enough mistakes up to this point to last a lifetime.

He forced the thought away with a shake of his head and took a step backwards, searching for a delicate way to say no.

"Yeah," he said. "Maybe we can all play as a group."

Cara raised one eyebrow. "The person you're already sort of seeing wouldn't want you playing alone with me?"

Antonio wondered what Fran would think of Cara. It had been a while since he'd seen Fran. The last time they spoke, she'd told him she wanted to get back together. But he hadn't been able to forgive her at that point.

Now he was ready.

"It's complicated," he said, shoving a hand through his windblown hair and wondering how far into this he should go. Probably not far. But there was no sense in lying or brushing her off. They were both part of the same friend group now.

"I'm trying to get back together with my wife. Well, ex...almost-ex wife," he said, stumbling over what to call her. "We separated a few months ago."

A moment of processing happened before she said, "Ah."

Antonio nodded.

She mimicked his despondent nod.

"Well, I hope it all works out for you," she said, looking awkwardly around like she couldn't run away fast enough but also didn't want to offend him.

"Thanks," he said. "Good luck with your breakup."

She gave him a small smile that didn't reach her eyes. "Good luck with your makeup," she said, and with an awkward little wave, she turned on her heel and headed deeper into the parking lot, away from the door to Keller's.

He watched her go, telling himself he was being a good friend to Max and keeping an eye on his little sister. In all honesty, though, he couldn't look away, and it was only when she disappeared from sight that his mind shifted from her to his own problems.

He was so deeply lost in thought that he didn't even notice his cousin arrive until the sound of his voice snapped him out of it.

"Tonio?"

He spun to find Nico there, looking at him as if he'd just been licking the ground.

"Who was that?" he asked, his face twisted in shock.

"No one."

Nico called him out with a single look.

"Just a…"

What the hell was she?

"A friend's sister. An acquaintance. Nobody."

"Well, 'Nobody' was pretty cute," he said with a smirk.

Antonio shook his head even though he full-heartedly agreed. Cara was cute. And sexy. He wasn't sure how she was pulling off being both at the same time.

"It's been a year since Fran left you. It's okay to think a girl is cute."

Antonio shook his head. "It's been seven months. And we're getting back together."

"You are?" Nico asked, pulling back in shock. "My mom said Uncle Reg told her that Fran wanted you back and you told her no."

Antonio winced. "I'm so sick of being everyone's gossip."

Nico shrugged. "You're the only one going through something right now."

"Maybe you could just fuck up your life somehow and take some heat off me."

"No can do," Nico said with a laugh. "But I *will* let you take all my money tonight."

"I was going to do that anyway," he said with a laugh. "Come on, let's eat."

Antonio walked with his cousin into Keller's. One good thing about hitting rock bottom was knowing there's only one way left to go.

· · · ● · ● ● · ● · ·

Love or Leave, Cara and Antonio's story, is the last installment in the Mapleton Series—and it's one you won't want to miss. Packed with secret fake dating, humor, and the fast-paced, slow-burn tension you love, this book also features a heartwarming **series epilogue** told from all your favorite characters' points of view.

Grab your copy here: https://mybook.to/BelTb PE

www.ingramcontent.com/pod-product-compliance
Lightning Source LLC
Chambersburg PA
CBHW030517190726
48283CB00006B/1668